# The Witch
# of
# Napoli

———

## Michael Schmicker

PALADINO FICTION
AN IMPRINT OF PALADINO BOOKS

www.MichaelSchmicker.com

ISBN-10: 0990949028
ISBN-13: 978-0-9909490-2-2

Cover: Andy Carpenter/ACD Book Cover Design
Interior design: Mark Bernheim/52novels
First Palladino Fiction Edition published 2015

**E-book Edition**
Published by Palladino Books
Available online from Amazon, Barnes & Noble, Apple iBooks, Kobo, Smashwords

**Audio Edition**
Produced by Audiobook Creation Exchange/ACX
Available online from Audible.com, Amazon.com, and Apple iTunes
(Spring 2015)

*To Patricia above all*

*"I shall not commit the fashionable stupidity of regarding everything I cannot explain as a fraud."*

– Dr. Carl Jung
Speech to the Society for Psychical Research (1919)

# 1

A lessandra is dead.
　　Sunday's edition should fly off the news-stands, with the photos Giorgio shot, the stuff we discovered in Lombardi's diaries, the interviews we did with the Vatican and the police, the comments we've gathered from the rich and famous throughout Europe.

When I got back from the burial last night, the editorial offices at the *Messaggero* were dark, but the lights were burning bright in the print shop and the presses were thundering away. I climbed up the stairs to my office and found a copy boy waiting outside the door with the front page, the ink still wet. I hung my hat and coat on the hook, then sat down at my desk to study it. Antonio did a good job on the lead.

> Dateline: Rome, Italy, April 20, 1918—Alessandra Poverelli, the fiery, vulgar, Neapolitan peasant who levitated tables and conjured up spirits of the dead in dimly-lit séance rooms all across Europe, whose psychic powers baffled Science, captivated aristocracy, and enraged the Catholic Church, has joined the Spirit World herself at age 60. *Requiescat in pace.*

A bit melodramatic? Perhaps. But after four years of this damn, endless war, and the Kaiser's troops threatening Paris once again, our readers are desperate for a little scandal and amusement, and as the editor of the *Messaggero* I pride myself on giving the customer what he wants.

Alessandra got what she wanted too.

When the consumption finally claimed her, I made sure she was buried as she wished—here in Rome, not Naples, and quietly and privately, without any religious mumbo jumbo. I rode in the hearse with her corpse out to the city cemetery, accompanied by Maria, the nurse who took care of her the last month of her life. A light rain was falling, and the team of horses plodded up the muddy hill, her pine casket covered by a sheet of canvas in the back of the wagon. When we got there, two gravediggers were standing under a dripping oak tree smoking cigarettes. They quickly tossed their butts and doffed their hats and asked when the priest would be showing up. The hole was ready and they obviously wanted to get it over with quickly so they could return home.

"There won't be any priest," I told them.

They looked bewildered. "*Signore*, no prayers either?"

"No prayers."

They shrugged and clambered up onto the wagon to haul down the casket. Maria huddled under her parasol, sniffling into a handkerchief, as they lowered the box into the ground. Before they grabbed their shovels, I walked over and tossed into the grave the famous photograph I had taken of Alessandra back in Naples so many years before. In minutes, they had filled the hole, leaving a brutal, black scar on the earth which Spring will quickly heal. It's going to take me a lot longer.

Here's to Alessandra, the witch of Napoli—wherever she finds herself now.

# 2

I owe her.

Alessandra was my first photograph for the *Mattino*—the assignment that launched my newspaper career. Of course, she owed me as well—my photo made her famous. She could finally escape Pigotti and get out of that shithole Naples. She never forgot that.

Did I ever tell you how we first met?

In the Spring of 1899, my uncle Mario owned a photography shop in Naples, and he hired me to lug his camera up to Vesuvius and take photos for him, which he printed and sold to German and French tourists. He paid me five *centesimi* for each postcard he sold, but everybody was hawking the same scenic views, and I was always hungry. So I convinced him to shoot some dirty pictures, like the ones he smuggled home from Paris. Our best seller was a girl wearing a nun's cornette, with a rosary dangling between her two *cioccie*—it sold like crazy. We doubled our sales, but *zio* Mario didn't double my fee. He was a cheap bastard. A month later, a sub-editor from the local paper, the *Mattino*, stopped by the shop, thumbed through the photos, and asked if I wanted to work for the newspaper.

"He works for me," uncle Mario told him.

"The hell I do," I said. "I quit." I was 16 years old.

When the *Mattino* sent me out to do that first story on her, Alessandra was almost 40 years old. She was performing weekly séances at the apartment of Dr. Ercole Rossi, a professor of philosophy at the University of Naples and the head of the Spiritualist Society of Naples. He was her principal admirer at that time. She was a medium. Mediums talk to the dead, passing on messages from spirits on the Other Side to family and friends they've left behind in this world. When you're from Naples, you believe in these things, and the town was starting to talk about her.

Alessandra was special—what Spiritualists call a *physical* medium. She could talk to the dead, but she could also levitate tables, make things fly through the air, and do other spooky things. Professor Rossi attended one of Alessandra's séances, watched a chair waltz itself across the floor without anyone touching it, and converted to Spiritualism.

Rossi wrote a letter to the *Mattino* about what he witnessed, and Venzano, our editor, sniffed a good story. The séance and table-tilting craze was sweeping Europe. D.D. Home was entertaining royals in England with his psychic tricks, and the Pope was issuing papal bulls warning us about talking to spirits, so why not do a story on our own Alessandra.

"Get a shot of her with Dr. Rossi," he told me. "Then get back right away. I want it in the morning edition."

At 7:30 that evening, I knocked on the door of Rossi's apartment and the maid led me into the parlor where Rossi and a small group of older, well-dressed men and women were gathered in a circle, exchanging introductions and pleasantries. When Rossi spotted me, he excused himself and walked over.

"So you're the boy from the *Mattino*?"

"Yes, sir," I replied. "Tommaso Labella."

"I'll let you decide where you want to take your picture. The séance is scheduled to begin at eight, so you need to set up your camera right away."

I was unfolding my tripod when we heard a commotion and footsteps hurrying down the hall and Alessandra burst into the parlor.

"Late again! *Buona sera* everyone!" She yanked off her hat and tossed it onto a chair, then bent over and buttoned her boot before popping up again, clapping her hands together. "*Andiamo!* Let's get going!" Pigotti, her thuggish manager, had followed her through the door, a cigarette in his thin lips.

Alessandra's bright eyes swept the room, searching for Rossi, her host, and fell on me standing next to my camera. Rossi had warned her the *Mattino* was preparing a story. She opened her arms in welcome and headed over to me.

"You are from the newspaper, no?" she demanded.

Across the room, Pigotti glowered at me.

I felt my face go red and stammered out my name. Taking both my hands in hers, she pulled me close and whispered in my ear.

"Please make me look beautiful."

Then she winked at me.

I felt dizzy.

We Italians say when you fall hard for a woman at first sight, you're struck by a *colpo di fulmine*—a lightning bolt. I can tell you it's true. I have no idea what Alessandra looked like when she was young. When I first showed up in her life with my camera, she had already lost her girlish figure. She wore that petit bourgeois, black silk dress she always favored for the séance room, which did her no favors, but she exuded a raw, animal magnetism that left boys like me tongue-tied, and made men ignore their wives and crowd up close.

But it was her eyes that really hypnotized men.

Lord Carraig sent French astronomer Alan Bonnay a letter shortly after he met Alessandra for the first time. "Her large eyes, filled with strange fire, sparkled in their orbits, or again seem filled with swift gleams of phosphorescent fire, sometimes bluish, sometimes golden. If I did not fear that the metaphor were too easy when it concerns a Neapolitan woman, I should say that her eyes appear like the glowing lava fires of Vesuvius, seen from a distance in a dark night."

She certainly used them to her advantage. Unlike most women, she didn't drop her gaze when she talked with a man. She *looked* at you, and you could read whatever you wanted into that. She didn't care.

I was utterly bewitched that night.

I wasn't a virgin when Alessandra showed up—I was sixteen, after all—but my sexual experience was limited to Coco, the skinny, pimply-faced girl who helped run uncle Mario's shop. She was constantly flirting with me, so one day when he left early I invited her into the store room. It was the first time for both of us. It took me forever to get her blouse over her head, she lay there stiff as a board with her eyes scrunched closed, and as soon as I came she pushed me off her and broke into tears. I didn't know what was going on. She was afraid I had made her pregnant and she begged me to marry her, threatening to tell her brother if I didn't. Every time uncle Mario left the shop, she would start to cry and throw things at me, accusing me of ruining her, and I was a heartless bastard, and her brother was going to come over to the shop and cut off my balls. A month later, she found out she wasn't pregnant and wanted me to take her to the cinema so we could fool around.

Alessandra was the first *woman* in my life.

I felt a sudden surge of jealousy when she turned her attention to Dr. Cappelli, a fellow professor from the university who assisted Rossi with his psychic explorations. He was tall and handsome, with an engaging smile, and an amateur magician to boot. The two of them sat knee-to-knee in a corner as Cappelli demonstrated a coin trick that left her laughing and searching his sleeve. Pigotti marched over, yanked her to her feet, and shoved her over to where I was setting up. He returned to his post at the door, glaring at Cappelli.

I posed Alessandra sitting on an arm chair in the parlor, flanked by two elegant fan palms and holding Rossi's white cat in the lap of her black silk dress. When I leaned forward to square her shoulders to the camera, I could feel the heat of her body, and her dark hair touched my cheek. She looked up at me.

"I've never been photographed before, Tommaso," she confessed. "Do you think I look ugly?"

At first I thought she was teasing me, and then I realized she wasn't. I stared at her dumbfounded. I wanted to shout, you're the most beautiful woman I've ever met. Instead, all I could say was "I think you look very nice."

She reached out to touch my hand. "*Grazie*," she said softly.

No matter how beautiful women are, they're always worried that they aren't attractive enough. They need to be reassured. A few don't, but even they appreciate the attention.

The minute I fired off the photograph, Rossi began herding everyone towards the séance room. I didn't know if I would ever see Alessandra again, and it frightened me. As Rossi was closing the door, I stopped it with my foot.

"I could set up my camera in the séance room," I suggested boldly. "If anything happens, I can capture a photograph of it." Behind him, I could see Alessandra settling down in her chair and the other sitters taking their places around the table. Rossi shook his head.

"Impossible. These manifestations happen very quickly and rarely last more than a few seconds."

"That's all I need, sir." I replied. "A second."

Rossi hesitated, hand on the doorknob. He seemed to mull it over in his head. I held my breath.

"Wait here," he said finally.

He retreated inside. Through the door, I could see him huddling with Alessandra and Pigotti. Pigotti didn't look very happy, but Alessandra threw a smile my way. Finally, Rossi returned to the door. I could come inside, but I had to remain in the corner with my camera, I wasn't to speak, and I couldn't take a photograph unless Rossi gave me a signal.

So I hustle in my equipment, jam myself into the corner, and load my flash gun. Pigotti crowds in next to me, the stink of his body strong, his hooded eyes fixed on Alessandra. Six people hold hands around a small, four-legged card table, a turned-down oil lamp providing the only illumination. It's gloomy, shadowy, and hard to see. I strain my eyes. A clock on the wall quietly ticks away the minutes, *tic, toc, tic, toc.* Maybe 30 minutes pass, and despite the enthusiastic prayers at the start, absolutely nothing happens. Other than Alessandra's coughing, the room is dead silent. I'm running out of time to get the photo and get back to the paper. Suddenly the table jerks forward, and the woman in front of me lets out a gasp. Then another sudden jerk. I watch dumbfounded as the table slowly tilts backwards on two legs and balances there, a toy music box skidding off and bouncing across the floor, sounding a note. More gasps and cries. I'm ready to shit in my pants.

Alessandra cries out, "Spirits, we know you are here. Show us more!" The table returns to four legs, remains there for several seconds, then slowly begins to rise into the air. The sitters scramble to their feet, trying to keep their hands on the top of the table. Then it hangs there, motionless.

"*E' fatto!*" Alessandra screams. It's done!

"Now!" cries Rossi.

I fire the flash, and in that split-second burst of illumination I see the table suspended in the air, a meter off the floor. *Maronna!*

The woman in front of me collapses, the table crashes to the floor, and the gas lamp is quickly turned up. Alessandra is bent over, pale and panting hard, her head in her hands. She finally turns and vomits into a pan. Rossi mops the sweat from her face, and the hostess gives her a glass of water which she drools from her lips, then Rossi goes over to Pigotti and pays him the fee.

As I'm hurrying to fold up my camera, I overhear these two withered English biddies who attended the séance gushing over the miracle they just witnessed.

"She's the spirit medium we've been looking for," gushes the first.

"I agree," sniffs the second, "but why would God use such an uneducated, immoral woman for His divine work? Besides, she smells like a goat." And they laughed.

They were damn lucky Alessandra didn't hear them. She would have thrashed them.

When I developed the plate in the darkroom that night, I immediately knew I had the photograph which would make my name. The next morning, Venzano summoned me into his office, and handed me a copy of the paper. My photo was splashed across the front page. Right below it, in tiny, six-point type, was my name. *Photo by Tommaso Labella.* It was my first byline in the business, and it appeared in the newspaper on March 26, 1899.

* * *

Almost 20 years ago, now. It's hard to believe.

This morning, before Antonio started assembling the big Sunday special on Alessandra, I called him into my office, closed the door, reached into a drawer, and pulled out my private file on her—copies of Huxley's reports, Lombardi's correspondence with other scientists, hundreds of newspaper clippings.

"Look through this," I said. "You'll find a lot of good stuff. But check with me before you use anything."

I explained to Antonio how I chronicled Alessandra's rise to fame every step of the way, crouching in corners of séance rooms, eavesdropping on conversations, scooping up tidbits of information to share with Venzano. I was never a pest. I keep secrets when necessary, and I always made sure my photos flattered her, right to the end. She was vain, like all women, and had a scar on her forehead which she did her best to hide with her hair. I never showed it in my photos. She told me she fell off a donkey cart as a child, but I know Pigotti gave it to her.

"We understood each other," I told Antonio.

She knew where I came from, and how far I had to climb to get to the top, just like she had to. People see me now, editor of the powerful and influential *Messaggero*, showing up at *The Barber of Seville* with a beautiful *contessa* on my arm, dining with Roman nobility, dressed in Castangia suits and drinking Veuve Clicquot. They don't know I started at the bottom. But I had ambition. I wanted to sit in the editor's seat, to "earn my bread by the sweat of my pen," as Aretino famously put it. So I educated myself, shooting photos for the *Mattino* then sneaking into the Biblioteca Nazionale on Saturday afternoons to read Manzoni and Leopardi, learning how to pen an elegant sentence, and memorizing lines from Dante and Boccaccio and Petrarca to impress my superiors.

"You've probably never heard of Petrarca," I teased.

Antonio looked up from the file he was thumbing through and laughed. "Let me hear you spout a few verses."

I struck a pose, my hands outstretched, reaching for the stars.

*Era il giorno ch'al sol si scoloraro per la pietà*
*del suo factore i rai...*

Antonio recognized it right away. He had spent a year at the university. "Petrarca's love sonnet for his unattainable Laura, no?"

"*Bravo*, Antonio," I replied. "I've used his poetry to coax more than one lady into bed."

He grinned. "Including Alessandra?"

I shook my head. "I tried a few lines on her when we first met, but it sailed right over her head. She never heard of Petrarca. We always laughed about that. We were two *bricconi* from Naples who fooled the world. But we never forgot where we came from."

What I didn't share with Antonio, or anyone else at the newspaper, was that I also ended up with her private diaries—38 notebooks, written in her childish, semi-illiterate scrawl, in a dialect only we Neapolitans understand, describing what she saw and did and felt in her extraordinary life, who she slept with, her feelings and desires, her memories and secrets. She trusted me to tell her story.

I tell you this in confidence: Hachette in Paris has approached me to write her biography—for 1,000 francs—but I turned them down, and I'll tell you why. It's a new century. The cinema is the rage now. I will give it to Pathé Frères and let them tell her story. The magic of film for a woman who produced magic right in front of our eyes.

The lower classes will flock to the theatres to see her story because she was one of *them*, their Cinderella, the poor girl who escapes poverty and humiliation and ends up wearing the glass slipper—she led the life *they* dream about, but will never taste. They'll also come because they're dying to know like the rest of Europe—was their heroine a fraud? Did she do it with tricks and wires and sleight of hand, or did she really have supernatural powers?

The answer may surprise you.

# 3

Alessandra was a nobody.

She came from this little goat-shit village in Bari.

I've seen the dump with my own eyes. Shortly after I first met her, she returned home to visit her father's grave and I jumped at the chance to tag along.

It was a hot, sticky day, and I stood in the shade of a dusty cypress tree fanning myself with my hat as she searched around for his grave. She finally stumbled across it, overgrown with brush, the headstone knocked flat. She let out a loud curse, fell to her knees, and began ripping out the weeds, sweeping the earth, and propping the tombstone back up. She had brought some of his favorite Turkish cigarettes and a bottle of grappa and was arranging them in front of the stone when we heard a noise. I looked back and saw a gaggle of old crones marching up the dirt road, led by the parish priest, yelling and screaming for Alessandra to get out of town, calling her a witch and a whore. Alessandra let out a howl, jumped to her feet, grabbed a stick, and chased them all the way back to the village. Alessandra wasn't afraid of anybody in this life but Pigotti and the Devil.

Satan was still real to us back then, when she was born.

As a child, she saw eyes glaring at her in the darkness, and was frightened one night when invisible hands stripped off her bedclothes—a tidbit I made sure Antonio included in his story. She was born left-handed, a sure sign, and always wore a *corno* on a silver chain around her neck to protect her from the *malocchio*, the evil eye, just like I do. This was despite Lombardi's protestations that it made her look like some superstitious hick. The truth is, she *was* superstitious. She believed in omens and curses, and tried one on Huxley when things went sour for her in England.

Alessandra's mother was a *strega* who practiced the "old religion," what some people call witchcraft. Fortunately, the newspapers never found out.

When Alessandra was born, her mother refused to have her baptized.

"The village priest showed up at our doorstep with his bucket of holy water, demanding to douse me, but my mother slammed the door in his face," Alessandra told me. "After that, villagers looked at us strangely. One boy used to throw stones at me after school, and scream that I was going to hell. Old women sitting in the piazza would cross themselves whenever they saw my mother approaching." I could see pain in her eyes as she spoke.

"It must have been pretty tough," I said.

"I didn't have a lot of friends, and the taunting never stopped. The summer I turned five, I came home one day and fell on my knees and begged my mother to let me be baptized. I just wanted it to stop, to be like everyone else. She told me she couldn't, but that I would understand someday. I ran to my bedroom and flung myself on my bed and sobbed. My father came in to console me, but I drove him away.

"Late that night my mother came into my room and woke me up. She told me we were going to the forest. I said, 'Why, mama?' and she just smiled at me. I dressed and followed her outside and we made our way through the village. The streets were dark and silent except for the murmur of crickets and the occasional half-hearted bark of a dog woken by our footsteps. Once we got outside the walls, my mother took off her sandals and told me to do the same. She put them in the small bag she carried and we set off again. The night air was wonderful, filled with the fragrance of lemon flowers. And above my head—so close I felt I could reach up and touch it—was this full moon. It was so beautiful it made your heart ache.

"My mother sang softly as we walked along—strange songs I never heard her sing at home, but which were sweet and filled my heart with happiness even though I couldn't understand the words. But when we reached the forest, I began to be afraid. 'Maybe a fox will eat us,' I said, and I clung tighter to her. Once again my mother just smiled at me. She sat down, and she pulled me into her lap and held me in her arms and sang another song, and as we sat there a fox trotted out of the shadows and sat down at the edge of the trees and looked at us. I felt like my mother was singing to him, and he was listening to her. And when she finished and fell silent, he turned around and slipped back into the darkness, and I no longer felt afraid.

"We followed this winding path for a long time until we reached a small clearing in the forest where a tall, old tree stood. I waited there until my mother came back with these small mushrooms and we ate them, and then she took my hands in hers and we started to dance under the moon. As she twirled me around, my feet left the ground and I was flying through the stars spinning above my head and my heart was bursting with love for my mother, and the next thing I remember I awoke on the grass in the crook of her arm, her soft brown eyes smiling down at me. I looked up and asked her what happened and she said I was of the blood, like her, and her mother, and she would explain everything at the right time."

I stopped Alessandra. "Of the blood?"

"The Old Religion. You're born into it."

"So you're a witch?" I laughed.

Alessandra glared at me. "Don't joke about things you know nothing about."

I held up my hands. "Sorry."

Alessandra was silent for a long time, then she sighed.

"Shortly afterwards my mother fell sick. She sent me back to the forest to find a special herb she needed to get well, and I looked and looked but couldn't find it, and she got sicker and sicker. Then one morning while I was sitting at her bedside she told me she had seen a peacock feather in her dream, and knew her time was short. I didn't understand at first, but that evening she called me and my father to her and told him to take care of me. That scared me and I cried and begged her not to leave me, and she took my hand and drew me close, and looked at me for a long time, then whispered 'We will see each other again.'"

Alessandra looked away. I said nothing.

"All these spirits I talk to," she said bitterly. "I always hope to hear *her* voice. But I never do."

When she was only 13 years old life screwed her a second time. One evening when we got drunk together—she could drink me under the table—I asked her about her father and tears welled up in her eyes. I was surprised, because Alessandra wasn't a woman who cried easily.

"Bastards!" she said, wiping a tear from her cheek. "Damn them all!" Then she told me what had happened.

It was a hot, summer day and she was up in the hills, flirting with a boy named Giuseppe as they tended their goats. While they're up there fooling around, the King of Naples's soldiers ride into her village, looking for her father who made the stupid mistake of publicly supporting Garibaldi during the revolution. Father Angelo, the village priest, tells them where to find him, piously assuring them that the Church supports the monarchy. The soldiers chase down Alessandra's father, beat the shit out of him, drag him back to town, and the captain of the horsemen, an English mercenary, orders the villagers to assemble in the village square to watch his execution.

Alessandra shouldn't have known what was happening to her father—she was way up on the mountain—but she had her mother's "gift."

"I had just grabbed Giuseppe's hat and put it on my head," she told me, "and we were laughing, and then out of nowhere I suddenly felt this incredible rush of panic, and I screamed, 'Something happened to my father!' and I jumped up and started running for home. I didn't know how I knew—I just knew. I ran as fast as I could, my heart pounding, running and stumbling and falling and crying as I ran because I knew he was in great danger."

When she got there, she found her father standing against the church wall, facing a firing squad.

"I started scratching and clawing and biting the soldiers, screaming for someone to help me, before I finally realized they were all cowards—every one of them—and no one was going to help me. My father was going to die."

But not before the captain had some fun with her. He reached down, yanked her into the saddle by her hair, lifted her dress and pretended to hump her doggy style to roars of laughter, then twisted her head around, forcing her to look in her father's eyes as he gave the order to fire. After the volley, the bastard dismounts, strolls over to the jerking body, pulls out his pistol, and gives Alessandra's father the *coup de grace*, splattering his brains against the wall. Then Father Angelo sanctimoniously mumbles a prayer and tosses holy water on the bullet-riddled corpse.

Christ, she was just thirteen years old.

She's lost her mother, and now her father's a bloody pile of rags and buzzing flies. She's an orphan, alone in this world. OK, that's life, you have to get over it and move on, and she did, but she never fully trusted anyone after that.

The heart turns to stone, as Dante says. You've got to look out for yourself because no one else is.

After the soldiers left, and villagers dug a hole for her father, the prick Angelo arranges for his fat housekeeper to take Alessandra into their little love nest. That's when spooky stuff starts to happen. A knife on the kitchen table levitates into the air and flies at the housekeeper. A wine bottle suddenly explodes in the priest's hand as Alessandra glares at him. The housekeeper accuses her of being possessed by demons, and Father Angelo performs an exorcism on Alessandra before packing her off to an orphanage in Naples run by nuns.

A nobody ends up a nobody.

# 4

That should have been the end of her story, but it wasn't. Instead, a rich, expatriate British couple, the Croppers, childless and bored with dressing up their dogs, visit the orphanage, discover her and decide to adopt her.

Alessandra despised them. And why not? An Englishman had killed her father. But she was suspicious of all foreigners. Her father taught her how the Spanish and French and Austrian turds used our country like a cheap whore for centuries before Garibaldi tossed them out on their ass. Besides, she had lived all her short life in the country.

"I was like a wild animal, a forest bird," she told me later, "and these foolish *stranieri* foreigners wanted to make me into a prissy English girl. They dressed me in pinafores and starched blouses, demanded that I take a bath every day, and comb my hair, and use a fork at the table. When I refused, they scolded me and I cursed them back in Italian."

The Croppers dabbled in Spiritualism, and one evening Mrs. Cropper needed more sitters for her circle. Alessandra was pressed into service, sullenly took her chair, and phantom raps and spooky levitations dramatically increased. Not every night, but enough for the wife to suspect Alessandra might be the one attracting the spirits. She let Alessandra skip her hated piano lessons in return for spending evenings at the séance table. At this stage in her career as a spirit medium, Alessandra didn't fall into mesmeric trances, and

Savonarola hadn't shown up yet—that stuff came later—but she did hear spirit voices inside her head and parroted their messages to the eager sitters crowded around the table. And when she didn't hear them, she quickly learned to make things up.

The English couple gushed in letters to their friends about their little "Sandra" and her most extraordinary and varied supernatural powers. But soon their tone changed, as Alessandra started experimenting on her own.

"I got bored sitting for hours around the table," she confessed, "so I started asking the spirits to play tricks on the other sitters. I just closed my eyes and wished hard, and things happened." How they happened, she didn't know. Unlike Lombardi, Alessandra never tried to understand her psychic powers. Where they came from—God, the Devil, or her own mind like Lombardi believed—she didn't care.

One evening, Mrs. Cropper and her circle of friends begged the hovering spirits to produce an "apport." An apport is a gift from the spirits—a flower, or coin, or ring that materializes out of thin air.

After fifteen minutes of fervent singing and praying, they heard a loud thump, turned up the lamps, and discovered a dead rat lying on the table.

"Two of the women fainted on the spot," she laughed. "You would have loved it, Tommaso."

But the group eventually became suspicious of her and started leaving her out. The final time she was invited, the gas lights were turned up after the séance ended and a gentleman sitter discovered his wallet missing. The next morning, the maid found it hidden in a tin box under Alessandra's bed. Alessandra brazenly blamed mischievous spirits for teleporting it there. After six months, the Croppers finally threw up their hands in despair. They locked Alessandra in her room, packed up her belongings, and sent the cook off to the convent to tell Mother Superior they were returning Alessandra in the morning.

That night, Alessandra escaped the house.

"I had a second key," she admitted. "I was sneaking out every night when they were asleep to see this boy. The night I ran away, I broke into the kitchen and stuffed my dress pockets with their silverware. I sold a spoon whenever I got hungry."

She found work as a laundress, and got married at 15. Her first husband was only a year older than her. She was madly in love with him, but he didn't put bread on the table. To keep them from starving, Alessandra started holding séances herself. There were a lot of dead for her to talk to. Cholera swept through Naples all the time, and every family had lost a child to yellow fever or typhoid fever and hoped to make contact one last time. Mothers besieged her seeking assurance that their little boy or girl was safe and happy on the Other Side. A few were simply looking for a supernatural thrill, hoping to hear a rap, or feel a phantom touch or watch a table levitate in the air. They paid Alessandra what they could—a cup of goat milk, a lemon, something stolen from a house they cleaned—and it helped keep them alive. But one day she came home and found her clothes in the street. Her husband had gambled the rent money, lost it, and had taken off, leaving her with nothing. Someone told her to talk to Pigotti. He could help her.

"They told me he had money and liked pretty women," she told me. "I was desperate so I moved in with him."

It was a terrible mistake.

# 5

Alessandra is beyond his reach now, thank God.

Pigotti took over her show and her bed but he was insanely jealous. He couldn't stand the thought of her sitting in a darkened room holding hands or pressing her leg against other men. He wasn't dumb; he saw how men undressed her with their eyes. But he liked the money more.

I should have been afraid of him after that first séance, but I was cocky, sixteen, and crazy in love with Alessandra.

I finally came up with a scheme.

I made a print of her with the cat—after cropping Rossi out of the picture—and mounted it in a pretty walnut frame, then sent her a message through Rossi offering her the picture and suggesting we meet for lunch. I waited nervously for her response, worried that I had appeared too aggressive, but a few days later received a scribbled note telling me to meet her that night at eight o'clock in the Piazza del Plebiscito. I snuck out of work early and hurried back to my apartment to press my white dress shirt, brush off my suit jacket, and pat a few drops of cologne water on my face before catching the tram to the piazza.

It was a beautiful April evening, the sky turning pink from the setting sun and a large crowd of smartly-dressed ladies and gentlemen already strolling the arcades and enjoying the cool sea breeze up from the harbor. I got there early and dodged my way through the clopping horses and the slowly circling carriages to the Caffè Gambrinus, expecting to see uncle Mario outside the entrance, in our usual spot, selling postcards. He wasn't, but Marcello was still there waiting tables.

"Aren't you the big shot now, working for the *Mattino*," he teased when he took my order. "You better leave me a big tip."

"Important people expect superior service," I laughed. "A *caffè nero*, and make it quick."

I sat there enjoying the show, one I never got tired of. Foreigners flock to the piazza to tour the royal palace which fronts the square, shopping for hats and gloves, lava and coral cameos, and copies of ancient bronzes. They always proved entertaining. As Marcello gabbed away in my ear, I sipped my coffee and watched a knot of German tourists, clutching their Baedekers and pestered by beggars and bootblacks, make their way towards the grand fountain to see the dancing dogs. Trailing behind them was a pair of Carabinieri, smartly dressed in their cocked hats and black and red police uniforms, watching for pickpockets. The Germans paused in front of an ice water vendor to inspect his tub of snow and lemons, and the eager proprietor hastily filled a tin cup and pushed it toward one of the ladies. But her fat husband shoved the cup away, and started shaking his finger at her—undoubtedly scolding her about drinking the local water. The insulted vendor jumped up to defend his refreshment, gesticulating wildly and pleading his case to the ragged crowd which quickly surrounded them. The embarrassed Huns finally broke through the ring of gawkers and hurried off, but not before Herr Professor stepped in some horse shit, which left everyone laughing.

At 7:30, the bells tolled in the basilica of San Francesco across the square, and they turned on the gaslights encircling the piazza, illuminating the twilight evening with a necklace of light. Newsboys from the *Piccolo* descended on the square like a flock of noisy crows, hawking the evening edition. We had stuck it to them with the Alessandra séance story. The *Piccolo*'s editor was furious with his reporters for not picking it up before we got it. I bought a copy, lit a cigar, and thumbed through it, killing time. When the bell finally sounded eight, I warned Marcello to hold the table for me and hurried across the piazza to the church to look for Alessandra, her photograph in a wrapped box tucked under my arm.

A puppeteer had set up his theater on the church steps, and a group of laughing street urchins were watching beak-nosed Pulcinella deliver a lesson with his cudgel, but Alessandra was nowhere to be found. I wandered around to the side and looked out to a garden, dimly illuminated by the gas lamps from the piazza, and spied a solitary figure sitting on a bench.

"Alessandra?" I called out.

"Tommaso?" came the soft reply.

I hurried over and greeted her. She wore a plain black skirt, a shawl thrown around her shoulders, and the veil of her hat covered her face. I was overjoyed to discover she was alone.

"Come," I said, handing her the box. "I have a table reserved for us at the *Caffè Gambrinus*. You can open it there, where the light is better."

"No, let's stay here," she whispered.

I sat down next to her as she opened the package and pulled out the photo. She let out a little cry. "Oh, how beautiful," she said. Then she lifted her veil to inspect the photo more closely.

My stomach turned over.

"Jesus!" I gasped.

Her right eye was swollen completely shut, her puffy face a mass of black and blue bruises. I moved my fingers towards her battered face and she pulled back.

"Don't," she said. "Please." I felt sick.

"Your husband?" I demanded.

She laughed bitterly. "He said I was flirting with Professor Cappelli, so he taught me one of his lessons." She stared at the photo in her hand.

Men always slap their wives around, but Pigotti had really laid into her. "You'll look fine in a few days," I lied. "Does he do this often?"

"Usually he leaves my face alone. It's not good for business. But that doesn't stop him from having his fun." She hesitated, then unbuttoned the sleeve of her blouse, pulled it back, and shoved her arm forward.

"Oh Christ," I exclaimed.

Running up her left arm were several ugly, red welts, scabbed over. Cigarette burns. I felt rage rise up inside me.

"Leave him!"

"Don't you think I tried?" she shot back angrily. "He always finds me and drags me back."

"You can hide at my place."

"Do you know what he would do to you?"

"I'm not afraid of him." I said.

"You should be," she replied wearily. "You don't understand—he's Camorra."

"Jesus." I cradled my head in my hands. The night of the séance, I had noticed a tattoo on Pigotti's forearm—a hand holding a stiletto. So that's what it meant.

The Camorra ran Naples back then—they still do today. The city is divided into twelve *quartieri*, with a boss for each, and you don't mess with them. Ever. They don't just kill you; they torture you before they kill you. They own the police and the politicians. They fix the lottery, and run the whorehouses and the gambling dens, and everyone pays them off to stay in business –porters, cabmen, dockers, butchers, hawkers, storekeepers. Even the *Mattino* had to pay them so they could sell their papers in the city.

"Then get out of Naples." I said. "Go back to your village."

"Never! I'm never going back there."

She turned back to the photo in her hands, studied it carefully, and her face softened. "You're a sweet boy, Tommaso. Thank you."

"But you can't go on like this," I protested. "You have to get away."

"I will," she said fiercely. "I'm going to Rome."

# 6

That's when she first told me about her crazy scheme.

When Rossi first approached her to do séances, Alessandra negotiated a weekly fee of five *lire*, but lied to Pigotti and said they offered four. She was secretly pocketing one lira from each séance. She had already squirreled away 20 *lire*, hidden in a slit inside the straw of her mattress. When she saved up enough, she said, she was going to escape to Rome, rent a small room all her own, with a flowerpot on a sunny windowsill, and live all by herself, and when she got old and fat she'd get a cat like Rossi's to keep her company.

It was incredibly risky. You don't do side deals when your partner is Camorra. You end up in a gutter with your throat slit. And even if Pigotti didn't find out and kill her first, it would take her forever to save up the money, and besides how would she live when she got there—broke and without friends? She'd end up in a rat-infested tenement there too, begging for work just like a thousand other peasants from the South.

It was never going to happen, but I didn't have the heart to tell her that. *La speranza e' il pane dei poveri*, as we say in Naples. Hope is the bread of the poor.

"Everybody's leaving Naples these days," I said, trying a smile. "I've been thinking of going to America myself."

Just then, we heard loud male voices. Alessandra jerked around.

"Oh God, no!" she cried. "He's coming! Hide, Tommaso!"

I looked at her bewildered. "Who's coming?"

She shoved the photo into my hands and pushed me towards the shadows.

"Run!"

I ran to the side of the garden, jumped the hedge, and threw myself flat on the ground. Peering through the bushes I saw two men round the corner of the church wall. One was Pigotti. Next to him was a squat, beefy man who looked out into the garden.

"There she is," he growled. He pointed towards the bench where Alessandra sat rigid.

"Fucking bitch!"

Pigotti flew down the steps and sprinted across the grass, cursing loudly. When he got there, he yanked Alessandra off the bench.

"What the hell are you doing here?" he screamed. She jerked her arm away.

"I told Vito," she shot back. "I went to the cathedral to light a candle."

"Then why the fuck are you out here in the dark?" he snarled. "You come here to see someone? Where is he?"

He shoved her down on the bench and wheeled around, his fists clenched, eyes darting around the garden. "I'll kill him!"

I buried my face in the dirt, trying to make my body as flat to the ground as I could.

"Vito!" I heard Pigotti shout.

"Boss?"

"Find him! He's around here somewhere."

I peeked up and saw Vito heading towards the hedge, holding a big stick in his hand. I looked towards the piazza. I could outrun Vito, but then Pigotti would know, and he would kill Alessandra—I was sure of it. I turned around and crawled on my knees as fast as I could down the hedge and deeper into the darkness until I bumped into a wooden cart. I pushed my way under it and lay there motionless with my hand stuffed into my mouth, praying he wouldn't find me.

I could hear Vito coming down the opposite side of the hedge towards me, whacking the bushes with his stick. When he got near me, he stopped and listened. I could hear his heavy breathing. I curled up tighter, terrified my foot was sticking out. He jabbed into the hedge and his stick struck the cart. I could hear the bushes creak as he leaned over the hedge. I shut my eyes and held my breath.

After an eternity, I heard him grunt, the bushes creaked again, and he moved on. Finally he yelled back to Pigotti.

"Nobody around, boss."

I slid out from under the cart and peered through the hedge to see Pigotti staring hard at Alessandra, trying to read her face.

"Lucky for you," he finally grunted. He lit a cigarette, yanked her to her feet and shoved her towards the church. "Get moving."

I looked down and I had pissed my pants.

# 7

Camillo Lombardi changed everything.

Short, goateed, little Jew. But he was smart, I'll admit that. When he died, they saved his brain in a jar so scientists could study it.

The week after the séance at Rossi's home, Lombardi announced he would be giving a big, public lecture in Rome on the topic of "Science, Evolution, and Spiritualism." Venzano immediately recognized the opportunity. *Mattino* readers were hungry for more stories about Alessandra and her supernatural powers, so he bought Rossi a train ticket and sent him to Rome to attend the lecture. His job was to intercept Lombardi after the talk, show him my photograph of Alessandra levitating the table, and convince him to come to Naples to investigate her. The *Mattino* would pay Lombardi's expenses, and in return would get exclusive rights to the story.

Lombardi's position on Spiritualism was well known. He had attended three séances in Florence at the invitation of Dr. Lauro Nobile, head of the Italian Spiritualists Society, and concluded the medium was suffering from what he called female hysteria. As for the mysterious rappings and furniture levitations, they were most likely produced by trickery. His blunt dismissal, published in his book *Studies on Hypnotism, Trance States and Credulity,* made headlines across Europe.

His reputation in the field of psychology rivaled Freud's at that time. The two trained in Paris under Charcot, who conducted experiments using hypnosis on women suffering from hysteria. His entertaining shows at the Salpêtrière clinic drew the *beau monde* of Paris. Afterwards, Freud returned to Vienna to study the nervous disorders of rich housewives and Lombardi became the youngest full professor ever appointed to the University of Torino. He taught abnormal psychiatry and ran an asylum for the criminally insane.

Lombardi was 45 when he first met Alessandra. He was short and slightly pudgy—a gourmand who enjoyed rich food and had the money to indulge—but he dressed smartly and sported an ebony walking stick with a winking Chinaman decorating its ivory knob. He spoke four languages fluently—not only Italian, but French, German and English as well, and could switch from one to the other without missing a beat.

But he was also insufferably brash and abrasive, and collected enemies as fast as he did admirers. His students loved him, but a clique of older professors despised him. When the archbishop of Turin publicly denounced Lombardi in *La Stampa* for aggressively promoting Darwin in his classes, Lombardi famously countered in a letter to the editor that Darwin's books weren't even on the *Index Librorum Prohibitorum*. If the Pope didn't object, why should His Excellency? His "impertinent and unwarranted" retort earned him a written reprimand from the Rector of the university. He tossed it in the trash.

Before Rossi left for Rome, he called Alessandra and me to his home to share the exciting news. Alessandra was already there, chatting away with Cappelli, when I arrived. I hadn't tried to contact Alessandra since the night at the Piazza del Plebiscito. Pigotti scared the shit out of me, and I doubted Alessandra saw me as anything more than just a sweet kid. But seeing her again still made my heart race.

Rossi was cautiously optimistic he could lure Lombardi to Naples.

"He's a scientist, and your photograph is scientific evidence he can't easily dismiss," he told me. "In any event, I'm already scheduled to be in Rome that week for a meeting, so it's worth a try." He turned to Alessandra. "If I convince Professor Lombardi to come, it's up to you to convince him spirits exist. Do that, and you can triple your séance fee. The aristocracy of Naples will clamor to sit with you."

Alessandra was giddy when we left Rossi's apartment. My God, did I understand what that meant? she demanded. She *would* get out of Naples. She *would* get to Rome.

"Tommaso, it's going to happen," she gushed. "I know it will. And all because of your photo." She grabbed my face and gave me a kiss. I felt my face turn red, but she was already hurrying down the street to catch the tram.

# 8

L ombardi was a real showman.

Rome's *Messaggero* newspaper published a detailed account of his extraordinary lecture in their morning edition the following day. I saved a copy in my files. Here, let me read it for you.

### Rome, Monday, April 12, 1899

———

### Large Crowd Throngs Teatro Valle
### for Darwin Lecture

———

### Lombardi Dismisses Spiritualism
### and Afterlife Claims

———

Over four hundred attendees, graced by the presence of Her Royal Highness Queen Margherita, crowded into the Teatro Valle last night to listen as the celebrated professor of psychiatry Dr. Camillo Lombardi of the University of Torino presented a vigorous defense of the theory of evolution advanced by the English naturalist Charles Darwin.

At exactly 8:00 P.M., the red velvet curtain was slowly drawn back, the electric lights came up, and Professor Lombardi appeared, center stage, standing in front of a small table. Two skulls sat on the table in front of him. A hush fell over the crowd as he began his lecture. The Bible was a wonderful book, Lombardi assured his audience, filled with sage advice on how to live an ethical life, but the story of God's creation of Adam and Eve in a Garden of Eden was a fairy tale. The fossil record clearly shows we're just smart monkeys.

Dr. Lombardi picked up the first skull and presented it to his audience. "This," he announced, "is the skull of an African ape." He studied it for a moment, then lifted up the second skull. "And this," he declared, "is the skull of an African bushman. I believe even those of you in the back can notice the similarities." The audience erupted into laughter, and Professor Lombardi proceeded to deliver a most lively exposition of the modern, scientific theory of evolution by comparing the craniums and jawbones of the African and the ape, while quoting extensively from Darwin's scientific treatise *On the Origin of Species by Means of Natural Selection, or the Preservation of Favoured Races in the Struggle for Life.*"

At that point, Lombardi reached under the table, pulled out two more skulls, and lined up all four in a neat row. He's got you. You're thinking—what the hell is all this about?

Resting his palm on the first skull, Dr. Lombardi declared, "Here is the ape, from which we are all descended." Then he moved in succession down the line of craniums. "And here is the Hottentot, representing the black race; and here the Chinaman, representing the yellow race." He paused before lifting up the fourth and last skull, gazing at it with a brooding pose before concluding with the words. "And this is the pinnacle of evolution, the Caucasian, representing the white race."

The audience goes crazy, whistling and cheering. Lombardi pauses, takes a sip of seltzer water, then pulls off the *tour de force* of the whole evening.

Assuring his audience that the superiority of the white race is scientifically measurable, Dr. Lombardi clapped his hands twice, a horn sounded behind the curtain, and a man dressed in a hunting jacket with a fowling piece resting on his shoulder marched out on stage and handed the professor a bag of birdshot.

Dr. Lombardi removed the top of the monkey skull, filled it with shot, poured the pellets back into a measuring glass, and announced an amount of 350 cubic centimeters, which represents the capacity of a monkey's brain. He then measured the Hottentot's brain cavity which held 1100 cubic centimeters, then the Chinaman's brain at 1200 cubic centimeters.

Silence fell over the audience as Dr. Lombardi finally turned to the last skull on the table, that of the European race. In the balcony seats high above the stage, one could observe well-dressed ladies and gentlemen raising their lorgnettes to their noses and leaning forward in their plush seats in eager anticipation of the results. The shot rattled into the cranium with a tic-tic-tic noise, Professor Lombardi transferred the birdshot into the waiting measuring cup, then announced the results.

"Ladies and gentlemen—1350 cubic centimeters."

"*Quod erat demonstrandum*," he announces, and bows to the audience. The white race rules the world because we have the biggest brain. Again, people go absolutely crazy. Finally, the applause dies down, and a lady raises her hand, demanding to know if Lombardi believes women are inferior to men.

Professor Lombardi patiently explained that the average male brain is 14 percent larger than that of the female of our species. "Whether one likes this or not, it is a scientific fact, which leads us to the inescapable conclusion that men are indeed superior to women in terms of their intellect and reasoning power." Here he deftly paused a second, then added "though our wives may disagree." After the laughter subsided, Dr. Lombardi explained that evolution has adapted women for life in the home, as wives and mothers, where love is more important than logic. The young lady, a devotee of *Signora* Mozzoni's suffragette movement, persisted in her pestering questions until she was escorted from the hall by two burly ushers.

But Rossi wasn't there for a lecture on evolution. He wanted to hear Lombardi talk about mediums and

Spiritualism. Unfortunately, when Lombardi finally got to it, his comments were disappointing—brief and dismissive.

After a thirty minute intermission, Lombardi returned to the stage to address the topic of the Spiritualist movement now sweeping Europe. Darwin's theory of evolution has exposed Christianity's claim that humans are special, he explained. We are simply evolved apes, and like apes we have no "soul" that survives death. The soul is simply an emanation of the brain, and when the brain dies we return to dust like the brain. As a result, troubled believers are flocking to séances, desperately seeking proof of a non-existent afterlife. Yet any clever trickster can manufacture vague "messages" from the dead, and produce furniture levitations in the dark for a gullible audience eager to believe. Dr. Lombardi stepped forward, his powerful voice filling the hall. "Ladies and gentlemen, we have a choice. We can remain in the darkness of primitive superstition, or we can embrace the light of Science. I choose Science." His plea was greeted with a fresh volley of cheers.

Professor Lombardi acknowledged that the Spiritualist phenomenon presented some mental mysteries worthy of scientific attention. He proceeded to describe for his audience a most unusual séance he attended, featuring the well-known English spirit medium Madame Guppy. When she fell into her mesmeric trance, a deep, male voice emerged and carried on an intelligent conversation with him for almost an hour. The voice claimed to be that of a 15th century Welsh pirate named John King. Science, however, had a simpler answer, based on the recently discovered phenomenon of the secondary personality. But the hour was getting late, he apologized, and thus he would have to save this topic for a future lecture. "Until then, you might amuse yourself by reading Mr. Stevenson's new novel, *Dr. Jekyll and Mr. Hyde.*"

Dr. Lombardi ended his educational lecture, and a most entertaining evening, with a blunt dismissal of Spiritualism. "There is always room in my asylum for people who believe they can talk to the dead or levitate a table, but there's no room in Science for such nonsense."

The moment Lombardi finished his final bow, Rossi was on his feet, heading for the stage.

# 9

I was back in the darkroom at the *Mattino* preparing some new photographic plates when one of the reporters knocked on the door and shouted that I had someone waiting for me in the lobby.

I threaded my way through the crowded newsroom with its clattering typewriters out to the front desk where Rossi stood clutching his carpet bag. He had come straight from the train station. I broke into a big smile and hurried over to him.

"So Lombardi's coming?" I asked eagerly.

Rossi shook his head. "No."

I stood there in disbelief, my mouth open. I knew it wouldn't be easy, but I had truly expected Rossi to pull it off.

"What happened?"

He grimaced. "He left before I could catch him."

"Before you could catch him?"

"As soon as he finished, I pushed my way through the crowd, but by the time I reached the stage he had left."

I found chairs next to a window looking out onto the street and Rossi put down his bag. "Did you pursue him?" I demanded.

"I did. I ran round the back to the stage door and got there just in time to see his carriage disappear down the street. I rushed back to the hall, seeking someone who might know what hotel he was staying at, but nobody knew."

I felt sick to my stomach. All I could think of was Alessandra. She would be devastated.

We sat there in silence.

Finally I stood up. "Well, you gave it a try," I said.

"Maybe it's not over yet," Rossi replied. He pulled a sheet of paper out of his bag and thrust it into my hands. "Not if we can get this published in the *Mattino*. Can you help?"

He handed me the paper and I sat back down and started reading. It was a clever public challenge to Lombardi, drafted by Rossi on the long train ride home.

Rossi started by flattering Lombardi—I attended your recent lecture in Rome, professor, and found it exceptionally interesting and educational, etcetera, etcetera, especially your scientific investigations into Spiritualism. Then he introduced Alessandra.

> *Here in Naples, we have a woman who belongs to the humblest class of society. She is nearly forty years old and very ignorant. But when she wishes, be it by day or by night, she can divert a curious group for an hour or so with the most surprising phenomena. Firmly held by the hands of the curious, Alessandra levitates furniture, holds it suspended in the air like Mahomet's coffin, and makes it come down again with undulatory movements, as if they were obeying her will. She produces raps and taps on the walls, the ceiling, the floor far distant from her. She can make musical instruments—bells, tambourines—positioned in a corner of the room far beyond her reach play without touching them...*

I looked up. "You saw her do all that?"

"I did."

I turned back to the letter. Rossi understood that Lombardi would be skeptical of such preposterous claims, of course, so he was enclosing a newspaper story with an amazing photograph—mine—clearly showing a table suspended in the air, a full meter off the floor, with no wires, strings, or other contraptions visible, and the medium's hands, knees and feet not touching it in any way. It was the sacred duty and crowning glory of Science to investigate the unknown with an open mind. Failure to do so would erode the public's faith in Science, etcetera, etcetera.

> *The editor of the* Mattino, *Signor Venzano, assures me that his photographer, Tommaso Labella, is a sober, honest employee not known for playing tricks, and the newspaper will be happy to make available for your personal inspection the original photographic plate.*

That would be the first thing Lombardi would want to do. A lot of photographers were into tricks like double exposures to fake a ghost, which were really popular back then. I had produced a few myself when I worked for uncle Mario.

I returned to Rossi's letter. Since Lombardi found Mrs. Guppy's trance personality quite interesting, he is sure to find Alessandra's equally fascinating.

> *In addition to levitations, Signora Poverelli often falls into a mesmeric trance and "spirits of the dead" speak through her, most representing themselves as relatives and friends of the sitters, eager to pass on a message of hope, the location of a lost bracelet, or to beg for-*

*giveness for some misdeed they perpetrated in*
*life. On occasion, however, Alessandra is also*
*possessed by a spirit claiming to be the notori-*
*ous Fra Girolamo Savonarola, the Dominican*
*monk and heretic burned at the stake by the*
*Church in 1498.*

"*Maronna!*" I exclaimed. "You've actually seen this spirit?" Up until then, nobody had told me about Savonarola.

"Yes. Three times, now." Rossi stared out the window for a moment, lost in thought, then he turned to me. "But I'll tell you—each time it's frightened me. I don't like the idea of being in the same room with him."

"With his spirit."

"No, I mean with *him*," Rossi shot back. His vehemence caught me off guard. "He takes over her body, he possesses her." He shuddered. "He's *alive* again—and when Savonarola was alive, he was nasty." He shook his head in disgust. "He was a Dominican—his Order *ran* the Inquisition. When he shows up, you just feel this sense of…of menace."

I kept looking to see if he was pulling my leg, but he wasn't.

I heard a shout, and a pack of newsboys dashed through the lobby, papers under their arm, racing out to the street to hawk the noon edition. One boy bumped into our table, tripped over Rossi's travelling bag, and skidded across the marble floor, tossing a *scuzza* to us before jumping up and pursuing his friends. I looked up at the large clock above the reception desk. 10 AM. I needed to get back to work, but I also badly wanted to learn more about Savonarola.

"Was he really that evil?"

Rossi frowned. "Twisted might be a better description. He preached the love of God but burned people alive. I know more about him than I want to."

"You've read a lot about him?"

"In my second year at the university, I came across a poem he wrote called *De Ruina Mundi*—the Destruction of the World—and I decided to research his life for a paper I had to write. He knew how to frighten people. Late at night, when I was sitting in the library all alone, reading his sermons, I would start thinking of my own sins, imagining the punishment that awaited me, and I would actually start to tremble with fear."

"But why would the Church burn him at the stake? Scaring people is what priests are supposed to do."

"Priests aren't supposed to get into politics. That's the Pope's job." He looked at me. "What do you know about medieval history?"

"I read some poems from that period. That's about it."

He settled back in his chair. "The Medici family and their allies ran Florence when Savonarola began preaching there, and he went after them for their lavish, decadent lifestyle. In 1493 he prophesized that Florence would fall to an invader and, as God or luck would have it, the following summer Charles VIII showed up at the city gates with a French army eager to sack it. Savonarola convinced him to spare the city, and the awed Florentines replaced the Medici with Savonarola. He and his followers formed a government that would operate the city under the laws of God, not man."

Rossi paused. "Have you ever been to Florence, Tommaso?"

"No," I admitted. "But I've seen post cards."

"Today, everybody visits the Piazza della Signoria in Florence to gawk at Michelangelo's statue of David. In 1495, everybody flocked to the piazza to gawk at Savonarola. He drew crowds of 10,000 people, haranguing them for hours with his apocalyptic sermons and hellish visions of the End Days."

Rossi shook his head.

"He ordered prostitutes and sodomites burned at the stake. He recruited a children's army of 5,000 young boys and sent them door to door, frightening citizens into giving up to the flames of his *falò delle vanità*, his bonfire of the vanities, their playing cards and chess games, and lutes and recorders, their copies of Boccaccio's salacious tales, and their Renaissance paintings which glorified man's body instead of his soul. After one of Savonarola's sermons, Botticelli himself was so scared he tossed some of his artworks into the fire. The Last Judgment was coming any day, and he had been painting naked pagan goddesses."

Rossi shook his head. "Madness." He seemed lost in thought for a moment, then finished his story.

"Eventually people tired of his piety and sermons and began to rebel. They smeared shit on the altar in his cathedral, planted explosives under his pulpit to try and assassinate him as he preached, and eventually he needed an armed escort of a hundred men to travel around the city. When cardinals in the Curia tried to rein him in, he called the Church the "harlot of Rome," and denounced the pope as the Devil incarnate. Finally Alexander VI had enough and excommunicated him."

Rossi smiled grimly. "Then the citizens of Florence extracted their revenge. They hung Savonarola in chains from a wooden cross and burned him alive over a bonfire built on the exact same spot in the piazza where he had burned their worldly vanities. They jeered and spit and poked him with sticks as he screamed in agony. They kept the fire blazing for three hours, till his flesh was blackened and charred, then they broke the bones into little pieces, burned them to ashes and threw them into the Arno while citizens lined up on the Ponte Vecchio and pissed on them as they floated by."

Rossi looked at me. "He died filled with hatred for humanity—our sins, our weaknesses, our disbelief. Now he's back."

"But what can he do to us?" I protested. "He's just a spirit."

"For Christ's sake, Tommaso!" Rossi glared at me. "Have you forgotten what you saw the other night? If a spirit can lift a table off the floor, it can also hurl a vase across the room at your head. If a spirit can touch or pinch you in a séance, it can also slap or punch you. I don't like Alessandra calling on him. "

"Does she call on him often?"

Rossi scowled. "Whenever no other spirits respond. I've warned her to stop. She's never seen her twisted face with Savonarola's fiendish eyes staring out of her own sockets, or heard the venom spewing out of her own mouth. She's in a trance when he's possessing her, and when she recovers she remembers nothing. All she knows is that she produces her most spectacular feats when she allows him to take over her body."

He pulled his watch out of his vest pocket and shot a quick glance. "I'm late. I have a class to prepare for this afternoon and I need to get going. Can you read the final paragraph?"

I turned back to the letter. Rossi had wrapped it up nicely before finally baiting the hook with a few shekels.

> *The Spiritualist Society of Naples would like to invite you to visit us and investigate Signora Poverelli. We suggest that you attend three séances, as you did with Madame Guppy. We are prepared to pay your travel and hotel expenses, as well as an honorarium. We believe she is genuine, but if she turns out to be a fraud or a hysteric in your opinion, we believe you'll still find her quite entertaining.*

Rossi held out his hand. "My apologies for taking so much of your time. Can I leave this to you to handle?"

"Sure," I promised. "Count on me."

He reached under the table for his bag. "Even if Lombardi comes, Alessandra may perform poorly. But I've spent enough of my time and money on this." He put on his hat.

"If she fails, I'm done with her."

## 10

L ombardi's answer arrived a week later.
Venzano called Rossi and Alessandra to the newspaper and his secretary, Julieta, who everyone knew was his mistress, ushered us into his elegant, private office on the fourth floor of the *Mattino*.

I idolized Venzano. He had style. He always dressed smartly, a white walrus moustache accenting his tailored dark suits and polished black shoes. He collected the *macchiaioli* long before the Paris art world discovered them, and he cultivated exotic orchids from South America. A long-stemmed, purple cattleya from Costa Rica graced his desk. I learned a lot from him.

After we were seated, he leaned across the desk and handed Rossi a telegram he had received that morning from the *Mattino*'s correspondent in Torino. Alessandra and I waited nervously as Rossi silently read it. When he finished, he turned to Alessandra.

"I'm sorry, Alessandra" he said.

I watched the color drain from her face as he read the telegram to her.

> *Lombardi rejects offer Stop Not coming Quote Naples not exempt from Newton law of gravity Don't believe in miracles Do believe in mendacity credulity of common man Unquote.*

Alessandra snatched the telegram from Rossi's hand.

"No!" she shouted. "He must come. He must!" She crumpled up the telegram and flung it to the floor.

I jumped up. "Don't worry, Alessandra, we'll think of something."

Rossi bent down and retrieved the telegram, then passed it back to Venzano.

"Alessandra, it's over. He's not coming."

Venzano folded up the telegram. "Professor, do you have a comment we can run with the telegram?"

"Perhaps later," he replied, reaching for his hat. You could hear the resignation in his voice. Alessandra and I followed him out to the street where she refused to let him go.

"Professor, if we can just get him to come…" she pleaded. "Once he's here, I can convince him. I know I can! I know it! We can't give up. We'll talk about it after the service this week, yes?"

That's when Rossi dropped his bombshell.

"Alessandra, we're discontinuing the weekly séances."

"No!" she cried. "But why?"

"Some members object to the cost."

"But you can't! Oh, you can't! It's such a small amount."

Rossi stared at her for a second, then clasped her hands in his. "I'm so sorry about Lombardi, Alessandra. The failure is mine. I do believe you would have convinced him."

Rossi bowed then disappeared into the chattering lunch crowd thronging the street. I steered Alessandra over to a bench and helped her sit down.

She was silent for several minutes, staring at the ground. Then she looked up, tears in her eyes.

"Pigotti found the money," she whispered.

"What money?" I said.

"The money I was saving for Rome. He noticed the slit in the mattress."

"Oh God, Alessandra! What did you say?"

"I told him I was saving it for his birthday, to buy him something special. That I stole it from Rossi's wallet during a sitting."

"Did he believe you?"

"I don't know. He slapped me hard, then he took the money. It's all gone, Tommaso."

I tried to think of something to say, but I couldn't. I mean, what *could* you say? Her dream was over. At least Pigotti hadn't discovered the whole truth. She would have been dead.

A beggar woman cradling a dirty-faced child approached us with her hand out, and I tried to shoo her away. The city was filled with them, and you can't help them all. But Alessandra called her back, dug into her purse, found a few *soldi*, and handed them to her. Then she stood up, and extended her hand.

"Thank you for everything you have done for me, Tommaso. You've been a true friend."

"What will you do now?" I said.

"I don't know," she replied wearily. "Maybe Dr. Cappelli can help. His family has money. And I know he likes me."

"Will I see you again?" I asked.

She looked at me for a long time, then a soft smile appeared on her face. "You're a sweet boy, Tommaso. You're going to make some woman very happy someday."

Then she was gone.

# 11

I hid in the darkroom all afternoon, my head in my hands, thinking of Alessandra.

Try as I might, I couldn't come up with anything. Sick to my stomach, I was reaching for my hat to go home when Doffo stopped by to find out what had happened at the meeting.

Venzano had hired him a month before I joined, hoping his drawings would put more bite in our editorial pages, especially the war we were running against the mayor and his cronies. People were dying from eating rotten meat because the Camorra ran the slaughterhouses and owned the inspectors. At the time Venzano offered him a job, Doffo was working up in Rome as a cartoonist for a small Socialist weekly that couldn't always pay him.

He was skinny, near-sighted, and a *ricchione* with a boyfriend in the Vatican, but he was fearless. He studied Daumier in art school and had an acid pen. He worked hard at his craft. The Dreyfus affair was big news that year, and he followed *La Libre Parole* closely—studying how their cartoonist exaggerated the Captain's big nose, gave him a slouch, put him in ridiculous situations.

A light suddenly went on in my head.

"Doffo! Follow me," I said.

"Where?"

"To Venzano's office."

"Why?"

"I'll tell you on the way. Let's go."

I knew Venzano desperately wanted to keep the Alessandra story alive. He had a great business sense, and he understood what sells papers. He also had a soft spot for me—he saw a little of himself in me—and so when we arrived he waved us into his office. I wasted no time pitching my idea.

"We'll shame Lombardi into coming," I explained excitedly. "Let Doffo do a cartoon suggesting he's afraid to test Alessandra."

Venzano gave us an amused look, then nodded at Doffo. "Alright, what can you do with it?"

Doffo thought for a moment, then took the pencil from behind his ear and started drawing. I watched in fascination as he sketched out a woman in long flowing robes, which he labeled "Science," holding the torch of "Knowledge." She was scowling down at Lombardi, who's hiding under her skirts. The caption read "Lombardi Investigates the Spirit World"

I wanted to humiliate Lombardi. "No, make Lombardi a cat, hiding from a little mouse—Alessandra." Doffo grinned and quickly redid the sketch. Venzano stroked his moustache as he studied the drawing, then smiled. "Finish it up, and we'll run it next to Lombardi's telegram."

"Front page?" I suggested.

Venzano laughed. "Get out of here, both of you."

# 12

Lombardi's visit to Naples started off poorly.

He was still smarting from the *Mattino* cartoon when he stepped off the train at the Napoli Centrale station. Before leaving Torino, he had announced to a reporter from *La Stampa* that he would be attending one séance only, and he expected to be disappointed.

Rossi had booked him into the Palazzo, a short walk from the Main Post Office, a decent hotel but hardly *de luxe*. He should have known better. Lombardi wasn't some ghetto Jew. He came from a wealthy family, and besides, Northerners always look down on the South.

When I showed up at the hotel at eight the night of the séance, I found Lombardi in the lobby giving Rossi an earful—his room was too hot, mosquitoes buzzed him all night, the service was embarrassing, the hotel food both atrocious and suspicious. Rossi used my arrival to extricate himself and went off to find a bellman to call a carriage. When it finally swung by to pick us up, I hopped up in the front seat next to the driver and Rossi followed Lombardi into the back seat. Rossi leaned forward and tapped the driver's shoulder.

"Do you know your way to Corso Vanucci?"

The man hesitated. "*Si, Signore*, I do. Is that where you want to go?"

I looked back in surprise at Rossi. I had presumed the séance that evening would be held at his home near the university. Instead, we were headed for the Basso-Porto, a seedy part of Naples, down by the docks. I started to say something but he shot me a look and I kept my mouth shut.

"Yes," he repeated. "Corso Vanucci. Number 48."

"As you wish, *Signore*."

He snapped his whip and the horse trotted off. Lombardi and Rossi chatted away as I racked my brain, trying to think why we would be headed for that disreputable gehenna, then it hit me. The night I took the photo at Rossi's house, Alessandra told me she lived down by the docks.

We were headed for Alessandra's place.

We made our way across town, down the Corso Garibaldi past the railway station till we came to the Reclusorio, the city poorhouse, where we turned left onto Strada Marinella which runs southeast out of town, following the curve of the bay. Rain had swept the city that afternoon but by evening it had stopped and the heat and humidity had soared. The stink of rotten garbage soon mixed with the smell of stale fish, tar and salt air. The city sewer, built after the terrible cholera epidemic of '84 which killed 12,000 people and turned Naples into a mortuary, empties into the mud flats there. Lombardi pulled out a handkerchief and pressed it to his nose.

"I say, Professor, isn't there a more pleasant route to our destination?" he demanded.

The streets got progressively narrower and dirtier, and Lombardi fell silent. We finally arrived at Corso Vanucci. Dingy, flat-roofed, three-story tenements hung with laundry lined the narrow street down to the quay and the warehouses. The gaslights had already been lit, and we made our way down the rain-dampened cobblestones, the carriage forcing grumbling vendors to move their stands and press against the wall as we passed by. In the shadow of a doorway, a whore solicited a drunk, and a mangy dog nosed through a pile of garbage, hunting scraps to eat.

When the driver halted his carriage in front of Number 48, the astonished Lombardi turned to Rossi.

"Certainly you don't live here?"

But Rossi had already jumped out of the carriage. He shoved some money in the cabman's hand and started walking briskly towards the apartment. Lombardi hopped out and hurried after Rossi. He caught up with him at the curb, and grabbed his arm.

"I was told the séance would be held in your home. I demand an explanation!"

Rossi looked at him evenly. "This is where Alessandra lives, Professor."

"This is ridiculous!"

"You offer her one opportunity to perform. Fair enough. She feels most comfortable in familiar surroundings, and she chooses to demonstrate her powers here."

"That's outrageous! This is no place for a gentleman. I insist you take me back to my hotel."

Rossi shrugged his shoulder. "You can come with me or remain here on the street."

A pack of ragged, dirty-faced boys came running up to Lombardi and started yanking on his sleeve, begging for money. Lombardi raised his walking stick and they scattered, laughing and flinging rude gestures at him. Lombardi stood there for a moment, looking around. The carriage was gone. He had no choice. He muttered an oath, grimly gripped his cane like a club, and followed us up a dark, narrow staircase smelling of piss and garlic to Alessandra's third floor dump.

Give Rossi credit. It was a spectacular gamble, but he had gotten Lombardi there.

But could Alessandra deliver?

# 13

Pigotti was waiting for us at the door.

He nodded at Rossi, who had been there before, but he eyed Lombardi suspiciously.

The apartment was small and cramped—a parlor-kitchen with a small, high window open to the stink of the public latrine in the courtyard below, and off the parlor a bedroom. For Lower Town, it was a palace—most poor bastards in that part of town rent eight, ten to a room with no windows, sleeping on dirt floors with their chickens and pigs. But Pigotti ran the lottery and the gambling in the neighborhood for the Camorra, and could afford better.

Two elderly women I didn't recognize were seated at the table chatting with Alessandra when we stepped inside. A kerosene lamp burned brightly on the table, casting harsh, deep shadows in the corner of the room. Alessandra stood up as we entered.

Lombardi probably expected a gypsy fortuneteller, wearing bright colored skirts, and sporting bead necklaces and silver rings and bracelets. Instead, Alessandra was dressed completely in black. Her dark hair and the black, high-neck collar of her plain silk dress framed her pale, consumptive face, drawing your attention to her liquid eyes. She wore no jewelry. Alessandra stepped forward, offering her hand.

Lombardi was still fuming from Rossi's trick. "So, you're the woman who levitates tables and talks to dead monks?" he said sarcastically. Alessandra's eyes flared at his rudeness, but Lombardi had already turned his attention to the two women—*Signora* Damiano, president of the Spiritualist Society of Naples, and her companion who served as the Society's secretary.

Damiano grabbed his hand and pressed it to her ample bosom. "Professor, we believe you will witness miracles tonight which will change your mind about the question of survival," she gushed.

"*Signora*," he replied coldly," You have one night to produce your miracle. I'm not coming back here."

He turned to Rossi and told him he wanted to inspect the apartment. There wasn't much to inspect, but Lombardi did a thorough job. When he finished with the bedroom, he returned to the parlor and asked Rossi and me to turn the table and chairs upside down. He took the lamp, got down on his knees, and peered through his pince-nez looking for hidden wires or mechanical devices. Finally, he walked over to the kitchen window, closed the shutters and locked them.

"Can't you leave it open a bit?" Damiano pleaded, fanning herself. "We will all die of heat in here." A sirocco wind was blowing the week Lombardi visited, and the heat and humidity was oppressive. She looked to Alessandra for help.

"Professor," Alessandra said, "would you agree to ...."

Lombardi whirled around "No, I don't agree to," he snapped. "I didn't agree to a test in your apartment, but I'm given no choice." He stared hard at Rossi. "I am not a fool. I find this whole arrangement exceedingly suspicious."

He held out his hand. "Now, if someone will kindly give me the apartment key. I will lock the door and hold the key—after *Signor* Pigotti here is ushered out."

Pigotti's jaw dropped. For a second, he was speechless then you could see the color rise in his face. He stepped up to Lombardi, and dangled the key in his face.

"I remain in the room during all séances," he said in a soft, menacing voice.

I would have pissed in my pants. Amazingly, Lombardi didn't flinch. Maybe when you work with the criminally insane, like Lombardi did, you learn how to read them. Whatever, my opinion of Lombardi changed that night. He locked his eyes on Pigotti, his voice calm, measured.

"If you remain in the room," he replied, "I leave." He held out his hand again. "The key please."

Rossi had backed away. Alessandra thrust her hand out.

"Give me the fee. Quickly!"

Rossi pulled it from his coat pocket and handed it to her. Alessandra pushed past me and shoved the money into Pigotti's hand.

"*Caro*, take it! Take it!" She grabbed the key and pushed him towards the door.

Anger and avarice contested briefly on Pigotti's face before he finally jammed the money in his pocket, glared at Lombardi, and stalked out. Alessandra immediately slammed the door, locked it, and handed Lombardi the key.

"There. Are you satisfied now?"

Lombardi ignored her. He assigned us seats, starting with Rossi, who was ordered to sit at the opposite end of the table, furthest from Alessandra. Lombardi himself would sit next to Alessandra, controlling her right hand and knee. He wanted me to sit on her left, controlling her left hand and knee. He didn't care where Damiano and her friend sat. When we were all in position, he reached over and turned up the lamp. "It will remain at full illumination during the séance," he announced.

*Signora* Damiano rose to her feet.

"That's impossible!" she protested. "Bright light frustrates the work of the spirits, and can be dangerous to the medium."

"I'm sorry," he replied curtly. "Those are the requirements for my participation."

"Surely, Professor, you will not object to half-light?" Rossi pleaded. "I assure you that you will find the illumination adequate for your purposes."

Lombardi shrugged, and reached for his bag. "Then I am ready to return to the hotel."

"*Basta!* Enough!"

It was Alessandra. She marched over to the door and yanked it open.

"Get out! Enough of your insults, your rudeness, your suspicions. Get out!"

Everyone looked at Lombardi. My heart was in my throat. If Lombardi walked, her dream was over. Damiano and her circle would wash their hands of her, and Pigotti would dump her on the street. But you could only push Alessandra so far.

Lombardi stared at Alessandra for what felt like an eternity, then surprised everyone by folding his cards.

"My report will note that illumination was marginal," he announced stiffly. "I suggest we begin."

Everyone was exhausted, and the séance hadn't even begun.

# 14

I was looking forward to holding Alessandra's knee under the table.

We all joined hands, bowed our heads, and *Signora* Damiano led us in a *pater noster*—except Lombardi of course, because he was an atheist. I mumbled along. You always do a prayer before every séance to beg God to protect you from evil spirits. As Rossi said, When you summon the dead, you're opening a door to the spirit world, and you never know who will step through. You hope it's your dead grandmother, not Jack the Ripper.

When Damiano finished, she pulled a small, silver tea bell out of her purse and placed it in the middle of the table. Any spirits hovering around the room would be invited to announce their presence by moving or ringing it, she told Lombardi. Of course, spirits could use raps, taps or touches as well, but the bell seemed to attract the spirits' attention, and the Society always used it in its séances. Lombardi was instantly suspicious. He insisted on examining it carefully before returning it to the table himself. His skepticism was becoming extremely annoying and tiresome.

At last, Lombardi nodded to Rossi who turned down the lamp, everyone settled back into their chairs, joined hands, and Alessandra started the séance.

"Spirits, we know you are here," she intoned. "Give us a sign."

I didn't bring my camera that night. Venzano had wanted me to photograph the séance, but Rossi vetoed it. The Mattino could interview Lombardi after the séance. He didn't want extra pressure on Alessandra, because she was already nervous. Cappelli had promised to join the circle that night, but at the last minute had to go to Palermo on business. Alessandra wanted me to take his place. She knew I believed in her. I had seen the table levitate. I had even photographed it. Alessandra was convinced believers increased her psychic powers.

I did my best. I closed my eyes and tried to will the spirits to show themselves, but I didn't really know how, and eventually I gave up and opened my eyes again.

The lamp cast a flickering pool of light on the table. Everybody's fingers were resting lightly on the top, like we were instructed. *Signora* Damiano and her assistant sat there with their eyes shut, simpleton smiles on their expectant faces, their bony, hands clutching Rossi's. Across the table from me, the lamplight danced on Lombardi's glasses. His eyes were wide open, his watchful attention alternating between the bell on the table and Alessandra, who fidgeted uneasily in her seat. You could see the concentration on her face, her eyes scrunched shut, whispering to herself, straining to summon up the dead.

The minutes passed.

You never know what will happen at a séance. Sometimes you sit there in the dark, holding hands for an hour and nothing happens. The room was stifling, everyone was sweating, and the smell of Lombardi's cologne hovered in the fetid air.

I was delighted to hold Alessandra's hand. She had delicate long fingers, like a pianist, soft and warm to the touch. Occasionally she would squeeze my hand, but it didn't mean anything. She was in constant motion, shifting her position, giving out soft sighs. My other hand rested on her knee. I was supposed to make sure she didn't use her knee to lift the table. I could feel her leg through the silk of her dress. I wondered what Lombardi felt as he held her other knee in the dark. I imagined Pigotti, kneeling outside the door, eye glued to the keyhole, going crazy.

After fifteen, twenty minutes of nothing happening, Damiano and her assistant spontaneously launched into a hymn, hoping to increase the "psychic energy" in the room, but Alessandra angrily shushed them. She closed her eyes and resumed her whispered pleading. "Spirits come. Spirits come!"

Across the table from me, Lombardi wore a smug look on his face—even making a show of pulling out his pocket watch to check the time.

In the apartment next door, a couple started arguing. The voices on the other side of the wall got louder and angrier, then we heard a dish shattering, screaming and cursing, a slap, then a woman bawling. Then kids joined in the wailing.

Alessandra finally opened her eyes, and locked her frowning gaze on the bell. As she did, she swept her hands towards the bell, then slowly drew them back towards herself, commanding the bell to come to her.

"*Vieni! Vieni!*"

I shot a glance at Lombardi who observed impassively from his seat. The bell was a good half-meter beyond her extended fingertips, making it impossible to reach, and no tablecloth to pull on to tug the bell towards her. Lombardi let her drag his hand along with hers, an amused look on his face.

Suddenly the bell jerked forward, almost toppling over.

Everyone saw it, even Lombardi. Alessandra gave a sharp cry of excitement and frantically redoubled her efforts, dragging our hands along with hers towards the bell. She was shouting now.

*"VIENI! VIENI!"* Come! Come!

We all crowded around the bell, faces flushed with excitement, even Lombardi. But as quickly as it happened, the show was over. The bell refused to move any further.

Alessandra let out a howl of frustration.

We had been sitting there for almost an hour. At the end of the table, Rossi slumped despondently in his chair. I felt terrible for Alessandra.

"Shall we call it a night?" Lombardi announced.

Everyone looked to Alessandra.

"No!" she replied.

"Alessandra, maybe it's time..." Rossi started.

"NO!" she shouted. "Not yet."

Everyone sat back down, unsure of what else to do, and the séance continued.

I took control of her hand and knee again. Tired of the whole night, I shut my eyes and let my mind wander. She was sweating from her exertions, and I could feel the heat from her body. I imagined myself slipping my hand under her dress, running it up between her thighs, and playing with her *fica*. After a while, I could feel a bulge in my trousers which I couldn't touch but which continued to grow and stiffen. Now we were in bed, and I was on top of her, and she was moaning and I could hear her calling out my name—"Tommaso...maso." Then Alessandra's leg shifted again, snapping me out of my fantasy, and I realized she was whispering to herself.

"*Babbo.... Babbo....*" Father. Father.

She was calling Savonarola.

Down at the end of the table, Rossi's eyes were fixed on Alessandra, and he looked scared.

# 15

It all happened so quickly.

Alessandra's hand suddenly went limp in mine. She slumped against my shoulder, slid off and fell forward, striking the table with her face, and lay there motionless, a thin tickle of blood coming from her forehead. She didn't appear to be breathing. Panicked, I looked to Rossi but he shook his head—leave her alone. Across the table, Lombardi reached for her wrist.

"We need to check her pulse."

"No!" Rossi shot back. Lombardi hesitated, then sat back.

A shudder ran the length of Alessandra's body, then she began to jerk and twitch violently, her head banging against the table. Once again, she lay there lifeless, unmoving. I let go of her hand and, as I released it, the fingers on her hand slowly began to curl up into a claw, and what looked like blisters appeared on her skin. I thought I was hallucinating. I reached forward and touched the hand, and suddenly—I can't explain how—I found myself there, on the Piazza della Signoria, in the jeering crowd, watching him twist and burn, smelling his fat sizzle, hearing his screams of agony.

I recoiled in horror, fighting the urge to vomit, and as I pushed away from the table Alessandra's head jerked up.

Her eyes had rolled up into her head.

When they rolled back, they were no longer Alessandra's.

The dull green eyes staring back at us were heavy-lidded, almost reptilian. From her throat came a deep, menacing growl—a *man's* voice.

*"Oh ye of little faith!"*

Lombardi drew back, surprise and confusion on his face.

"Alessandra?" he said.

*"Alessandra's not here, Jew,"* the voice hissed. *"You see the world through human eyes. You're blind to the world of spirit, like all unbelievers. What shall I do to open your eyes?"*

As we stared in amazement, the small, silver bell rose slowly into the air and hung there in the gloom, tinkling softly, *ting, ting,* as if taunting Lombardi.

"It's a trick!"

Lombardi lunged for the bell. As he fell forward onto the table, the bell shot across the room as if flung by an invisible hand, smashing against the wall.

Lombardi stood up and shook his fist at Alessandra.

"It's all a trick! I know it is! How do you do it?" he demanded.

*"You're filled with pride, like all academics,"* the voice snarled. *"Unwilling to trust your own eyes. O unbelieving and perverse generation, how long shall I suffer you?"*

Lombardi jerked backwards as an invisible hand slapped him hard, knocking him clear off his feet, his glasses flying off his face.

My heart was in my throat. Rossi kept his eyes glued on Alessandra as he reached down, retrieved them from the floor, and passed them back to the dazed Lombardi. I sat absolutely motionless, praying that Alessandra—or the demon that possessed her—didn't turn its eye towards me.

*"I allow this only because my beloved daughter Alessandra begs me,"* the voice spat out. *"Someone from this side wants to talk with you."*

In the gloom directly behind Lombardi's chair, a gray, formless mist seemed to slowly materialize, gradually taking human shape, like a photograph being developed in the darkroom—blotches of grey, then the first faint edges emerging from the depths, a suggestion of something coming forward, then slowly resolving itself before your straining eyes into a figure—a body, arms, legs, and finally a head.

An old woman.

The vaporous apparition leaned down and started gently stroking Lombard's hair, and I could hear it whisper something in his ear. Lombardi uttered a cry and whirled around.

"Mama! Oh, mama!" he cried.

A luminous hand with exquisite delicacy applied itself to his lips, preventing him from continuing. The figure bent down and gave him a kiss on the head. Lombardi grabbed the spirit's hand, but it seemed to melt into his own, and the phantasm started to lose its shape, dissolving into a grey smoke.

Lombardi gave a wail, snatched the oil lamp from the table and thrust it into the shadows, but the spirit was gone. He frantically swung the lamp in a circle, and as the light passed Alessandra's face, she let out a scream, striking the lamp with her burned claw, and knocking it from his hand. The lamp smashed to the floor, snuffing out the light, and we were pitched into total darkness.

In the blackness, I could hear Lombardi sobbing.

# 16

Lombardi called us all to Rossi's office the following morning.

I had slept fitfully, my dreams haunted by Alessandra's grotesque transformation, and woke up groggy. Nobody knew what Lombardi would do next.

I caught an early tram to Piazza Amore and hurried up Corso Umberto to the university. The sun was up and the street sweepers were already hard at work. It promised to be a hot and muggy day, but the air was cool along the tree-lined boulevard. When I reached the university, I found the broad steps fronting Rossi's philosophy building packed with protesting workers and students. A flag of the Italian Socialist Party fluttered from a second story window, which meant it was Filippo Turati's boys. On the top step, a thin, bearded man in rolled up shirtsleeves paced back and forth, leading the crowd in a chant.

"Free Passanante!" Free Passanante!"

Giovanni Passanante was one of us, from Naples, a kitchen cook who hated popes and monarchs. In '78 when King Umberto visited Naples, Passanante attacked him with a knife during the parade, but the assassination failed and he was sentenced to life in prison. I'm not an anarchist, but you have to understand, people were desperate back then. The old order had collapsed and things were worse in the South than before Garibaldi.

I maneuvered my way through the crowd and climbed up to Rossi's third-floor office where I found him and Alessandra leaning out the window, cheering on the demonstrators down on the street. Rossi pointed down at a bushy-bearded young man who was reading out a list of demands. "Niccolo Raffa—one of my philosophy students," Rossi said proudly as he closed the window.

Alessandra looked fantastic. Her luxurious black hair that morning was pinned back with a tortoise shell comb, a white linen scarf encircled her neck, and a silver bracelet hung from her left wrist—so different from the night before. Alessandra never wore jewelry when she performed a séance. She believed Savonarola would be angry because he disapproved of female vanities. But the spirits had retired with the dawn, and her eyes were bright with excitement. She knew she had performed spectacularly. After she came out of her trance, Rossi had told her everything.

She paced the room. "Where is he?" she pouted. "He's late."

My eyes wandered around Rossi's office. It was large, pleasant, book-filled room, flooded with morning sunlight from three tall, curtained windows, the air stale with tobacco smoke, black walnut bookshelves climbing to the ceiling, filled with tomes and antiquities. Rossi noticed my gaze linger on a small marble bust on his desk. He smiled.

"Thomas Aquinas. One of the more distinguished alumni in our university's 600-year history. A Dominican, like Savonarola—but a philosopher who celebrated reason instead of a twisted piety."

A loud knock interrupted him. Alessandra gave a cry and hurried to the door. Professor Lombardi rushed in.

"I apologize for being late," he announced. "But I had to make my way through the commotion on your doorstep. We have our own share of these disturbances in Torino these days."

Rossi steered Lombardi to a high-backed, leather chair before offering him a coffee. Lombardi waved it away. He had dark rings under his eyes and he looked like he had slept in his clothes. He put down the leather portfolio he was carrying, slumped into his chair, then took a deep breath, as if to compose himself.

"I must apologize for my unprofessional behavior last night," he began. "I assure you I do not normally act that way. I have spent the night trying to reconcile what I observed last evening with my lifetime of scientific training." He rubbed his forehead as if trying to erase what he had witnessed at Alessandra's apartment.

"I am quite familiar with the subconscious mind, and the manias and hysterias it easily falls prey to, not to mention the tricks and limitations of human perception. But I freely admit to being baffled—even astonished—at what I observed with my own eyes last night."

Behind his desk, Rossi broke into a smile. Next to me, Alessandra moved to the edge of her chair, her hands clasped tightly together, nervously biting her lip. Lombardi pressed on.

"Like all of you, I observed the bell rise up off the table, and hover in the air, then fly across the room. The light was dim but adequate, and I could discover nothing attached to it. I also felt a powerful blow to the face, without observing the perpetrator of that phantom blow. These are facts, and I am treating them as such. Perhaps the human mind has unknown powers Science has yet to discover—telekinetic powers which are available to us in exceptional situations, or peculiar states of mind."

Lombardi gazed across the room, as if recalling something, then turned to Rossi.

"I will share a story with you, Professor," he said, "an experience which has perplexed me for many years. It may or may not have a bearing on this matter." He paused, gathering his thoughts, then launched into his odd story.

"My youngest brother was always sick as a child. Three times a day, he had to swallow a foul-smelling medicine which he detested—a thyroid extract—which the maid served to him in a silver spoon, part of an antique tea set from Austria which my mother inherited and cherished.

"After several months of this, my brother finally refused to take another spoonful. The maid was afraid of disobeying my mother, but couldn't force him to drink it, so she held it out and waited for him to relent. My brother told me that he stared at the spoon, and felt a burning anger inside him, and the spoon began to turn hot in the maid's hand, as in sympathy with his feelings, then the spoon handle began to curl up. She dropped it and fled the room, and was dismissed shortly afterwards by my mother who believed she had carelessly bent it.

"My brother showed me the spoon. I didn't believe him, and accused him of trickery, but he never changed his story. Indeed, after that, he submitted meekly to the medicine—frightened, as he confided to me, of seeing something scary happen again."

He paused to clean his spectacles with his handkerchief, then returned them to his nose.

"I reluctantly confess to another unusual experience I had last night—an astonishingly vivid hallucination of what appeared to me to be my deceased mother. I attribute this to the fact that the anniversary of her death is fast approaching, and she has understandably been in my thoughts." Lombardi sighed. "However, this visual hallucination was also accompanied by an auditory hallucination—I distinctly heard my mother's voice. Such a combination is not unknown in the literature, but exceedingly rare."

Lombardi nodded towards Alessandra.

"There was of course the possibility of ventriloquism on the part of *Signora* Poverelli, but that suspicion collapsed when the voice in my ear spoke to me in the native dialect of my race, and addressed me by an affectionate, pet name known only within my family. Though I cannot accept the existence of spirits, I admit to having no explanation for these facts."

"Professor, *we* saw the spirit too." Rossi insisted. "How do you explain that?

I chimed in. "I heard the voice. A woman's voice—an old woman."

Lombardi shook his head. "The psychological conditions conducive to a collective hallucination were strong last night. You desperately wished to see a miracle, and therefore you did." He paused. "What I cannot understand is that I certainly did *not*, yet fell ill to the same hysteria."

Rossi pressed him. "And your explanation for Savonarola? Do you honestly believe that was Alessandra speaking to you last night? That she's capable of counterfeiting such a voice and manner?"

"I don't believe in voices from a Spirit World," Lombardi replied. "I believe Savonarola is simply a primitive, secondary personality of Miss Poverelli's."

Alessandra leapt to her feet.

"*Basta*! You and your stupid theories. You know nothing about the spirit world."

"And you know nothing about Science," Lombardi shot back. "Sit down!" He reached into his portfolio and took out a piece of paper.

Alessandra remained standing, her eyes blazing.

# 17

Alessandra wasn't prepared for Lombardi's stunning offer.

He closed his portfolio and looked at her. "I have a proposition for you."

"And what is that?" Alessandra returned, eyeing him suspiciously.

He took a deep breath. "I said I *believe* Savonarola is a creature of your mind. But even if I'm right, I have no explanation for the bell, or my mother's hallucination. I want you to come to Torino to be studied by me, for six months. For your service, you will receive room and board, and a fee of 3,000 *lire* upon completion of that service."

We let out a collective gasp.

Three thousand *lire* was a lot of money. You could live in Naples on that for several years—or you could escape to Rome and start a new life.

Alessandra was speechless.

"A generous offer," Lombardi continued, "but it comes with an equally generous number of conditions." He sat back in his chair and stared at Alessandra. "I'm risking my professional reputation by undertaking this investigation. You frankly risk nothing. To earn your fee, you must earn, and maintain, my trust. My requirements are spelled out in this agreement. They're not negotiable."

He handed her the agreement, then sat back in his chair.

"First, you will live in the staff dormitory at my asylum during those six months, under the supervision of my chief female warden. You will not leave the premises, nor receive visitors, without my prior approval. Is that understood?"

Alessandra nodded.

"Second, you will make yourself available for testing by me or anyone I invite to test you, under whatever test conditions I propose, whenever and wherever I choose. After I conduct my own tests, we will spend the summer touring the Continent. This will allow professional colleagues of mine, in Vienna, Munich and other cities, to conduct their own tests. I will, of course, cover all your travel expenses.

"Third, you will act like a woman of good breeding. I expect you to control your temper, and speak politely at all times. If you're caught drunk, in a compromising situation, or involved in a scandal of any kind, your employment will be immediately terminated. You will also forfeit the fee—all 3,000 *lire*. This way we both have something to lose. Do you accept?"

Alessandra eyed him calmly. "Four thousand," she replied.

"Three is more than generous. I will also be paying your room and board."

Alessandra waved the agreement at him. "You'll find an excuse to dismiss me when the time comes to pay my fee."

"I'm a gentleman. My word is my bond."

"And I'm from Naples. Four."

A thin smile appeared on Lombardi's face. "You're an unusual woman, *Signora*. You would do well at the card table. Agreed—but one slip-up and you will find yourself back in Naples without a *centesimo*."

Alessandra flashed me a triumphant smile, grabbed Lombardi's pen, and laboriously scratched out her name on the contract. Lombardi passed it to Rossi who affixed his signature as witness, then turned to Alessandra.

"I expect you in Torino within the month. I will arrange a train ticket for you."

"I'll return with you."

Lombardi raised an eyebrow. "That's not possible. I leave for Torino tomorrow. You will need to secure your husband's permission for your employment in Torino. I am sure that will take some time, though I trust you will be successful."

"I'll have it by tomorrow."

Lombardi stared at Alessandra, then waved his hand. "As you wish. A ticket in your name will be left at the station master's office. Ask for the *capostazione*." Rossi passed him the signed contract and the professor slipped it into his portfolio.

"Please understand, *Signora* Poverelli. My offer of employment is for you alone. Your husband is not to follow you to Torino, to visit you while you are in my employ, nor attempt to attend any of the sittings I will arrange. If he shows up, you may consider your employment terminated."

We all crowded around Alessandra to congratulate her, including Lombardi. He was smiling now. The negotiations were finished and he had his precious scientific experiment in hand.

"Will you be making a statement to the newspapers?" Rossi asked.

"Yes," Lombardi replied. "I meet *Signor* Venzano at the *Mattino* at noon to deliver this statement." He pulled a paper out of his jacket pocket and handed it to Rossi. "In it, I describe the levitation of the bell and the phantom blow to my face, but at this point I am not prepared to reveal the hallucination I had of my mother."

Outside the window, the protestors had started singing *Inno dei Lavoratori*, the workers anthem, then the singing abruptly stopped, and I suddenly heard shouting and then the clatter of horses' hooves on pavement, followed by loud screams and curses.

I raced over to the window and stuck my head out. The police were stampeding the crowd, bashing protestors with their clubs and sending them running for their lives. Several students already lay bleeding on the ground. I watched a policeman draw his saber and urge his steed up the steps in pursuit of Rossi's student, Niccolo. He ducked into the building just as Rossi joined me at the window. In the hall outside Rossi's office, you could hear the sound of running feet. Rossi turned to Lombardi.

"*Signore*, for our safety, we must all leave this building now, quickly."

We followed Rossi down the back stairs and ran out into the courtyard where we found students grabbing rocks and sticks and hurrying back into the building. Lombardi paused to catch his breath, panting from the exertion. Rossi urged us forward. I looked over at Alessandra and there was fire in her eyes.

"We should stand with them, Tommaso!"

She reached down, grabbed a stone from a pile, whirled around, and stood there defiantly, then let out a yell and flung it towards the gate which the police were battering down.

"Free Passanante!"

I started laughing. I yanked her hand and we started running again.

"God, I'm going to miss you, Alessandra!" I said.

# 18

Lombardi's conversion sent a shock wave through scientific circles in Europe.

The *Mattino* ran his statement in the evening edition, and I kept a copy. Here, I'll read it to you.

> I am aware that my decision to pursue the investigation of *Signora* Poverelli will cause a stir of surprise and incredulity in the scientific and academic community. If there ever was an individual in this world opposed to the claims of spiritism by virtue of scientific education and, I may add, by instinct, I was that person. I have made it the indefatigable pursuit of a lifetime to defend the thesis that every force is a property of matter. But I glory in saying that I am a slave to facts. There is no doubt in my mind that genuine psychical phenomena are being produced—levitations and movements of objects most likely produced not by spirits of the dead but by some as yet undiscovered power of the human mind.
>
> I see nothing inadmissible in the supposition that, in hysterical and hypnotized persons,

the stimulation of certain centres of the brain, which become powerful owing to the paralyzing of all the others, may give rise to a transmission of cerebral or cortical forces which can be transformed into a motor force. In this way, we can understand how a medium can, for example, raise a table from the floor, pinch someone by the beard, strike him or caress him—phenomena frequently reported during séances. Do we not see the magnet give rise to an invisible force which can deflect a compass needle without any viable intermediary? What is needed is the development of instruments to establish the reality of this occult force. We were unable to detect the existence of the X-ray until science gave us photography and the vacuum tube. Once we had the necessary instruments, doubt was dispelled.

As for my scientific colleagues, there surely will be doubt. Let us seek the truth together. I will be making arrangements for *Signora* Poverelli to be scientifically tested in my laboratory, and I challenge other scientists to do so as well, with the results of these tests—whether favorable or unfavorable—to be shared with the public upon completion.

Say what you want about Lombardi—the guy had a pair. He knew he would be accused of bringing witchcraft within the domain of science, but when he made up his mind, he didn't back down. He was ready for a fight.

Me, I was ready for a drink. Alessandra was heading to Torino, leaving me behind. After we escaped Rossi's building, Alessandra headed home and I accompanied Rossi and Lombardi to the *Mattino,* feeling miserable. Doffo stopped me in the hall and begged me to tell him what happened at the séance, but I told him to fuck off and locked myself in the darkroom. Shortly after lunch, he pounded on the door.

"Venzano wants to see you."

"Get lost!" I shouted through the door.

"Fuck you, then. I've given you the message."

I opened the door, expecting him there, but he had already disappeared. I walked up to the fourth floor where I found Julieta, Venzano's secretary, impatiently waiting for me.

"What took you so long?" she hissed. "Follow me."

Lombardi and Venzano were having a cigar when I entered the office and took a chair. Venzano looked at me with an air of amusement, then turned to Professor Lombardi.

"A rascal, Professor, but intelligent, hard-working and ambitious. I'll miss him."

I looked bewildered at Lombardi who studied me for a moment then floored me with his announcement.

"I want you to come to Torino to serve as my photographer to document my investigations and experiments with Alessandra."

I looked over at Venzano, my heart racing. He had a huge grin on his face. He leaned forward in his chair.

"The pay is double what I can offer, Tommaso, and I would have lost you anyway in a few years. Besides I'll still get something out of your worthless hide for a few more months. Professor Lombardi has agreed to give the *Mattino* first crack at any stories and photographs he shares with the public."

"Does Alessandra know about this?" I stammered.

"Not yet," Lombardi said. "If you accept, she will be informed. But before you decide, there is one other duty I will expect you to perform for me. I don't pretend to understand Alessandra. We have nothing in common. You're from Naples, you understand her, and I've observed enough people in my profession to recognize that she trusts you, perhaps even likes you."

My face turned red, but I said nothing.

"She's a woman," he resumed, "and like all members of the weaker sex, is governed by her emotions. It will be your job to make sure that she doesn't get homesick and quit, or get in trouble during the six months I need to investigate her. After that, I don't care what happens to her."

He picked up his cigar. "Do we have a deal?"

I could hardly believe my ears. "You can count on me, Professor," I replied.

I pumped Lombardi's hand, thanked Venzano, and took off. As I passed Julieta's desk, she was bent over putting letters into a filing cabinet, her pretty rump in the air begging for a pinch. It was my lucky day, and hers.

"*Arrivederci, cara*" I said, as she jumped up to slap me. "I'm off to Torino."

# 19

I didn't know how Alessandra would escape Pigotti, but I knew she would die before she would miss the train.

I got to the station as the sun was coming up, determined to surprise her.

The Piazza Garibaldi fronting the Napoli Centrale was already filled with carriages when I got there, and the station was crowded and noisy, with people hurrying here and there, shouting to each other, dragging boxes and trunks, frantically searching for their train. I wandered around hopelessly lost until an old porter pushing a luggage cart directed me to the office where Lombardi had left my ticket. After the yawning clerk passed me the envelope, I opened it and stared at the ticket for a moment, feeling a bit disoriented and a little scared. I had never been outside Naples. I wondered what Alessandra was feeling.

I jammed the ticket deep into my trousers in case there were pickpockets around and headed into the main hall to buy a coffee. A sleepy waiter took my order and I sat there, my bag safely wedged between my feet, wondering how I could best surprise Alessandra. Lombardi had bought Alessandra and me second class seats in the same compartment, so I decided I would board the train early, and be sitting there when she showed up. Or maybe I should hide behind a pillar and jump out when she came running up. I nursed my coffee and passed a half hour playing with various ideas before finally deciding to wander around and see the shops. The train didn't leave until 9:00, and it wasn't even 7:00 AM.

I was half way across the main hall when I heard a shout.

"Tommaso! My God!"

I turned around and there was Alessandra, sitting on a bench, clutching a battered portmanteau. Her hair was a mess, and her eyes puffy, but she had a huge smile on her face. She jumped up from the bench and spread her arms in welcome.

"You've come to see me off?"

"When on earth did you get here?" I laughed. "I was planning to surprise *you*."

"I slept here last night." She steered me to her bench and combed her fingers through her hair. "I look like a mess, I know. But I've been busy."

She looked around, then reached in her bag, pulled out a tin box, and cracked open the lid just enough for me to peek inside. The box was stuffed with *lire*. I stared at the money, then back to her for an explanation.

"I got all my money back, Tommaso," she said triumphantly. "The money he stole from me."

"The money you hid in the mattress?"

She started laughing. "And *his* money too."

My jaw dropped. "Jesus Christ, Alessandra, he'll kill you!" Grabbing her own money was bad enough. Grabbing Pigotti's was insane. He was probably already looking for her.

I glanced nervously towards the station entrance, half expecting to see Pigotti charging through the door in hot pursuit. I grabbed her bag and hustled her off the main concourse and into a side hallway leading to the public lavatories.

"Does he know you're headed for Torino?" I demanded.

"No," she shot back. "I'm not stupid, Tommaso."

"He didn't ask you what happened at the meeting in Rossi's office?"

"When I got home, he was waiting for me. I told him that Professor Lombardi wanted to conduct some more séances with me—here in Naples. " Alessandra looked away for a moment, and when she turned back to me, I could see the rage in her eyes.

"He said he was doubling the fee, then he grabbed me and threw me against the wall, and said I was a whore, and a bitch, and he knew what I was doing in the dark with Lombardi and Cappelli, and when I stopped making money for him he was going to kill me."

She shoved the tin box back into her bag.

"Well he'll have to find me first," she said fiercely. "And I'll have a knife ready, and maybe I'll kill him instead."

"How did you manage to escape?"

"He went out drinking with his friends, and I grabbed my clothes and the money box and came to the train station, and slept here." She grimaced and rubbed her shoulder. "God, Tommaso, that was a hard bench."

A nanny towing a young girl glanced at us curiously as she headed down the hall to the women's lavatory. I handed Alessandra her bag.

"Wait till you see your cell in Lombardi's asylum," I teased.

She finally noticed my bag.

"What's that?" she said.

I thought fast. "A bag Lombardi wants you to take to Torino for him."

I walked her to the track and when the conductor finally called 'all aboard', she took my hand.

"Thank you for everything you've done for me, Tommaso," she said. "If only you could come with me."

86

I pulled the ticket from my pocket.

"Maybe I will."

Alessandra looked at the ticket, then at me, then let out a whoop of joy and smothered me in her arms, dancing me around the platform.

"You and me, Tommaso! We're in this together!"

The whistle blew and the train started to pull away from the platform.

"Get on! Get on!" I laughed. We ran alongside, passengers gawking out the windows as I pushed her up the steps, threw our two suitcases on, and leapt aboard just before the platform disappeared. Alessandra ran to our seat, yanked up the window, and stuck her head out.

"*Arrivederci*, Napoli!"

It was goodbye forever, as far as she was concerned. She was never coming back.

The train picked up speed, the dirty streets and dingy tenements of Naples slipping backwards, the city falling behind, until we burst free onto a sunlit plain of orchards and vineyards and turned north for Torino.

For one brief moment in time, we were both on top of the world—we were both getting out of Naples, and setting out together on a grand adventure. For Alessandra, Rome was no longer an impossible dream, and I had a shot at my own dream. I would be spending the summer touring Europe, with Alessandra in the next hotel room and Pigotti stuck in Naples. It was a long shot, but a boy could get lucky.

# 20

Lombardi's manservant was waiting for us with a carriage when our train pulled into Porta Nuova station in Torino. Lombardi took Alessandra straight to the asylum where his staff warden, *Frau* Junker, a stocky German woman with short-cropped hair, welcomed her with a scowl. The building reminded me of a prison—which it was for the patients. Three stories, with bars on the windows, a great iron door opening into a dark, empty, grey, stone courtyard where several miserable souls wandered about gesturing and talking to themselves. This was going to be Alessandra's home for the next six months. Lombardi's valet handed Alessandra's valise to the warden. I hopped out to accompany Alessandra to her new living quarters, but Lombardi ordered me back in the carriage. He was impatient to get home.

Alessandra turned to me with a nervous look. "Tommaso, promise you'll visit me often."

"I'll be here so often you'll be sick of me," I promised, squeezing her hand. "We Neapolitans have to stick together."

When our carriage pulled up at Lombardi's house, I found a small room prepared for me in the servant's quarters. It wasn't much, but it was more cheerful than Alessandra's situation. Lombardi's mansion was impressive—a large, two-story home with a porte-cochere and a well-tended, formal garden filled with rosebushes just beginning to bud. He employed three domestics in the house, and they all spoke

French. Lombardi's wife was a cold, peevish shrew from Geneva who ran the house with an iron fist. I stayed out of her way and so did Lombardi. As we Italians say, the husband is like the government at Rome, all pomp; the wife is like the *mafia*, all power.

Three days later, a maid handed me a letter from Cappelli for Alessandra, and one for me from Rossi, back in Naples. Pigotti had come around, looking for Alessandra, and seemed surprised that she had gone to Torino. He told Rossi he urgently needed to contact her. Could I send Rossi her address in Torino? He'd pass it on.

I figured the chances of Pigotti showing up in Torino were slim. It was a seven-hundred kilometer train trip, and guys like him didn't even know how to buy a ticket. But she *did* take his money, and added insult to injury by running off with Lombardi. He would seek revenge. Just to be safe, I made up a fake address and posted it back to Rossi.

The first month at the asylum was rough on Alessandra. I can't count the number of times she threatened to quit and I talked her out of it. Cappelli was also sending her long letters every week, which I delivered to the asylum.

Lombardi suspected mediums were evolutionary defectives, preserving genetic traits found in our primitive ancestors, including the caveman's magical thinking and a susceptibility to trances. He ran Alessandra through a series of bizarre tests, assisted by *Frau* Junker, whom we nicknamed the "Kaiser." He clamped a metal device on her head and spent a day measuring her skull, penciling in the centimeters, logging the slope of her forehead, the angle of her jaw, the width of her eyes. He drew blood, made her pee in a bottle to examine her urine, repeatedly pricked her with needles to test her sensitivity to pain, and shone lights in her eyes because some mediums were epileptics. He filed everything away in his notebook.

> "*She has the hyperaesthesic zone, especially in the ovary. She has the hole in the esophagus that women with hysteria have, and general weakness in the limbs of the left side. She exhibits a persistent cough from tuberculosis, a disease endemic in Naples. It is easier for her to be magnetized than hypnotized. Methodical passes of the hand over her head can free her from headache, and quiet her agitation of mind, and upward magnetic passes can provoke her in a state of semi-catalepsy, just as passes in the reverse direction can remove distortions of her muscles and paresis.*"

Did Alessandra feel anything different or special just before a levitation? Lombardi dissected the mystery.

> *She experiences a desire to produce the phenomena; then she has a feeling of numbness and the gooseflesh sensation in her fingers; these sensations keep increasing; at the same time she feels in the lower portion of the vertebral column the flowing of a current which rapidly extends into her arms as far as her elbow, where it is eventually arrested. It is at this point that the phenomenon takes place.*"

Alessandra the laboratory rat.

One day, she casually mentioned that after every sitting her hands felt like they were burning—like they had been dipped in lye. Lombardi pounced on it. Rontgen has just discovered the X-ray and Lombardi wondered if her hands radiated some form of undiscovered energy. Alessandra was forced to spend a boring afternoon pressing her hands to unexposed photographic plates.

Weeks passed before he finally sent out invitations to the scientific and academic elite of Torino to attend a presentation on Alessandra.

The day of the talk, we set out early in Lombardi's carriage for the city. The June sun was up and shining, and the morning fog had burned off, but the air was chilly and my teeth were chattering. I was brought along to answer any questions raised about my famous photo, which *La Stampa* had run, but Alessandra stayed at the asylum. Her stomach had been acting up all week, and she begged off.

I pulled my jacket tight, and jammed my hands in my pockets, marveling at the snow-covered Alps in the distance. I regretted not having a camera—I could have sold the shots to Uncle Mario. As we trotted along, the scenery slowly changed from wheat and rice fields to an industrial area with lots of factories, and finally the city itself. Everything was new and exciting. Unlike Naples, the city was clean, with wide boulevards, broad and straight and lined with elegant shops. I couldn't keep my eyes off the women walking in and out of the stores. They were beautiful—tall and slender, with blue eyes and pale complexions, elegantly dressed, with an air of sophistication about them. You don't see women like that in Naples.

We crossed the Po at the Vittorio Emanuele Bridge and, just as we entered the piazza, a loud horn suddenly sounded behind us, spooking Lombardi's horses which reared up, nearly tipping over our carriage. I spun around and saw the first automobile in my life. It was a Fiat 3.5 CV—one of the first machines Agnelli ever built. I never dreamed that one day I would own an automobile myself.

The talk wasn't until that evening, and Lombardi spent his day at the university, polishing his address, while I spent mine haggling in shops, selecting a camera and ordering the photographic supplies I needed for the tour. Lombardi spared no expense when it came to his scientific investigations, and I ended up with a new Underwood Tourograph camera—better equipment than I had back at the *Mattino*.

We arrived at the Minerva Club at seven o'clock that night. It's a distinguished-looking building fronting the Piazza Mafalda, just a door down from the winter residence of the Royal House of Savoy. Professor Carlo Gemelli, our host, was waiting for us in the library with a glass of sherry in his hand, watching the staff busily arranging high-backed leather armchairs in a semi-circle around a polished table in front of the fireplace. Gemelli taught physics at the University, but he came from a noble family and had money. You needed both to get into the Minerva Club. Lombardi was a Jew, so he couldn't join, but he had successfully treated Gemelli's wife for melancholy, earning Gemelli's gratitude and the invitation.

"Expecting a small turnout, Camillo?" Gemelli inquired, signaling to a waiter for another sherry. Lombardi handed his hat and cane to a servant and flopped down into a chair.

"We might get thirty." He pulled a list out of his vest pocket and studied it, a look of disgust on his face. "Lots of regrets and excuses."

Most of Lombardi's university colleagues had begged off. He was already the butt of whispers and jokes—most suspected the whole thing was just a clever ploy by Lombardi to set himself up with a Neapolitan mistress he could enjoy after hours. Lombardi's wife certainly wasn't happy about his new scientific interest. Daniela, their pretty upstairs maid, told me she overheard them loudly arguing about Alessandra the evening we arrived.

"Did Dr. Renard respond?" Gemelli asked.

"Yes. He's coming."

A waiter appeared at Lombardi's elbow with a sherry. Gemelli raised his glass.

"Bravo! It's not often we mortals get to rub elbows with a Nobel Laureate. He's a physiologist. I'm still astonished he's interested in this stuff."

"Renard's privately funded a small institute in Paris to quietly pursue his investigations. Rossi says he's enlisted some of his medical students from the University of Paris to help him recruit mediums to test. The French are ahead of us in this game, Carlo, but we can catch up."

Gemelli laughed. "I'll leave the mysteries of the human mind to you and Dr. Renard. I'm interested in the workings of nature." He put down his glass and pulled out a cigar. "I've been corresponding with Marconi recently, and it occurs to me that maybe electromagnetic radiation is somehow involved in this queer levitation business—though I'll be blunt: I suspect trickery."

I stood in the corner of the room and carefully observed the two of them as they bantered back and forth—how they sat back comfortably and confidently in their chairs, how they held out their empty glasses, knowing a waiter would immediately respond, how they cut the tip off their cigars, and how they lit them evenly around the edge with a match. If you want to be a gentleman, you have to strut like one—one is treated the way one carries oneself. Nowadays, of course, I'm a member of the Circolo Canottieri here in Rome, but back then the only way people like me entered the Minerva was through the delivery door. When I went to take a piss, I discovered even the water closet had a marble floor.

When I returned, the room had begun to fill up and a half-dozen additional guests were crowded around Lombardi. A bell rang, and the doorman announced a new arrival.

"Professor Giovanni Sapienti, and guest."

Lombardi hurried over to shake the astronomer's hand. Sapienti was famous for his observations of Mars, and his presence that night was another small triumph for Lombardi.

Sapienti's eyes twinkled. "Professor, I bring you another sympathetic ear tonight." He turned to the portly, balding middle-aged gentleman at his side. "May I introduce my close friend, Dr. Ettore Parenti, Director of the Egyptian Museum here in Torino. He is fascinated by occult mysteries."

Parenti stepped forward and bowed. "Like you, Professor Lombardi, I enjoy digging for the truth among the dead."

Gemelli laughed. "Always prepared with a *bon mot*, Ettore. I hear you're off to Cairo to open another tomb this summer?"

Before Parenti could respond, the bell sounded again.

"The Honorable Dr. Alexander Baranov, Imperial Counselor to Tsar Nicholas II of Russia." I was in awe. Russian nobility, Nobel Prize winners, world-famous astronomers—believe me, it was an unforgettable night for a nobody from Naples like me.

Baranov, sporting a long white beard and a chest full of medals, hobbled over to Lombardi to introduce himself. Baranov was in his seventies, and a big name in Spiritualist circles where he was known for his investigations into telekinesis. Baranov's wife was a spirit medium herself. Baranov hosted D.D. Home when the famous medium visited Russia in happier days, and entertained the Tsar's family with his table levitations. At one séance in the Tsar's apartment, Home spoke with some invisible spirit then went over to the fireplace, used his hand to stir the embers into a flame, knelt down and picked up a burning coal, and held it in his bare hand for thirty seconds, before returning it to the fire, leaving everyone astonished.

"I hurried down from St. Petersburg as soon as I received Professor Rossi's telegram," he declared, offering a trembling hand to Lombardi. "I understand from Professor Rossi that Dr. Renard will be here tonight—accompanied by Nigel Huxley, unfortunately. I give you fair warning."

Gemelli raised an eyebrow in mock concern. "Is this Huxley someone we should keep an eye on? Pinch the silver?"

Baranov grimaced. "Far worse than that, I'm afraid—at least for Professor Lombardi here. He's the grand inquisitor for the London Society for the Investigation of Mediums in England, and he takes no prisoners. We've clashed many times. He believes all mediums are charlatans and frauds." Baranov turned to Lombardi. "You would be wise, Professor, to keep him at arm's length until your experiments with Alessandra are completed."

Gemelli looked at Lombardi. "Sounds like an unpleasant fellow. Who invited him?"

"Renard." Baranov interjected. "Huxley is on his way back to England from India, and is staying as a guest of Dr. Renard in South France for a few days. Renard asked if he could bring him along."

"India? What on earth was he doing there?"

Baranov grimaced. "Back from the hunt. Pursuing poor Madame Dubrovsky. God help her." We heard a commotion in the hall outside, and Renard made his entrance.

Followed by Baranov's nightmare.

## 21

Nigel Huxley was a *stronzo*, a turd.

All Englishmen are—they enjoy humiliating other people. Huxley viewed Italy as a country stinking of stupidity, superstition and criminality.

Everyone turned and stared when Huxley entered the library.

Tall, athletic, and impeccably dressed, he moved with the confidence of someone used to competing and winning. When they shook hands, Huxley towered over Lombardi. It was a dogfight between them right from the beginning. Lombardi was smart, but Huxley was his intellectual match. I later learned Huxley graduated summa cum laude in law from Cambridge where he eviscerated opponents in debates. The English rarely bother to learn any other language but their own—why should they, they run the world—but Huxley was an exception. He spoke impeccable French and Italian, and passable German as well.

Huxley was also a street fighter. He relished a bare-knuckle scrap. He rowed for Cambridge, and once broke an opponent's nose in the boxing ring. Huxley pursued his investigations with the devotion of a monk. Women threw themselves at him, but he never married. He lived alone in a tiny bachelor's suite at the Athenaeum Club in London— one small bedroom and a sitting room—but it didn't matter since he only slept there. His days were spent on the hunt, and he channeled all his energy into his investigations. He had a genius for detecting the mechanics of fraud.

"Professor Baranov tells us you're just back from India where you were hotly pursuing some woman," Gemelli said to Huxley. "Perhaps you could entertain us with the story before we begin our formal program tonight." He looked over at Lombardi. "That is, if Professor Lombardi here would be gracious enough to delay his presentation a bit longer."

Baranov glared at Huxley. "As entertaining as Mr. Huxley's tall tales may be, I believe we have all gathered here tonight to hear Professor Lombardi talk about Alessandra."

Parenti jumped in. "I don't know about you, sir, but I'm still young enough to handle two women in one night. Come, Mr. Huxley. Let's hear a bit about this mysterious *femme fatale* who's captured your attention."

Everyone turned to Lombardi. I could see he was annoyed at the request, but he nodded and Huxley took command of the evening.

"A dried up old mummy would be a more accurate description, Professor," Huxley smiled, "but I found Madame Dubrovsky to be an ingenious—one might even say gifted—impostor.

"Her great grandfather served as a General in the army of Catherine the Great, but she inherited a mystical streak, wasting her childhood in his library reading fairy tales, French grimoires, and the mystic Dostoyevsky. After a brief, failed marriage to the vice-governor of Armenia, she escaped to Constantinople where she met up with a Russian countess and the two traveled arm in arm through Egypt and the Middle East."

Parenti gave Huxley a wink. "Devotees of Sappho, eh?"

Huxley smiled. "Respectable women are not attracted to mediumship, Professor. I find them invariably odd in terms of their sexual appetites. But they eventually separated, and

Madame made her way to the caves and jungles of Hindustan, where she found a little, brown-skinned guru and started receiving messages from spirits who called themselves…" Huxley paused to light his cigar, cleverly holding us in suspense before deadpanning "…the Ascended Masters dwelling in the sixth dimension." He waited for the laughter to subside. "Curiously, these exalted spiritual beings preach a rather disappointing stew of communism, free love, and suffragette nonsense, which our priestess of Isis turned into a queer religion and a profitable book business."

"I object, sir!" Baranov interjected angrily. "Jesus preached the same message of sharing our wealth with the poor in the Gospels."

Huxley knocked the ash off his cigar. "Forgive me, Doctor. I'm a lawyer, not a theologian. But I believe you're mixing up Saint Mark with Karl Marx."

"*Touché!*" roared Gemelli. Even I had to laugh at that one.

According to Huxley, Dubrovsky bewitched a wealthy American industrialist in London into bankrolling a salon and she set up court, smoking her opium cigarettes and entertaining London's upper crust at séances where messages of spiritual instruction from the Enlightened Ones mysteriously materialized in the darkness. After the lamps were turned up, Dubrovsky passed around these letters to her astounded sitters. Everyone in London was clamoring for an invitation. The Earl of Sussex attended a séance and suggested the *London Times* do a story on her, and the *Times* asked the Society to check her out first.

"So you somehow managed an invite?" Gemelli asked.

Huxley chuckled. "You don't turn down a request from the Society. The president's wife is a cousin of the Prime Minister."

The Society had been founded by a group of prominent Cambridge academics interested in metaphysics, and the society's board was loaded with influential, upper crust people, including the editor of the *London Times*. But shortly before the scheduled sitting, Dubrovsky decamped to India with her American millionaire.

It was too late. Huxley was after her.

The Viceroy of India had boarded at Eton with Huxley's uncle, and hosted Huxley in Bombay where he spent three months investigating her. He discovered one of Dubrovsky's Hindoo acolytes named Gandhi had studied law in London, and made his acquaintance. Through him, he befriended her personal staff and secretly put two of them on his payroll. They passed on to him copies of Dubrovsky's personal correspondence and Huxley matched her handwriting to the letters supposedly written by the Enlightened Ones from the astral plane. They also tipped him off to a secret trap door in the ceiling of the séance room in London which allowed Dubrovsky's confederates to drop the epistles down onto the séance table when the lamps were extinguished.

"Bravo, sir!" Gemelli exclaimed when Huxley finished. "Is every Englishman a Sherlock Holmes? Your race seems to have a passion for police work. Take a bow."

Huxley smiled. "They were a gang of vulgar tricksters in league with one another." He turned to Baranov. "It will all end up in my report."

Baranov reached into his coat, pulled out a telegram, and shook it in Huxley's face. "And so will my rebuttal, sir! Shame on you! Endorsing the scurrilous lies promoted by two discharged employees—for theft, mind you!—who were only too happy to slander Madame Dubrovsky. She has sent me her side of the story and I intend to make sure it is heard."

"I look forward to reading it," Huxley replied coolly. "Meanwhile, Professor Lombardi has been exceptionally patient, so I suggest we cede the floor to him."

# 22

Huxley could command an audience, but Lombardi matched him that evening.

He described his invitation from Rossi to come to Naples, and his dramatic sitting with Alessandra. Lombardi deliberately left out his mother's ghost, but his excitement was infectious as he described Alessandra's bizarre personality transformation, the bell suddenly jerking forward on the table, how it rose slowly in the air and hung there for at least three seconds, even sounding a note before being flung across the room by an unseen hand, and finally the stinging slap to his face from some invisible force.

"I freely confess, before I encountered *Signora* Poverelli I did not consider it worthy of the dignity of a *savant*, and a naturalist, to be present at such spiritistic séances. I shared that degree of distrust and suspicion which should always accompany the observation of the abnormal. Yet these telekinetic phenomena are incontestable facts—for I cannot deny what I have seen with my own eyes."

He looked around the room.

"However, let me be clear. I do not believe in the supernatural, spirits of the dead, or the absurd doctrines of Spiritualism. The force which moved that bell was not a spirit from a non-existent afterlife. It was produced by the mind of Alessandra herself."

He described Alessandra's unhappy childhood, including being forced to witness the murder of her father, powerless to do anything about it. "My hypothesis is that her repressed, inner rage, focused on an object or person, produces the telekinetic levitations, raps, pinches, and blows frequently reported during her sittings. But her most dramatic telekinetic effects are produced when this *soi-disant* Savonarola personality emerges."

He was used to dealing with psychopaths in his asylum for the criminally insane, but Alessandra's transformation was unsettling, even to him. He could understand why an earlier, superstitious age believed in demonic possession.

"Frankly, I wasn't prepared for the hatred which emanated from this Savonarola personality—a rage that was barely contained and, if let loose, appeared capable of wreaking severe injury."

He stared into space for a moment, then shook his head.

"Many years ago, on a hike through the countryside, I knocked at a farmhouse hoping for a glass of water. The door was flung open, and I was surprised by a vicious dog on a short chain, fangs bared, eyes burning, mere centimeters from my face. Fortunately, the dog's master had a good grip on his beast." He grimaced. "I did not get the feeling that *Signora* Poverelli had a secure grip on hers. I hope to explore this with Dr. Freud in Vienna."

Lombardi paced back and forth, throwing out questions which demanded Science's attention. Were mediums like Alessandra freaks of nature? Or were we all capable, in certain extreme mental states, of moving objects with our minds? Did weather—temperature, barometric pressure, humidity—have any effect on telekinetic powers? There was so much to learn! *Andiamo!* Let's go!

The crowd erupted in an ovation of approval, and Gemelli signaled to the waiters to serve the brandy. Lombardi returned his notes to his portfolio, then turned back to his audience.

"I'm sure some of you have questions. Shall we start with our host?"

Gemelli pointed his glass at Huxley. "I'll defer to our English guest. I'm curious what he has to say about all this."

Everyone looked at Huxley.

# 23

Huxley stubbed out his cigar, rose to his feet and walked to the front of the room. He stood there for a moment, as if collecting his thoughts, then launched his devastating cross-examination.

"The first question I suggest we ask is not *how* Madame Poverelli's telekinetic powers work, but whether she *has* any."

He looked around the room, a condescending smile on his face. "Are we dealing here with telekinesis ... or trickery?"

Lombardi stiffened.

Huxley fixed his gaze on Lombardi.

"I presume that Alessandra knew in advance that you would be coming to her apartment? Several days, or even a week before you visited her?"

Lombardi looked puzzled. "She was expecting me, yes. Professor Rossi told her."

"And the séance took place in Alessandra's apartment. Is that correct?"

"Yes. I was frankly surprised. I expected it to be held in Professor Rossi's home."

"And who changed the location?"

"Professor Rossi."

"Did he say why?"

"Yes. He said Alessandra felt more comfortable there, and she performed best in familiar surroundings."

Huxley raised an eyebrow. "So Alessandra knew in advance you were coming, and she picked the place for the séance, her own apartment—a place she is familiar with, a place she has furnished to suit her taste—or her needs...."

Lombardi turned red as it finally dawned on him where Huxley was leading him. "I'm not a fool, Mr. Huxley. I recognized the opportunity this gave to *Signora* Poverelli to cheat if she wanted to. I thoroughly inspected the premises before we began."

"So you inspected the premises for concealed doors, or hidden mechanical devices. Tell me, Professor—are you familiar with the magician's trade?"

"No," Lombardi shot back. "Are you?"

"Oddly enough, Professor, I am. I find that knowledge quite helpful in my business." He smiled, then continued. "Did Alessandra cooperate with you when you requested permission to search her apartment?"

"Yes. For the most part."

Huxley cocked his head. "Meaning?"

"*Signora* Damiano objected to having the window closed and locked."

"*Signora* Damiano, the head of the Spiritualist Society of Naples, and good friend of Alessandra's. But you wisely insisted, given that it provided access to the room from the outside?

"It was a reasonable request under ordinary circumstances. It was extremely hot and humid that night. But I felt it needed to be closed and locked for my purposes that evening."

"I applaud your caution, professor. Did your inspection before the séance began also include an inspection of *Signora* Poverelli's person?"

Lombardi shot him a look of disgust. "No. Is that something you regularly do in your trade, sir?"

Huxley turned to the group. "I'm sure all of us here to-night would enjoy such an assignment," he said. He waited until the laughter stopped. "Alas, most mediums are reluctant to allow men to play in their petticoats. That's why I always bring along a woman friend to perform the inspection. Women have been deceiving men since the Garden of Eden. They've had centuries of practice."

"Your suggested protocol is duly noted," Lombardi replied stonily.

Huxley smiled. "Indeed, we caught one clever vixen bringing to her sittings a bell which she would place on the table—for the 'spirits' to ring—while concealing a second bell in her skirt. In the dark, it's quite difficult to tell exactly where a sound is coming from."

Huxley paused for a second to let his audience ponder that troubling point, then resumed.

"And the illumination in the room…was the light adequate?

"Bright enough to observe everything clearly, including Alessandra's movements."

"But you were not observing in full light?"

"No."

"And I see you wear…spectacles."

Huxley picked up his brandy glass, took a sip, then put it back down on the table.

"So let me understand, if I may, Professor. Alessandra knew in advance you were coming, the séance was held in her apartment, you attempted an inspection… "

"*Conducted* an inspection! A damn thorough one!"

"My apologies….conducted an inspection of the apartment, though not an inspection of *Signora* Poverelli's person, who performed her magic in dim light… "

Lombardi exploded. "Damn you, sir! Enough! I know what I saw that night!"

Baranov hopped to his feet, "Hear! Hear!"

Lombardi stepped towards Huxley, his face flushed, and jabbed his finger in Huxley's chest. "Do you think I would risk my professional reputation if I weren't completely convinced of that? Knowing that people like you would be waiting to attack my observations, to ridicule me?"

Gemelli rose from his chair. "Gentlemen! Gentlemen! Please!"

Huxley raised his hands in mock surrender.

"Forgive me, Professor. I wasn't there, and you were. But if I were a betting man, I'd wager a hundred pounds that your Alessandra is a jumped-up trickster."

We all let out a gasp.

Huxley dropped his bombshell. "Did you know Alessandra's first husband was a street magician?"

Lombardi looked like he had been punched in the stomach.

"How would you know that?" he finally said.

Huxley nodded at Renard. Renard looked embarrassed.

"I was told that by Professor Rossi," Renard said. "I'm not sure how he learned that. But yes, that is what he told me."

Lombardi looked at Huxley. "Your point?" he said weakly.

"You don't find it both convenient and suspicious that your Alessandra was married to a magician—and has had twenty years to perfect the tricks she may have learned from him? I think the conclusion is obvious."

I felt sick.

"Objection, Mr. Huxley." Renard rose to his feet. "We can all agree that Madam Poverelli had the opportunity to cheat. But the possibility of fraud is not proof of fraud. The question is, did she? What would be helpful is for Madame Poverelli to demonstrate what she can do—under conditions acceptable to an investigator with your experience. May I make a proposal?"

He looked at Lombardi.

"Professor, you would be wise to learn more about Alessandra before you launch your public tour of Europe. If Mr. Huxley's suspicions are correct, it is far better to know now."

He turned to Huxley. "As Mr. Huxley here knows, I own a small, private island in South France, on the Cote d'Azur, where I have a summer cottage. I would be happy to host a private sitting there. Mr. Huxley has spent the week as my guest, so he is familiar with the layout of the building, and its isolation should appeal to his suspicious nature. If Alessandra is employing confederates, they'll have to swim three kilometers to assist her, with no place to hide when they get there."

Huxley smiled, and Renard continued.

"If Mr. Huxley is willing to spend a few more days as my guest, I suggest we meet on Ile Ribaud for a séance with Alessandra. Mr. Huxley will set the rules for the evening—I will act as the referee should you strongly object to some condition he imposes. With Mr. Huxley's permission, you may want to bring a photographer. Last but not least, gentlemen, we all agree to accept the results, whether favorable or unfavorable to our position. Do I have your concurrence?"

Huxley, slouched in his chair, waved his acceptance. "Agreed."

"Agreed" Lombardi replied grimly.

I wasn't listening.

My mind had already jumped back to the photograph I had taken of Alessandra and the levitated table, hanging in the air. After developing the plate, I had studied it with a magnifying glass for almost an hour, reluctant to accept what I had witnessed. But I couldn't find anything I couldn't account for—a wire, a string, a lifted knee or slyly placed finger. Nothing.

Except for a thin, faint, vertical shadow parallel with the table leg, where the flash bounced off—what? Something. But what? And did Alessandra have anything to do with it?

Suddenly I felt scared for Alessandra.

# 24

Huxley wasted no time coming after Alessandra.

He was a master at intimidation, and it was easy to understand how some little cockney trickster working the London séance circuit would pee in her knickers if he turned his attention towards her game. He expected to land a quick knockout punch.

When we arrived at the train station for the trip to Ile Ribaud, Lombardi hurried forward to the first class carriage to join Huxley and Renard. Sapienti had also decided to come along. Alessandra and I went to buy food. It was six hours to Genoa, and another 14 hours up the coast by boat before we could reach Toulon, and we were traveling second class. We weren't welcome in the dining car.

We boarded at the conductor's *tutti a bordo* and dropped into our seats, loaded down with our luggage and a big basket of bread and sausages. A plump woman and her three children followed on our heels and squeezed into the bench opposite us. Across the aisle, a small, wide-eyed boy dressed in Sunday clothes sat next to a fat monsignor who had his nose stuck in his breviary, mumbling his Hours. The remaining seats in the car were grabbed by a dozen sailors from the Royal Navy who had sloughed off their uniforms, pulled the window curtains, and launched a noisy dice game.

By the time the train reached Asti, we had a card game of our own going, and a picnic spread out on our laps.

Alessandra invited the mother and her kids to help themselves to our larder, which they eagerly did, the little boy playing the jew's harp between chomps of bread, his sister dancing along as she stuffed her own mouth. Alessandra always played *scopa* with reckless abandon, and I steadily piled up the points. I had just captured her Knave, and she was swearing like a sailor herself, when we looked up and there stood Huxley in a white linen suit.

He fixed his icy blue eyes on Alessandra.

"One must play one's cards wisely, *Signora* Poverelli—or suffer the inevitable consequences."

No *buongiorno*, no introduction. Nothing.

He turned to me. "If you will allow me to sit down for a moment … ?"

I jumped up from my seat and removed my hat. Alessandra looked confused.

"*Scusa, Signore,* do I know you?" she asked.

"No, but you shall," he replied.

As he stepped past me, I poked Alessandra. "*Signor* Huxley. The Englishman Dr. Lombardi told you about." She had never met him.

Huxley sat down, adjusted his trousers, languidly leaned back on the bench, and gazed out the window for a few seconds, watching the countryside pass by. Finally he swung around to face Alessandra, leaned in close, and whispered in her ear.

"I know your game. You're a pathetic fraud, and a waste of my time. You may fool Dr. Lombardi, but not me."

Alessandra's jaw dropped. So did mine.

He drew back and stared out the window again, not even deigning to look at us. "I've exposed a dozen cheats smarter than you. I know what you'll do, and how you'll do it." He nonchalantly brushed a spot off his suit. "If you try any of your silly tricks on Ile Ribaud, you will return to Naples a topic of amusement, not amazement. Do you understand?" As the color rose in Alessandra's face, Huxley picked up the Queen of Cups from the scatter of cards on the bench beside him, studied it, then rose to his feet and handed it to her. "My advice, *Signora* Poverelli? Fold your cards while you're ahead."

The show was over. He had dropped by, delivered his threat, and was ready to return to first class for a cigar and a glass of sherry, confident his preemptive strike had scared the shit out of her.

Instead, Alessandra grabbed the bread knife and leapt to her feet.

"*Vafanculo!*" she replied. Up yours!

Huxley blushed—he didn't expect *that* response, though he should have. You don't insult a Neapolitan to his face, and certainly not Alessandra. He looked at her calmly.

"Language one would expect from someone of your class."

I snatched the knife from Alessandra, scared she would use it, and shoved Huxley, knocking him backwards.

"Leave her alone!" I said. Huxley recovered his balance and turned towards me.

"Ah, the little photographer boy who created the fake photo. Tell me, how long have you been her confederate in this scam?"

I shoved him again, harder. "Leave her alone!"

He grabbed my elbow and yanked me up close. "You little guttersnipe!" he snarled. "When I'm done with her, perhaps you and I can go a few rounds in the ring. How does that sound to you?" My heart was pounding in my chest.

Alessandra jumped forward and slapped him in the face.

"*Cazzo!*" Prick!

Huxley glared at her, red-faced. Down the car, the sailors stopped their dice game and began to whistle and cheer her on. Let him have it, lady. Bastard! Asshole! Huxley turned and stomped back to his carriage. I had to physically restrain Alessandra from chasing him back to his car. She was spitting mad.

# 25

Alessandra was spoiling for another fight, but I wasn't. Lombardi had warned her about her temper, and the consequences if she couldn't control it. As the train pulled into Genoa where we would disembark to transfer to the ferry, I lit into her.

"Do you want to be sent back to Naples?" I shouted. "Your husband will kill you. You stole his money, for Christ's sake—remember?" I was pissed. "And think of someone other than yourself for once. If you're sent home, so am I."

That stung her. Whatever faults Alessandra had, she was loyal to her friends. For the rest of the trip, she made an effort to avoid Huxley, and we reached the Cote d'Azur without another scrap.

Renard's man was waiting for us with two boats at the small harbor in Hyeres when we finally arrived the next morning. In the distance, across the sparkling, blue water, the Ile du Grand Ribaud rose up out of the bay in the blinding, noon sunshine, white gulls lazily circling in the sky above. I could make out a small lighthouse on one tip of the flat island but nothing else.

Gaston and his young son Henri hurried forward to grab our bags. Lombardi and Sapienti looked uncomfortable and out of place in their dark suits and ties, but Huxley and Renard had already donned casual summer clothes and leather sandals. In his short-sleeved mariner's shirt, Huxley's athletic build was conspicuous. He would have killed me in a fight. I watched as he pulled a square, leather box from under the pile of luggage, swung it easily to his shoulder, and stepped sure-footedly into the boat, ignoring Gaston's offer of a hand. Renard followed, helping Lombardi and the unsteady Sapienti into their wooden seats at the bow.

Alessandra and I were assigned to Henri's skiff along with the luggage, my camera gear, and supplies for the weekend. The kid settled into his seat, grabbed the oars, and I untied the rope and shoved us off. Alessandra kicked off her shoes, closed her eyes and leaned back, letting the sun warm her face. Henri said something in French I didn't understand, and giggled. Alessandra let her hand play in the sparkling water as we headed out into the bay.

"God, Tommaso, I miss the sea." She unbuttoned the cuffs of her blouse but didn't roll up her sleeves. The cigarette burns Pigotti gave her were probably still there. "I used to walk down to the docks and watch the kids fish, and look out to the sea and imagine all the different places in the world the boats were going to."

I laughed. "You could have been a cook on a boat bound for Borneo."

She opened her eyes and grinned. "I know how to row, you know."

She hiked up her dress, slipped into the seat next to Henri, and grabbed an oar. Henri laughed, and the two of them started stroking together. I thought she would have us going in circles, but she pulled in rhythm and we powered right along. God knows where she learned that. Half way across the bay, we were closing on Lombardi's boat, and I'm sure she wanted to overtake them to thumb her nose at Huxley, but a wave caught her oar in a tangle with Henri's and we slid onto the beach a distant second. Huxley had already hopped out with his box and their gang had started up the beach.

In Naples, I never cared for the ocean. It stinks. Ile Ribaud was different. The scent of lavender infused the salt air, and white clouds floated in a blue sky above our heads as we scrambled up a steep, narrow footpath from the rocky beach. When we reached the top, Henri pointed to a low, stone cottage atop a small rise a sizeable hike from us. The island was mostly burnt grass and low bushes with an occasional olive tree, and the heat soon had us sweating despite the sea breeze.

Henri played guide, cheerfully babbling away in mixed up Italian and French, pointing out the sights—the lighthouse which Napoleon had something to do with, the small building next to it where he and his family lived—*"mon casa"*—and three shallow, rectangular ponds which we skirted along the way. I later found out they held poisonous jellyfish Dr. Renard used in his scientific experiments. I'm glad I didn't put my hand in the water.

Henri's mother, Capucine, was waiting at the door to greet us when we arrived, and led Alessandra to her room. Henri showed me to mine. As we passed by the verandah, I saw Lombardi and Sapienti had removed their coats and ties and everyone was busy lighting up cigars. Once our bags were dumped in the room, Henri headed back to the beach to pick up the luggage, Capucine busied herself in the kitchen, and Alessandra and I started for the verandah.

Renard intercepted us with his black dog Barbet, a large, friendly mutt who took an instant liking to Alessandra, jumping up and licking her face. Alessandra bent down and hugged him. Renard smiled and handed her the leash.

"Take him. He needs a walk," he said. "We're meeting with Monsieur Huxley to go over his requirements for the sitting tonight, and I don't think you're presence is welcome." He smiled. "Tell me, what exactly *did* you two talk about on the train? He was in a foul mood when he returned to his seat."

"He can go to hell," Alessandra shot back.

I winced. Renard looked at her quizzically.

"Alessandra, Monsieur Huxley has a right to be skeptical. He's uncovered the most shameful tricks played by the seemingly sweetest ladies. You need to earn his trust. And mine, too. But if you can produce the phenomena Dr. Lombardi believes he observed in Naples, you'll find no stronger champion than me."

Barbet let out a loud bark, tugging at the leash. Renard patted his head then pointed to the door. "Take Barbet to the beach, find a stick and toss it in the surf. He loves to swim."

I followed Renard out to the verandah, and found the others settled around a rough wooden table that Capucine had decorated with a vase of pretty wildflowers and a yellow bowl filled with oranges. Gaston was circling the group, a bottle of red wine in his hand, filling glasses. The view was superb. It looked back across a lovely bay crowded with holiday sailboats to the village of Hyeres and its white-washed houses running up a pine-covered hill crowned by a castle. The Brits had discovered the town years earlier, and half the street signs were in English.

Huxley ignored me as I pulled up a chair. Renard delivered a welcome toast, then turned the stage over to Huxley who pushed aside the flowers and placed his mysterious leather box in the center of the table. For the first time, I noticed it had a lock.

"Rule one in this business, gentlemen," he announced. "Never let the medium furnish the target objects." He removed a small key from his pants pocket. "Rule two. Never allow the medium access to them at any time." He sprung the lock and lifted the top. We all leaned forward as he pulled out a small silver bell and held it up for us to see.

"The test I propose is simple. I am challenging *Signora* Poverelli to duplicate the bell levitation she allegedly produced in Naples for Professor Lombardi here. Preferably, it will not be accompanied by a slap to the face similar to that suffered by Dr. Lombardi that night. If our insolent 'Fra Savonarola' attempts that outrage, she will get her ears boxed. But the test comes with a small twist.....

Huxley reached into the box again, and pulled out a small glass jar and a brush.

"....The bell will be coated with this carbon lampblack." He looked pointedly at me. "Anyone who manages to touch the bell will find a surprise left behind on their fingertips. Should any movement or levitation of the bell occur, we will stop the sitting immediately and I will conduct a careful inspection. Further, the bell itself will sit under this...."

He lifted out a large glass vase, flipped it over, and dropped it over the bell.

"...to discourage the use of strings, wires, sticks or other popular tools of the trade commonly employed by 'spirits' to move an object in the dark."

Renard leaned back in his chair, a look of amusement on his face. "Rather clever, Nigel."

"Indeed. Well done, sir," added Sapienti. Next to him, Lombardi sat in silence.

Huxley peered into the box. "Oh—and one final change to Dr. Lombardi's protocol in Naples." He pulled out a length of thin cord. "This time, *Signora* Poverelli will be tied to the chair, hand and foot."

Renard put down his wine glass. "Isn't that a bit too much, Nigel?"

Huxley bristled. "I never underestimate the acrobatic skills of these charlatans."

"But that presumes in advance that *Signora* Poverelli is a charlatan. Come, Nigel, your experimental controls are ingenious and quite formidable without the ropes. I'm not sure I would agree to be tied to a chair for two hours, unable to scratch my nose or shift my legs."

Lombardi spoke up.

"That's not the point. He wants to humiliate her." He stared at Huxley. "Don't you?"

Huxley returned his stare. "My sitting, my rules."

Lombardi stood up. "This is supposed to be a science experiment, not an Inquisition. But have it your way." He nodded to me.

"Tommaso, go get Alessandra."

# 26

Tommaso do this. Tommaso do that.

It was annoying, but you do what the boss says. The donkey gets hitched wherever the master wants. My neck was already sunburned from the row out to the island, and I fell on my ass when I slid down the slope to the beach. Alessandra had waded out into the water with Henri, her skirt tucked between her legs, playing fetch with Barbet. I shouted to her, but their backs were to me and the breeze was blowing onshore. I removed my shoes and socks, rolled up my trousers, and waded out. She finally saw me and they splashed back, chased by Barbet who shook himself off vigorously, soaking my clothes.

"You're needed at the cottage," I grumbled. I didn't like seeing Alessandra with Henri. You can't trust a Frenchman. "*Signor* Huxley has laid out the rules for the sitting and I'm not sure you're going to like them all."

"Tell me," she laughed.

As we walked back I filled her in. The lampblack and vase didn't bother her, but when I told her about the ropes, she stopped dead in her tracks.

"Never!"

She started pacing around in a circle, her fists clenched, then collapsed to her knees on the sand and let out a howl. I was completely bewildered. The ropes would be humiliating, but refusing would naturally invite suspicion. Her reaction didn't make any sense.

I slid down next to her, unsure of what to do. Her eyes were brimming with tears, and you could see she was trying to work something out in her mind, jabbing the ground with her stick, and rocking back and forth. She finally turned to me.

"Tommaso, I can't… … I won't. I'll return to Naples first!"

"But why?"

She swiped her tears angrily, jumped to her feet and set off running. Henri grabbed Barbet's leash and we hurried after her.

Lombardi and the others were still on the verandah, sampling a cognac Renard had trotted out, when Alessandra marched over to the table and grabbed Huxley by the arm.

"No ropes," she declared. "Or I go home."

Everyone stared at her in stunned silence. She looked like a madwoman, her face flushed, her hair wind-tangled, her eyes puffy. Huxley put down his snifter, looked at Lombardi, then back at Alessandra.

"You prefer to withdraw?"

"I won't be tied down," she repeated.

Lombardi spoke up. "She's not offering to withdraw. She's asking you to skip the ropes."

"No! My sitting, my rules. Or we can skip this whole charade and enjoy the weekend." He turned to Alessandra, a smirk on his face. "What are you afraid of, my dear?"

"Nothing!" she shot back.

"What are *you* afraid of?" Lombardi said, rising to his feet. "That she'll succeed? Use your lampblack and your vase, sir, and let's get on with it."

Renard reached over and rang the bell.

"Nigel, we've all come a long way. I for one would be greatly disappointed to leave without a test."

Huxley hesitated. He could insist, but it would be "bad form" as the Brits say—a mortal sin in Huxley's social circle. He swirled the Courvoisier in his snifter, swallowed it, and set the glass down.

"Fine with me."

That evening, Capucine served up a delicious seafood bouillabaisse for dinner, better than anything I ever ate in Naples. Renard kept us entertained during the meal with a humorous description of his visit to Stockholm to receive his Nobel medal, but Lombardi was distant and quiet. He seemed very nervous.

Alessandra wasn't—she had seconds and chattered away with Sapienti. As Capucine and Henri cleared the table, Sapienti invited us all outside to see the stars. Huxley begged off to go paint his bell and arrange the séance room. The sky that night was spectacular, and Sapienti, energized by Alessandra's flirtations, outdid himself pointing out various constellations and planets.

Afterwards, I headed to my room to fetch the tripod and camera for the sitting, since Lombardi wanted me to visually document the layout of the séance room before we began. As I passed the kitchen, Henri pulled me aside. Between his pantomimes and broken Italian, I finally understood what he wanted to tell me. While we were outside, Huxley had slipped into Alessandra's room and rummaged through our bags. Henri didn't know why, but I did. Huxley was looking for devices he was convinced we had brought with us.

# 27

At eight o'clock, Huxley locked the door and bolted the wooden shutters.

Gaston and his family had been dismissed for the night, and we crowded into the séance room. It was a tight fit. I set up my tripod in the corner assigned me, right behind Huxley's chair. Lombardi was banished to the end of the table along with Sapienti, and Huxley and Renard took their seats flanking Alessandra where they would control her hands and feet. I made sure the photo showed everyone's position, as well as the blackened bell sitting under the glass vase on the table. Huxley had placed the oil lamp on a small side table, the wick trimmed high. The room was definitely brighter than in Naples. Lombardi looked unusually somber.

None of them joined Alessandra in the opening prayer—Sapienti and Renard weren't religious, and Huxley wasn't about to pray with her—but Alessandra appeared confident.

Maybe she was overconfident, or maybe it was the brighter light, but she struggled from the start.

She fidgeted and sighed as she settled down, closing her eyes and calling on the spirits for several minutes, then re-opening them to stare at the bell—back and forth, back and forth she went. I stood behind Huxley, the camera squeeze bulb in my fist, ready to fire if anything happened. Maybe twenty minutes into the sitting, she turned to Huxley.

"You're holding my wrist too tight. It hurts." Huxley ignored her. A short while later, she turned to him again.

"I need a glass of water. Let go of me." She nodded towards a pitcher Capucine had stationed on the sideboard. Huxley shook his head.

"Dr. Sapienti can bring it to you."

"But I need to stretch my legs!"

Huxley smiled. "I'm sure you do."

It was clear Huxley wasn't going to let Alessandra out of his grip for a moment. I wondered when Alessandra would give up and call Savonarola. As Rossi said, when the spirits didn't show up, she inevitably called on him.

We didn't have to wait long.

Alessandra finally bent her head, closed her eyes, and began mumbling the disturbing incantation she used in Naples.

"*Babbo … Babbo! … Per favore! Per favore!*" Father! Father, please come!

Huxley partially blocked my view, but I anticipated everything that followed—the slump against Renard's shoulder, the head falling forward, the convulsions as the demon took possession of her twitching body, then …

Sapienti grabbed the table and gasped.

"My God! Look at her face!"

"*Disbelievers!*" A chilling hiss filled the room. "*You demand signs and wonders, even as the Devil prepares your place in Hell.*"

Alessandra's head swiveled to face Huxley, and once again I saw Savonarola's sickly, green eyes sweep the room. The heavy-lidded, reptilian gaze locked on Huxley.

"*My Alessandra begs, but I am tired of your games. I will show you nothing.*"

Huxley started clapping.

"Brava, *Signora* Poverelli. You really should be in theater. The voice! The facial contortions! The change of eye color—tell me, how did you accomplish that? I'm guessing a drop of methyl green slipped into the eye while we were distracted?"

The entity remained silent, its unblinking eyes fixed on Huxley.

Huxley looked around the table. "It's a show. Don't you see? That's all it is." He started to reach for Alessandra, and the green eyes burned brighter.

*"Do not touch my beloved!"*

The menace in the command was palpable.

Huxley hesitated, then drew back his hand. He seemed unnerved.

"Very well, *Signora*, have it your way. I expected it might come to this." He got up, walked over to the sideboard, poured himself a glass of water, then returned to his seat. I noticed a tremble in his hand.

"Let's play a game, shall we? You can be Fra Savonarola." He forced a smile. "At Cambridge, my alma mater, I had the pleasure of attending a most informative class in medieval Italian history. Unfortunately, it was some years ago, and I've forgotten most of it. Since you were there, I'm sure you can help me with a few facts ... ."

It was a brilliant trap. Huxley had obviously planned it in advance, and knew the answers to the questions he was about to ask. If Alessandra were play-acting, she was caught. She knew nothing about Italian history—she could barely read. Across from me, Renard had immediately picked up on it. So had Lombardi. Huxley took a sip of water.

"Now, you were born in Florence, if I recall correctly ... ."

*"Serpent!"* the voice hissed. *"You know I was born in Ferrara."*

The shock on Huxley's face was unmistakable. He stared at Alessandra, mouth open.

"I...I...yes, Ferrara..." he stammered. He took a deep breath, steadying himself.

"And you were the only child of..."

*"There were seven of us."*

Huxley sat there dumbfounded.

"Your mother's name?"

*"Elena."*

"Damn you! Your father?"

*"Niccolo."*

"Grandfather's name? Tell me that!"

*"Michele."*

"Enough of this!" Huxley yelled. "Rossi schooled you, didn't he? He's in on this. I should have guessed. But we're not here to test your memory." He pointed to the glass vase in the center of the table.

"Move the bell, damn you, or admit you're a fraud!"

The hooded green eyes narrowed, and a sneer appeared.

*"What if I move you instead?"*

Huxley's chair was suddenly yanked from under him, dumping him on the floor. As the chair flew backwards, it knocked over the tripod, and I ended up on my backside too. Sapienti stared at us. Lombardi had a triumphant grin on his face.

Huxley reached over and grabbed me by the collar.

"You! You did that!" he shouted, his face purple with rage. "You're working with her!"

"Nigel! Stop!" Renard scrambled around the table and separated us. "I saw Tommaso the whole time. He didn't touch your chair."

"The hell he didn't!"

At that moment, the bell rang.

Everyone turned back to the table. The bell was now outside the glass jar, lying on its side. Alessandra was slumped forward in her chair, face down on the table.

"Nobody touch it!" Huxley screamed, pushing us back.

He grabbed the oil lamp and examined the bell, searching for marks in the lampblack. Nothing. He seized Alessandra's hands and inspected her fingers. Again, nothing. They were clean. He turned to us, barely able to contain his fury.

"The chair was a diversion," he shouted. "We looked away, she moved the bell."

"But how?" Renard demanded. "There's no marks on the bell."

"They're clever—I warned you! That's why you use the ropes!" He slammed his fist on the table, and leaned down to Alessandra. "You think I'm some dumb, gullible Italian *paesano?* You're a fraud, and I won't let you get away with this."

# 28

On the train back to Torino, they argued fiercely.

Huxley was the odd man out. Renard and Sapienti had seen enough to join Lombardi's camp. Alessandra needed to be investigated by Science. Huxley would only agree to attend the press conference.

The day of the announcement, we picked up Alessandra at the asylum before heading to the Minerva Club. Lombardi wanted to keep her away from the press, but Renard convinced him he couldn't hide her forever. On the way over, Lombardi sternly warned Alessandra not to say anything.

"Dr. Renard or I will handle any questions from reporters," he said. He pointed his cane at her. "And stay away from Huxley. I don't want any incidents."

The library was jam-packed when we entered. A buzz of excitement filled the air. Renard had arrived early and was surrounded by a crowd. Sapienti and Gemelli were huddled in animated conversation in the back of the room, where a photographer from *La Stampa* was busily polishing his camera lens. I recognized a dozen other gentlemen in the audience who had attended Lombardi's first talk. Baranov had returned to St. Petersburg, but Dr. Parenti was there, and he hurried over when he spied Alessandra.

"And this attractive lady is undoubtedly *Signora* Poverelli," he declared, kissing her hand. "I understand you bested our English friend at Ile Ribaud. Score one for Italy!"

He reached into his coat pocket and drew out a tiny stone cat, carved in alabaster.

"For you, *Signora*. From a 3,000 year old tomb in ancient Egypt I excavated myself. The cat goddess Bastet—an amulet to protect you from your enemies, and bring you luck." He placed it in her hand and smiled. "You will need her. *Signor* Huxley hates to lose, and I suspect he will continue to pursue you."

"*Signore, mille grazie*," Alessandra exclaimed. "I... don't know what to say..." She stared at the pretty figurine in wonder. The only present Pigotti had ever given her was a black eye.

Parenti laughed.

"Just tell your boy Tommaso here to send me a photograph of you to put on my desk at the museum, so I can make my colleagues jealous."

In the front of the room, Gemelli was clapping his hands to shush the crowd and we grabbed two vacant seats as Renard and Lombardi stepped to the podium.

Huxley stood off to the side, stone-faced, as Lombardi recapped his earlier Naples sitting, and the two of them described what had happened on Ile Ribaud. They agreed that Alessandra's mysterious powers deserved further investigation. As soon as they finished, reporters started waving their hands. A newsman from the *Gazzetta del Popolo* jumped in first.

"Professor Renard, are you saying you believe in spirits?"

Renard grimaced.

"I'm saying I believe in the spirit of scientific inquiry. No more, no less. I've seen enough to conclude that something more than legerdemain *might* be at work here." Renard nodded towards the back of the room, and a sea of faces turned to look at us. "*Signora* Poverelli has volunteered to be tested and, believe me, she will be. Science has the tools and methods necessary to separate truth from fiction."

The reporter from *La Stampa* raised his hand.

"Does Mister Huxley share your view?"

"You will have to ask him," Renard replied, staring disdainfully at Huxley.

It was an awkward moment. Everyone had agreed before going to Ile Ribaud that they would issue a joint statement afterwards, but Huxley had reneged. For Renard, it was a betrayal he never forgave or forgot.

Huxley stepped forward. "The Society will issue an official report once I've had a chance to return to England and discuss my observations with our Board."

"Was there something you observed which raises a concern?"

Huxley had a trump card to play, and he played it.

"Frankly, yes. Unlike my colleagues Dr. Lombardi and Dr. Renard, I find it exceedingly suspicious that *Signora* Poverelli adamantly refused to be tied to her chair during the sitting. I submit there's only one logical conclusion to be drawn from her refusal."

You could see heads around the room nodding in agreement. Hell, even I had found her refusal troubling.

That's when Alessandra stood up. I tried to pull her back down, but she shook off my grasp.

"May I say a word?"

Up front, Lombardi frantically motioned for her to sit down, but she remained there. Huxley had an amused look on his face.

"Please do," he said.

Alessandra waited until all eyes were on her, then with remarkable aplomb she delivered the line that knocked

Huxley's complaint to the second page, and made her famous throughout Italy.

"You must understand, *Signore*—being tied up in a dark room with an English man would frighten any Italian woman. You risk not only your virtue but your purse as well."

A collective gasp rose up from the room, followed by a roar of laughter. Huxley stood there red-faced, as reporters stampeded for the door, hoping to be the first to get the quote on the street. A flash gun went off, blinding me. The *La Stampa* photographer had maneuvered his camera closer to Alessandra, catching her unawares. It was a great shot of her and ended up the next day on the front page—together with the saucy, verbal thump Alessandra had landed on John Bull.

# 29

I couldn't wait to tell Alessandra the exciting news.

Lombardi had made the announcement in *La Stampa* that morning. We were off to tour the Continent.

Alessandra's miserable month at the asylum was over.

We'd be staying in real hotels, where a doorman would bow to us when we arrived, a maid would plump our pillows each evening, and waiters in suits would inquire whether *Signora* preferred the apple tart or the pear tart.

Alessandra could finally tell the "Kaiser" to shove it.

I hurried down the grimy hall, careful to stay to the middle, beyond the reach of the inmates who lined both sides of the corridor, manacled to their chairs, yelling and spitting at me as I slipped past. Lombardi's asylum got the criminally insane—the ax murderer who talked to God, the mother who drowned her babies, the prostitute who slept with her client then slashed his face to ribbons with a razor.

At the end of the hall, a guard halted me and demanded my pass. Behind him I could see into the social room, where the harmless inmates, mostly women, were allowed to spend a half hour every day outside their cells. Heads shaved to combat lice, they slowly circled the room like a school of fish, shuffling along behind one another, making a cacophony of noises—moans and wails, jabbering and maniacal laughter. Someone spotted me, a cry went up, and the whole room rushed towards the door. The guard turned and waved his club and they fell back. He pointed me towards the staff quarters, and I gratefully escaped.

When I reached the dormitory, I found Alessandra sitting on her bunk, head down, vomiting into a chamber pot. I hurried over.

"You all right?" I asked. She wrapped her arms around her stomach, rocked back, and threw up again.

"Jesus, Alessandra!" I pulled out my handkerchief and wiped the sweat from her brow.

"I'm fine, I'm fine."

"You sure don't look like it. I really think Dr. Lombardi…

"No!" She nodded at the paper in my hand. "What's that?"

I held up the tour itinerary Lombardi had given me that morning.

"We're off to Paris."

"Paris?"

She took it from my hand, read it, then handed it back to me.

"Thank God. We can finally leave this hellhole…" She tried to stand up, but I pushed her back down.

"Not until tomorrow. And only if you feeling better."

"I'll be ready."

She bent over, clutched her stomach, and rocked back and forth, groaning.

"At least let Lombardi look…"

"No!" She angrily kicked the chamber pot with her foot. She lay back on the bed, her eyes closed. "It's the food they serve in this shithole, that's all."

A wash cloth sat in a bucket of cold water by her bedside. I squeezed it out, and wiped her forehead. The grimace on her face relaxed, and she opened her eyes and looked up at me.

"Sorry for the mess, Tommaso. Thank you." She closed them again. "Paris..."

I grinned. "...and Genoa, Geneva, Vienna, Munich, and Warsaw as well—*if* you can manage to stay out of trouble." Her eyes opened.

"What do you mean?"

"Lombardi says you're on probation."

"Probation? Why?"

"Jesus, Alessandra, you made Huxley the laughing-stock of Italy, and made Lombardi's life a lot tougher. He's already sent a letter of apology to the Society. He's praying it reaches London before Huxley does—and you better pray they accept it."

She raised herself up on one elbow. "But he insulted *me*!"

I dipped the wash cloth in the bucket. "You don't get it. Huxley works for the Society. The Society is like the Camorra, *capisci*? You don't want to piss them off. They run the show when it comes to investigating mediums. If they warn people to stay away from you, the academic community will turn its back on Lombardi. Most of them already have—in case you don't know. The only thing keeping Lombardi in the game right now is Renard and his Nobel prize."

I passed the cloth to her. "Lombardi's serious about this. If you embarrass him again, he'll dump you. He told me."

"So what am I supposed to do when someone calls me a cheat?"

"Shut up and take it. In four months you'll have your 4,000 *lire*—then you can head to Rome with enough money in your purse to start a new life."

I had delivered the warning Lombardi ordered me to give her, but I knew Alessandra wouldn't listen. She came from Naples, where honor trumped everything, even good sense.

She flung the cloth on the bed.

"I'll never let Huxley insult me, Tommaso. Never!"

# 30

The first elevator I saw in my life was in Genoa.

We all squeezed into the lift and the uniformed operator pulled the metal door closed. Lombardi offered Alessandra a seat on the red velvet bench but she was too excited to sit down. The operator hit the button and we jerked upwards. She grabbed my arm, and hung on tight. She had never ridden in one either.

Outside the wire cage, the lobby of the six-story, Grand Hotel Isotta in Genoa was bustling with English and German tourists eager to start their summer holidays on the Italian Riviera. Lombardi had deliberately chosen Genoa as his first stop on the tour. Alessandra would still be in Italy, where the language and the food were familiar, performing before a friendly audience.

For two *paesanotti* bumpkins like us, the rooms were like something out of *A Thousand and One Nights*. Lombardi traveled first class everywhere he went, and we always stayed in the same hotel as him. He wanted to keep an eye on Alessandra.

She flitted around her room, marveling at everything— the tropical flower prints on the wall, the enormous bed, the snow-white, crisply pressed sheets, and the private toilet.

"Can you believe this, Tommaso!"

She picked up the soap and sniffed it, then handed it to me. "It smells like flowers." She rubbed her face in the luxurious towels, then marched over to her bag, yanked it open and pulled out a dingy, gray rag and a block of hard brown soap. She had expected to stay in a cheap place, and brought her own from the asylum. She balled everything up and tossed it in the wastebasket.

"*Arrivederci!*" she laughed, and joined me at the window.

On the street below, a tram filled with people passed by in the late afternoon sun, the clang of its bell floating up to us as we leaned out, elbows together, and took turns pointing out the sights. We were high up enough to see over the surrounding rooftops and catch a glimpse of the Ligurian sea, a pale blue sheet of water spread across the horizon beyond the docks and wharves.

A knock sounded at the door and I walked over and opened it.

My surprise had arrived.

I gave the bellboy a tip and wheeled the cart into the room.

"Time to celebrate!"

"Champagne?—Oh my God, Tommaso!" she laughed. "Close the door! Hurry! Lock it!"

She sat on the bed as I poured two glasses, then handed her one.

She took her glass and gave me a mock pout.

"Tommaso, I'm surprised at you. You're always lecturing me to behave. Do you want to get me sent back to Naples?"

"This is simply to help remind you what you will lose if you screw up. Now, a toast….." I raised my glass. "To Alessandra and Tommaso. Two nobodies from Naples. But when we're done, the world is going to know our names."

We sat on the bed, drinking the champagne. She had had champagne once before, at a reception at Rossi's house. She loved the bubbles.

"This tastes delicious," she said. "Where on earth did you get the money?"

"A little trick I learned from you. I told Lombardi his darkroom equipment cost 700 *lire*, but it only cost 600. I pocketed the difference—but I bought this instead of stuffing it in my mattress."

Alessandra burst out laughing. "I can't think of a better place to hide money."

I topped up her glass. "Did you know that Lombardi and his wife had a big fight just before we left Torino?"

"About what?"

"You."

"Me?"

"She doesn't like the idea of him traveling alone with you. She was shouting and throwing dishes, and yelling that mediums were whores, and he was embarrassing her and ruining his reputation at the university. The maid told me everything the morning I left." I refilled my glass. "That's not all. She told him if he left with you, she was going to Budapest to stay with her sister, and threatened she might not return."

Alessandra laughed. "She can save her cups and plates. I'm just a science experiment to him. And all I want from him is my 4,000 *lire*."

There was a knock on the door.

"Alessandra? This is Professor Lombardi. Are you there? Professor Negri is waiting for us in the lobby." I panicked and jumped up to hide the cart in the bathroom, but she pushed me back down on the bed.

"Stay there," she whispered. "Don't move."

She turned towards the door. "Thank you, Professor. I'll be down shortly."

"I knocked on Tommaso's door. There was no reply. Maybe he's downstairs already."

She stifled a giggle. "He said he needed to check his equipment bags."

When we got to the lobby, Lombardi and Dr. Enrico Negri were enjoying a cigar and chatting away. Negri stood up and kissed Alessandra's hand. He was a short, jovial man with an aquiline nose and a peaked beard. He worked in the psychiatry department at the university, where he was Director of the Clinic for Nervous and Mental Diseases. He held up a small box and removed the lid. Inside was a silver medallion.

"*Signora* Poverelli, our fair city is the birthplace of Christopher Columbus." He handed her the box and bowed. "You are the leading our exploration to another New World, and we are simply your humble crew."

Lombardi smiled. "And when do we start our explorations, Rico?"

Negri wagged his finger. "No work tonight. Just dinner—and a chance for those of us in Genoa to enjoy the pleasure of this beautiful woman you've kept for yourself for too long, Camillo."

Negri wasn't looking for proof; his tests with a local Genovese medium had left him convinced. He was simply trying to understand how it worked. "I accept the phenomena as real," he had written in his book *Psicologia e Spiritismo*, "not only because they are reported by persons worthy of credence, even by scientists, but because I also have experimented."

That night, the three of us took a carriage over to Negri's second floor apartment in the Bocadâze, an old mariners' neighborhood just off of Via Aurora. Its large windows looked out to a small bay and a cobblestone beach crowded with small fishing boats. The evening was warm and the windows were thrown open, and you could hear laughter and chatter from the fishermen preparing to head out for some night fishing. Alessandra lingered at the window for a long time, staring out, contently sniffing the salt air and letting the breeze caress her face. She and the sea were lovers.

"What a wonderful place to live." she whispered to me. "When I'm in Rome, I'm going to spend my summers here, Tommaso." Typical Alessandra. She only had a few *lire* to her name, but she had the Midas touch when it came to turning destitution into dreams.

Negri was a bachelor, but his cook Gemma fed ten of us, crowded shoulder to shoulder in the small dining room. Most were professors or students from Negri's university, and Gemma outdid herself—pasta tossed with *bianchetti*, broiled *bronzini,* and a special surprise for Alessandra. When we finished the fish, Negri slipped into the kitchen, returned to the table with a plate in his hands, and placed it ceremoniously in front of Alessandra.

Alessandra clapped her hands in surprise. "A pizza?"

"Genoa's salute to Naples." Negri gestured towards the kitchen. "Gemma is hiding in the kitchen until she hears you like it."

The Genovese *faina* does look like a Neapolitan pizza—a thin pancake cut in triangles, but made of chickpea flour instead of wheat flour. Gemma had delicately seasoned it with rosemary and sea salt.

Alessandra took a bite and a big grin spread across her face. "*Deliziosa!*" She hopped up from her chair and headed for the kitchen. "*Signora*, I beg you, tell me how to make it."

Alessandra spent the rest of the evening encircled by a harem of admirers who peppered her with questions about her mediumship. Everyone drank a lot and laughed a lot. They teased her about her famous jibe at the Englishman Huxley. One of the guests, Professor Baldinotti, pulled out his little *du botte* accordion and played "Santa Lucia," and then a Neapolitan tarantella which got Alessandra up on her feet to dance and soon everybody was up and dancing and bumping into each other and falling down and Alessandra

ended the evening by singing Peppino Turco's famous Neapolitan song about the cable car up Mount Vesuvius:

*funiculì, funiculà 'ncoppa, jamme ja!*

That week, Alessandra produced table levitations four
nights in a row. During the second sitting, she invited Dr.
Pirelli, one of Negri's plump colleagues, to get up on *top* of
the table. He sat there, dumbfounded, as all four legs of the
table lifted off the floor for several seconds before crashing
back down again. All the time, my palm was squeezing the
flash bulb, I'm thinking "Now! Now!" but Lombardi was
too flabbergasted to speak, and we missed it. I should have
just fired the damn flash. It was unbelievable.

But Alessandra topped it on our last night in Genoa.

# 31

It feels like a cat is climbing my right arm towards my shoulder..."

"Somebody is tickling me."

"Something just pulled my beard!"

Everyone in the room that night was being touched, pinched and grabbed by invisible hands except me. The only thing I felt was a bead of sweat rolling down the back of my neck. Negri's laboratory was small and stuffy, the windows closed and papered over.

The room was pitch black. Alessandra was convinced that light discouraged the spirits, and Lombardi and Negri were curious to see what she could produce in total darkness.

Baldinotti, the accordion player, seemed to be the spirits' favorite target that night.

At one point, he declared, "I feel a hand fumbling in my jacket pocket....." He fell silent for ten seconds, then announced, "I don't feel it anymore..."

Alessandra's voice piped up in the darkness. "The spirits tell you to put your hand in the pocket."

"Certainly," Baldinotti replied. "I am now doing that.....I can feel my handkerchief....." Suddenly he exclaimed, "What the devil?...why, it's tied in a knot!"

Huxley would have claimed trickery—Alessandra had slipped out of her chair in the darkness and tied the knot, or switched handkerchiefs—but what happened next certainly wasn't.

Baldinotti saw it first. "Look! There! In the corner!" he exclaimed.

A faint, silvery ball of light—like in Naples when Lombardi's mother materialized—had emerged in the darkness. It grew in brightness then began to pulse, pushing five luminescent tendrils forward in the heavy, still air, which slowly resolved themselves into the five fingers of a hand. It was clearly a woman's hand, with long, thin, finely formed fingers, but it ended at the wrist—what Spiritualists call a partial materialization. It glowed with the phosphorescent light of a firefly. The spirit hand floated slowly across the room and halted next to Alessandra's right ear, faintly illuminating her face. The fingers reached out and gently pushed Alessandra's hair back, like a doting mother might do to her daughter, then came to rest on her shoulder, the fingers curling naturally and gracefully.

Our eyes by this time were well adjusted to darkness, and everyone could easily see the glowing hand on Alessandra's shoulder.

I blinked and rubbed my eyes. Your mind simply can't wrap itself around something so bizarre, so absurd, as a disembodied hand. There's nothing in your experience, your reality, to compare it to. But it was there—and it wasn't simply a hand wrapped in a white handkerchief, or a stuffed glove, or some cheap device made of pasteboard.

Negri, only centimeters away, raised his monocle and studied it.

"Can we photograph it?" he asked.

I had been so mesmerized I had completely forgotten I had a camera bulb in my hand.

"The spirits say no," answered Alessandra. "But you may touch it."

Negri passed control of Alessandra to Lombardi, then reached out and gently grasped the spirit hand, describing what he felt.

"I'm … I'm feeling a true hand … flesh … and bones are felt … the skin of the hand … warm … mobile fingers … fingernails … are all perceived … the hand gives off a light … I can see the bust and arms of *Signora* Poverelli … both her hands are held by Dr. Lombardi … "

The hand glided down the table, and when it reached Baldinotti it halted, and the palm opened up, inviting him to take it. He slowly reached up and laid his own palm gently on the spirit hand, and the ghostly fingers seemed to entwine his own, the light pulsing like the beating of a heart.

"Olivia … ?" He sounded startled. The light seemed to pulse brighter. "Oh, God—*Cara* Olivia!" He leaned forward and kissed the spirit hand, then laid his cheek against it and began to sob.

I never learned who Olivia was, and Negri left that part out of his scientific account, but Negri did have the courage to include the astonishing materialization in his report, and defended its reality till the day he died, despite the fierce ridicule he received from skeptics.

> *Absurd as the phenomenon of a materialized hand may seem, it seems to me to be very difficult to attribute the phenomena produced to deception, conscious or unconscious, or to a series of deceptions. It is inconceivable to suppose that an accomplice could have come into the room, which is small, and was locked and sealed during the progress of our experiments. We were making no noise, we could light up the room instantly. We must accept the evidence as we find it.*

It was a spectacular beginning to the tour, and Lombardi was ecstatic, but Alessandra paid a price for it. She did sittings six straight nights that week, and we usually didn't get back to the hotel until after midnight, and her cough seemed to be getting worse.

# 32

Alessandra didn't trust many people in her hard life. She was hurt too many times, and rarely let down her guard. But Zoe captured her heart.

When we arrived at her father's house in Lausanne, just outside of Geneva, the sassy, little six-year old ran to our carriage and thrust a bouquet of yellow daffodils into Alessandra's hand.

"*Buongiorno,*" she chirped, and performed a dramatic, sweeping bow. "*Mi chiamo Zoe.*" Then she giggled and looked back to her beaming mother.

It turned out that "Good morning" and "My name is Zoe" were the only words of Italian she knew, but fortunately for us her parents spoke multiple languages, like most educated people in Switzerland. Professor Theodore Fournier, our host in Geneva, owned a magnificent, two-story house right on the water at Lac Leman. He was the same age as Lombardi, and the scion of a prominent financier who controlled the *Banque Cantonale de Genève*. They lived like the Medici, spent a lot of time in Paris, and Fournier's wife Josephine decorated their house with Art Nouveau lamps and sculptures. Despite their money, they weren't stuffy people. Josephine painted and ran around with artists, and Dr. Fournier was unconventional enough to investigate Spiritualism.

After a lunch of rabbit with mustard, Zoe led Alessandra down to the lake to feed the wild swans, trailed by a servant carrying a silver bowl filled with pieces of bread, and I tagged along. Before we even got there, the swans started honking and paddling towards the shore, eager for lunch. There must have been a dozen birds surrounding us, racing forward to grab the bread, then scurrying away in an attempt to gobble it down before another swan stole it from them. Alessandra had moved down the shore a little to feed a solitary swan out in the water, and I had started for the dock to inspect their sailboat, when I heard Zoe scream.

"Mama! Mama!"

I turned around and saw three birds chasing Zoe across the lawn, nipping at her legs, and lunging at the bread in her hand. Josephine came sprinting down the lawn to save her, but Alessandra got there first. She swooped up Zoe into her arms and laid into the birds, giving a swift boot to the biggest and sending the squawking trio to flight.

After that, Zoe followed her heroine "Tante" Alessandra everywhere.

I never saw Alessandra happier in her life than those two wonderful weeks in Switzerland.

No matter how late the evening sitting ran, she would get up early the next morning to eat breakfast with little Zoe. One morning, I came down and found Alessandra on her hands and knees in front of Zoe who was perched in a chair trying to keep from laughing.

"Meow" went Alessandra. She pretended to be a cat, rubbing her face against Zoe's leg then looked up at Zoe with a sad face. "Me-o-o-w." Zoe covered her mouth with her hands, trying hard to keep a straight face, but she couldn't. She exploded in laughter and jumped into Alessandra's arms, kissing her, the two of them rolling on the floor. Josephine had taught Alessandra how to play Zoe's favorite game, "Poor Pussy."

Language was never a barrier between the two of them—they shared the language of the heart. One evening, I found Alessandra in the library, Zoe nestled in her lap, reading a children's story together. It was in French and Zoe would read a few lines then look at Alessandra who would nod her head and say something in Italian.

"You don't understand a word she is saying," I protested.

"It doesn't matter," she said. "As the French say, '*Pas de problème.*'" She laughed and hugged Zoe who stuck her tongue out at me and parroted Alessandra.

"*Pas de problème.*"

I looked at Alessandra. "What does that mean?"

"It means 'no problem,' silly." She tickled Zoe. "I learned it from my little *bambina* here."

Alessandra spent most of her free time with Zoe, playing with her little black and white terrier Antoinette, playing tea party in her bedroom, and sitting on the dock in the sunshine eating apples and kicking their heels in the sparkling water.

Lombardi always believed Zoe was primarily responsible for Alessandra's spectacular successes in Geneva. Alessandra's spirit soared when she felt loved, and her psychic performance improved dramatically.

After the success in Genoa, she and Lombardi seemed to relax a bit in each other's company. The first weekend we were there, Fournier took us all out for a cruise on the *Mademoiselle*, his magnificent, 25-meter sailboat—casually mentioning that it was designed by the British naval architect who built the Royal Yacht *Britannia* for the Prince of Wales. Their servants packed several baskets of cheese, bread and sausages to take with us, along with a half-dozen bottles of Valais white. Lombardi and Alessandra both loved their wine, and the two of them sampled liberally all the way across the lake to Évian-les-Bains, a pretty French town on the south shore with famous thermal baths catering to the rich. They toured the town with a bottle of Fendant and, on the way home, they sat together in the stern, well-lubricated, singing "Santa Lucia." It was a blustery day, with a stiff breeze, and half-way back Fournier handed the wheel over to Josephine and clambered forward to reef a sail.

Before he reached the bow, a gust caught the sails and we suddenly heeled hard over.

"*Merda!*" Alessandra yelled, and flipped head over heels into the lake.

Lombardi dove into the water, suit and all, paddling furiously to her rescue. By the time we came about to pick them up, they were both laughing and splashing each other.

"Grab hold!" I yelled, sticking my hand out to haul Alessandra aboard.

"Join us!" she shouted, and yanked me in.

I surfaced sputtering and Lombardi paddled over to crown my head with his straw hat. Then the two idiots started singing "Santa Lucia" again.

. . .

That evening after supper, I made my way down to the lake to look for my journal, which I had left in the cabin of the boat. I found it, and was climbing back up the steps to the deck when I heard voices. I popped my head out and saw Lombardi and Alessandra heading for the dock. In the deepening twilight, I could see they were walking close together, and he was holding her hand.

Curious, I slipped back down the ladder, and snuffed out the lamp. The night was perfectly still, and I could hear them coming closer, whispering to each other. Their footsteps echoed on the wooden dock and stopped, then Lombard's voice called out softly.

"Shall we sit here?"

"What a beautiful night, Camillo."

I slid over to a porthole and peered out. The two of them were sitting on the dock, their shoes off. The moon cast a long, silver shadow across the water. Out on the lake, a flock of swans silently breasted through the shimmering light. Alessandra loosened the comb from her hair, letting it fall to her shoulders, then leaned back and looked up.

"The stars!" she murmured. "Look at them."

Lombardi lifted his face towards the heavens, and they both sat there in silence.

She suddenly turned to him. "What month were you born?"

"Why?" he replied.

"Tell me."

"Alright...February."

"I thought so."

He reached for her hand. "You sound disappointed."

"You're water. I'm fire."

"Astrology?" There was amusement in his voice. "Don't tell me you believe in that unscientific nonsense, Alessandra."

She pulled her hand away and stood up.

"The Milky Way." She pointed her finger at the luminous arc of galaxies and stars that glittered above their heads, her finger tracing its majestic sweep across the zodiac. "Dr. Sapienti told me it has a million stars, Camillo. Can you believe that?"

"Come, then, sit down here beside me. We'll count them together."

Alessandra giggled. "Am I safe?"

"I haven't a drop of English blood in my veins. Your virtue is safe with me." Lombardi dusted the dock with his handkerchief, then reached up and grasped Alessandra's hand. "But if you're worried, I can send for Master Labella to play chaperone."

"I'll use your shoes." Alessandra positioned his shoes between them and sat down.

Lombardi grinned. "Hardly a credible barrier to intimacy."

"You told me you were a gentleman."

He laughed. "I was hoping you had forgotten." They fell silent again, gazing at the stars. Alessandra shivered, crossing her arms over her chest.

"I should have brought a sweater. The nights are so much colder than Naples."

"Here. This will help." Lombardi took off his jacket. "With your permission, *Signora*..." He pushed the shoes aside, reached over, and wrapped it around her shoulders, brushing back her hair. He returned the shoes. "See, a perfect gentleman."

Alessandra pushed the shoes away and leaned against him. He seemed surprised. He put his arm around her. "It's the mountain air."

Up at the house, you could hear Zoe singing, her voice floating down to us on the evening air. Lombardi's voice, low and soft, found the spaces.

"You've never been to Paris?"

"No. Is it nice?"

"It's the most beautiful city in the world. "The City of Lights – *La Ville Lumière*. You're going to love Paris, Alessandra."

"But I don't speak French." She sounded unsure.

"But I do. I can't wait to show you everything." He caught himself. "– and Tommaso, of course. The three of us. There's a restaurant near the Champ de Mars I want to take you to..."

"Tante Alessandra! Tante Alessandra!"

Zoe's voice broke the stillness, scattering the swans. "*Dove sei?* Where are you? *Dove sei!*" Zoe was running down the lawn, come to fetch her Alessandra.

Alessandra jumped up and grabbed her shoes. "Here, *bambina!* I'm here! Tante Alessandra is coming."

Lombardi sat there on the dock for a moment, then sighed, scooped up his jacket, and started after her.

It was clear he was falling for Alessandra.

# 33

Professor Fournier didn't believe in spirits.

Like Lombardi and every other scientist who tested Alessandra that summer of '99, he believed in the laws of physics—force, motions, and energy. The only thing he wanted to see Alessandra do was to levitate a table, or move a matchbox, or ring a bell—telekinetic effects that could be calculated, measured, photographed, recorded.

But Madame Aubertin believed in spirits, and she was desperate.

The evening we first arrived in Switzerland, a short, aristocratic-looking woman, about Alessandra's age, showed up at Fournier's house. She was dressed in mourning clothes and carried a little Papillon spaniel in a basket.

"Madame Aubertin is a friend of the family," Fournier explained, passing the basket to Alessandra. "And this is Phalene." The little dog licked Alessandra's hand and she took it into her lap, delighted to pet it. "Madame recently lost someone very close to her. She asked me if she could intrude on our experiments before we start, in hopes you could communicate with that loved one. I told her you would try your best."

Aubertin took a chair next to Alessandra, and lifted the black veil from her face. She had dark rings around her eyes, like she hadn't slept in a long time.

"*Signora*, I know you are busy, but if you could understand the pain I feel in my heart … "

Before Fournier finished his translation, Alessandra leaned over and embraced Aubertin.

"*Signora* … " She gestured toward the sitting room. "*Per piacere, venga*." Come with me.

Alessandra took charge of the sitting that night, holding one hand of Madame Aubertin while Josephine took the other. Fournier had never done a sitting to communicate with the dead, and was clearly skeptical, but he joined in the prayer, as did Lombardi for once.

"Spirits come!" Alessandra intoned. "Spirits come!" She closed her eyes and we all sat there in the dark, waiting for the spirits to show up. Next to me, head bowed, Madame Aubertin whispered her Ave Marias. I kept nervously glancing over my shoulder. Would the dead person suddenly show up behind a chair, like Lombardi's mother?

After perhaps ten minutes of silence, Alessandra suddenly spoke up.

"There is someone here," she announced. "A girl…. young girl … brown hair … short white skirt … ribbon … blue ribbon in her hair … "

Madame Aubertin 's eyes were open now, looking at Alessandra intently.

" … she is holding a stick and a … circle … wood? … She hits the circle, and rolls it … rolls it along, hitting it. Now she is smiling, pointing to the basket, to Phalene … .then she points to herself … her dog? … "

Tears were glistening in the corners of Madame Aubertin's eyes. Alessandra' s own eyes were still closed

" … She says her name now … Em … Em … Emma, Emme … ?

A tear ran down Aubertin's cheek.

"Aimee," she whispered. "Her name was Aimée."

"Aimée, yes, she is nodding….she points to her neck…no, her throat…something wrong….she swallows…it hurts…she is shivering…"

Aubertin was sobbing.

"She wants you to know she is all right…. she smiles…. she is standing next to an older man, old man…odd hat…he shows me something…a book…or notebook with writing inside….can't read the words…he puts the book in a bag…now he takes her hand…"

Aimee was Madame Aubertin's only child, just eleven years old when she died of diphtheria. The old man was Aimee's grandfather, who wore a beret and walked Aimée to school every morning.

That night before leaving Madame Aubertin embraced Alessandra for a long time, before pressing some money in her hand, but Alessandra refused to take it.

# 34

Alessandra could raise more than the dead.

During the two weeks we were there, she levitated a solid crystal vase of lilies, a music box, and a heavy, leather-bound dictionary. She also sounded a harmonica placed in a locked box, and stopped Josephine's mechanical metronome—once halting the pendulum swing for three full seconds.

And then there was the cuckoo clock.

Josephine wanted to get rid of it—"that old piece of junk" didn't fit in her modern house—but the clock had been in Dr. Fournier's family for a half-century and he wasn't about to dump it in the trash. All day long, the clock would chime at the hour, a little mechanical bird would pop out of a door at the top, flap its wings and tail and whistle two notes "Coo-Koo!" Then a music box inside the clock would play a little melody.

Alessandra and Zoe would count down the bongs together, then join the bird in flapping their arms and calling out "Coo-Koo!"

Fournier noticed their antics and, one evening after dinner as we all sat around the table, he pointed to the clock. It was 7: 55 PM. Could Alessandra use her telekinetic powers to stop the cuckoo bird from popping out of the little door when the hour struck?

"Do it, and we'll skip the sitting tonight," Fournier promised her. Lombardi smiled his agreement. Zoe jumped from her chair and ran to Alessandra.

"Do it, Tante Alessandra! Then you can play charades with us tonight."

Alessandra looked unsure.

"*Chi non risica non rosica,*" I teased. Nothing ventured, nothing gained.

A minute before 8:00, Alessandra pulled Zoe into her lap and glared at the clock. "I wanted the cuckoo to feel *afraid* to come out," she told me afterwards. Zoe imitated her, frowning, tiny fists clenched tight.

We sat there as the seconds counted down for what seemed an eternity before the minute hand finally landed on 8:00 PM. I held my breath as the hours sounded.

*Bong ... Bong ... Bong ... Bong ... Bong ... Bong ... Bong ... Bong* then ...

... nothing.

The door remained shut.

I stared at the clock. Alessandra had a big grin on her face.

Zoe grabbed Alessandra's hand. "Come Tante Alessandra! Let's go play charades."

"Go ahead," Lombardi laughed, shaking his head.

Fournier and Lombardi walked over and peered at the clock. The minute hand now showed 8:01. The rest of the clock was obviously working fine. Fournier tapped on the door, his amazement already turned to analysis. *How* exactly had Alessandra stopped the bird from coming out? Exerted a mental force on the door to keep it closed? Damaged the mechanism?

I left to join the charades. We could hear the two of them in the kitchen, parsing the possibilities. Josephina shouted to her husband to dismantle the clock and look inside.

"Maybe he won't be able to put it back together," she laughed, "and I can get rid of it."

An hour later, we all gathered in the kitchen and watched the clock. Nine bells chimed, the door popped open, the bird popped out, and the two tiny pipes inside sounded their duet.

"Coo-Koo."

## 35

L ombardi didn't want to invite D'Argent.

We were all sitting out on the terrace that Sunday when Fournier suggested his crazy idea. Zoe and Alessandra were playing tag on the lawn, and I was working my way through a French phrase book, though my eye kept getting drawn to the spectacular view. In the distance, the breathtaking, snow-capped peak of Mont Blanc rose up in the June sunshine. Dr. Fournier and the family always spent the Christmas holidays there skiing. Fournier looked up from his newspaper.

"A well-known Paris stage magician is in town. He's playing at the Théâtre de Genève."

Lombardi looked puzzled. "And…?"

"He's performed for Emperor Napoleon and the President of France. He says he attended séances in Paris, and investigated French mediums." He passed the paper to Lombardi. "I wonder if we…"

Lombardi looked at him. "You're not thinking of inviting him to a sitting, are you?"

"Maybe."

"That's absolutely mad. Why?"

"Why not? Alessandra's doing spectacularly well."

Fournier refilled Lombardi's wine glass. "We know Huxley's going to release his report on Ile Ribaud soon, and he'll make it sound like you were duped. What better way to counter that than have a famous magician declare Alessandra's real?"

"But what if she fails?"

"Possible. But look what she produced for Negri in Genoa. And she's done some amazing things this week, and she'll be doing the sitting right here, surrounded by people who believe in her."

Lombardi handed the paper back to Fournier. "No. It's too risky. I won't allow it." Fournier persisted.

"You took a terrible risk at Ile Ribaud, with Huxley breathing down her neck."

"I had no choice! Renard got me into it."

"And look what you got out of it! You got Renard to stand with you. What was that worth? I'll be frank, Camillo—you wouldn't be here if he hadn't given his imprimatur. " He leaned forward. "You already know what Huxley is going to say—she's just a clever trickster, that's all, and academics are easy to dupe. But if a professional magician tests her, and comes away convinced—or even comes away puzzled—you've got your riposte to Huxley's report, and a damn good one."

"We don't even know him. We would need an introduction... "

Fournier smiled. "I know the theater owner. He banks with our family. I'm sure he booked our Monsieur D'Argent."

Lombardi stared at his wine glass, silent. Finally Fournier spoke up.

"Why not let Alessandra decide?"

Lombardi sighed, then turned to me. "Tommaso, go get Alessandra."

# 36

Alessandra teased D'Argent's assistant shamelessly. Philippe was broad-shouldered and handsome—in his late twenties, I'd guess—with dark curly hair, cognac brown eyes, and a sense of mischief about him.

Alessandra flirted openly with men she found attractive. She truly enjoyed the company of men, but I think it was more than that. Pigotti was insanely jealous, and it was a way she could hurt him back. Huxley had already begun spreading the rumor that she was having affairs with both Renard and Lombardi.

D'Argent and Philippe flanked Alessandra during the sitting, controlling her hands and knees. Lombardi wanted me behind the camera. Six of them were crowded around a small table—a meter by a meter and a half, weighing maybe ten kilograms. A small oil lamp, lit and positioned on a side table, illuminated Alessandra's delighted face as she squirmed and fidgeted more than usual at the start, cooing away at Philippe—did he have a good grip on her knee? Would he like to move it closer? Did he want to interlace his fingers with hers for more control? Should she lean her shoulder against him? At the other end of the table, Lombardi looked annoyed.

Alessandra called the spirits, and five minutes into the sitting she made an announcement.

"I will do something just for you, Philippe. Bring your head closer to mine."

She placed her forehead on his and knocked together three times. Three loud, synchronous raps were heard coming from the séance table. D'Argent looked amused. I know what he was thinking—a clever trick, but easily explainable.

Alessandra pulled back, a mischievous smile on her face.

"And now I send you a kiss, *caro*."

She pursed her lips and smacked a kiss everyone in the room could clearly hear. Philippe immediately dropped Fournier's hand and touched it to his lips.

"I felt a mouth kissing me," he said to D'Argent. The surprise in his voice was unmistakable. Josephine had a grin on her face, but Lombardi glared at Philippe.

"Spirits, show us more!" Alessandra intoned.

Fournier spoke up. "I feel a vibration from the table."

Josephine chimed in. "Me too. Anyone else?"

D'Argent spoke up. "I feel it now. Philippe?"

"Yes." He sounded nervous.

Alessandra sighed dramatically, then leaned forward in her seat.

"For you, *caro*. Now I lift the table."

All four feet slowly rose off the floor, dragging everyone out of their seats. The table hung there, a meter above the floor, swaying gently.

"*Mon Dieu!*" D'Argent yelled.

He dropped to his knees and stuck his head under the table, as I fired the flash.

D'Argent is on all fours, his wide eyes staring up in astonishment at the table suspended above his head. In the background, Fournier and Josephine are still hanging on to the table, Lombardi is looking at Alessandra. Her head is flung back, one hand on the table, the other latched on to Philippe's arm.

It was a spectacular shot.

## 37

The *Tribune de Genève* spread the story across five columns. Lombardi himself couldn't have crafted a better headline.

### Madame Poverelli Mystifies Science

------

### Wonderful Spiritistic Manifestations Witnessed

------

### Professor and Professional Magician Fail to Detect Any Trickery

D'Argent delivered a verdict we knew would stagger Huxley. He described how he arrived skeptical, carefully inspected the room and the table, and retained tight control of Alessandra throughout the evening, but she had still performed a miracle.

> "I do insist that *Signora* Poverelli showed genuine levitation, not by trickery but by some baffling, intangible, invisible force that radiated through her body and over which she exer-

cised a temporary and thoroughly exhausting control."

Lombardi was ecstatic. So was Alessandra.

"Huxley can kiss my ass," she said.

Huxley certainly sucked a sour lemon. The three telegraphic monopolies—Agence France-Presse, Reuters, and Wolff—picked up the story from the *Tribune,* and newspapers across Europe ran the story of Lombardi and his bewitching protégé Alessandra. I earned a photo credit, but I already had my eye on a bigger prize.

I wanted to become an editor, and that meant I had to become a reporter first.

That night I sat down with a pencil and paper and wrote up what I had witnessed, just as if I had been assigned the story. "*A smirk on his mustachioed, Gallic visage, D'Argent took his seat at the séance table, confident he would unmask the Italian trickster.*" Lombardi and Fournier had judiciously avoided mentioning Alessandra's flirtations with Philippe, but I knew the *Mattino* audience wanted scandal. "*Philippe wiped his lips and leered at Alessandra. 'Your kiss is sweet' … *"

I dropped my dispatch in the mail the day we left Geneva, and within a week Venzano had telegraphed back. *Bravo, Tommaso. More stories. Sending 20 francs via Lombardi.*

I was now *Mattino* special correspondent Tommaso Labella.

# 38

Everyone clamored to test Alessandra after that. Lombardi made her mad by adding three more cities to the tour. We had been on the road for a month by then, and she had been counting down the stops left until we reached Paris, the end of the tour.

She was crabby and peevish, and performed poorly. For the first time, she wasn't dealing with Italians playing accordions and dancing around singing *funiculì funiculà*, or genial hosts taking her out for a Sunday sail. Her inquisitors were Germans—smug, pedantic, suspicious. Nobody in Italy likes Germans.

Heidelberg was blistering through a heat wave when we arrived, and the sitting room was oppressively hot. Professor Bloch was intrigued by Fournier's metronome experiment, and had rigged up a telegraph key to a revolving cylinder which recorded an electromagnetic signal on a sheet of blackened paper every time the key was depressed. He wanted to see if Alessandra could use her telekinetic power to depress the key and leave a mark on the paper. The humidity made Alessandra feel faint, and every few minutes Bloch would pull out a handkerchief and blow his nose, breaking her concentration. She finally produced a single click and a tiny squiggle, but it took her all evening, didn't impress Bloch much, and left her drained.

At the Austrian border, a suspicious inspector rummaged through our luggage, and it didn't get put back on the train in time, so Alessandra arrived in Salzburg without a change of clothes. Once we got to the university, Professor Glockner insisted Alessandra stand on a coal scale to measure her weight before and after each sitting—why, I don't know. "I'm not a cow!" she protested. They sparred with each other for three nights, with Lombardi playing the exasperated referee, and she didn't produce anything. When we left, Glockner handed her a peace offering of a box of chocolates, but she refused to take them.

On the train to Linz, she complained of stomach pains, and while Lombardi was off having a drink in the dining car we had a big fight.

"Alessandra, you got to see a doctor," I demanded. "There's something wrong."

"No!" she shouted. "It's the food. I hate German food!" She hugged a pillow to her stomach and glared at me. "*Porco Dio!* I'm sorry I even mentioned it to you."

When we got to the hotel, she headed straight to her room skipping her supper. After coffee, Lombardi sent me up to check on her.

I knocked on her door. No answer. I knocked again.

"Alessandra?"

"Who is it?" came an angry voice from the other side of the door.

"It's me. Tommaso."

I heard her cross the room, the lock turn, and the door opened a crack.

Her eyes were red and puffy.

# 39

I slipped inside.

Alessandra locked the door behind me, walked over and sat down on the bed. I came over and sat down beside her.

"I'm pregnant," she said.

She suddenly burst into tears, and buried her face in my shoulder.

I put my arms around her, my head spinning. Pregnant, Jesus!

Pigotti must have taken her right before she escaped Naples, a parting gift from the bastard. The thought of Pigotti on top of Alessandra made me sick.

The *cazzo* had managed to screw her twice. The tour was over. Finished. When Lombardi found out, he would send Alessandra back to Naples. He was a married man, and people were already whispering about his gallivanting around Europe with his dusky, Latin mistress. Would he even pay Alessandra her fee? That would cause talk. The scandalmongers would say he was paying her to be quiet.

Unless...what?

Unless they *were* having an affair—and *Lombardi* was the father.

The more I thought about it, the more it made sense.

They were simply using each other in the beginning. Lombardi needed her to win a Nobel Prize, and Alessandra was picking Lombardi's pocket, desperate to escape Naples. But Huxley's attack had pushed them together. Her success in Genoa brought them even closer, and by Geneva they were actually enjoying each other's company—drinking wine on the terrace, laughing about cuckoo clocks, cruising Lac Leman together sharing cheese and biscuits on Fournier's sailboat, him gallantly diving in the water, suit and all, to rescue her. Then there was the jealous glare Lombardi gave Philippe the night Alessandra flirted with him. The bouquet of roses Lombardi gave her after the *Tribune* story was published, the two of them enjoying a private *tete-a-tete* under the moonlight at the edge of the lake the night before we departed Lausanne.

How would Lombardi react when he found out? He wouldn't want the baby, that was for sure. Thank God he was a doctor. He could arrange something—do it quickly and quietly. I felt my heart rise.

Alessandra stared at the floor.

"It's all right," I said, squeezing her hand. "Everything's going to be all right."

"The father?" I finally asked.

She looked up at me.

"Dr. Cappelli."

# 40

"Cappelli?" I stammered.

She clutched my hand, her eyes brimming with tears.

"I was desperate, Tommaso. Dr. Lombardi had turned us down and Rossi was going to stop the sittings. I was afraid to tell my husband. So I went to see him." She let go of my hand, pulled out her handkerchief, and swiped at her eyes.

"Alessandra," I said, "you don't have to tell me about it, if you don't want to." I pulled her closer, and caught a tear sliding down her cheek. " It's over. It happened."

She stared at her handkerchief. We sat there in silence. The room hot and stuffy. A ceiling fan circled slowly in the gloom above our heads, doing nothing. I thought of going over and opening the window, but didn't want to let go of Alessandra's hand. In the lamplight, I could see the pain on her face. When she finally spoke, her voice was dull and flat.

"He told me to come in the afternoon. When I got there, he answered the door himself. The servants were gone. So was his wife. I knew then what he wanted, but I thought maybe I could get his help without doing…everything."

Her voice was a whisper now.

"He invited me into the drawing room, and I told him what Rossi said, that the sittings cost too much, and he was going to stop them. I asked him if he could help.

He went over to a cabinet and pulled out a bottle of liquor, and brought it back, and put it on the table. He poured two glasses, and told me he liked me a lot, and would pay for the sittings... if I would do something for him. "

She turned to me, her eyes searching mine, begging for understanding, absolution.

Suddenly, everything made sense—the "stomach ache" that kept her from going to the Minerva Club that night. Throwing up in the dormitory before we left for Genoa. The cramps she had in Heidelberg at breakfast. Same thing my mother had when she was pregnant with my brother Paolo. *Nausea mattutina.* Morning sickness.

And the letter Cappelli sent her shortly after we arrived in Torino –how Alessandra's hand trembled when I gave it to her.

"Dr. Cappelli knows, doesn't he?" I said.

"Yes."

"What does he want to do?"

"He doesn't want it."

"Maybe he'll send you some money for the... operation."

"He's moved to Palermo."

I put my arm around her shoulder and she leaned into me, the tears flowing now. Cappelli didn't give a shit. He got what he wanted. When you have money, you can fuck people and get away with it. It's always been that way. It isn't going to change.

I heard heavy footsteps coming down the hall and held my breath, afraid it was Lombardi coming to look for us. But the footsteps passed by the door and on down the hall. We waited until it was quiet again.

"What will you do now?" I finally said.

Her voice was fierce.

"I'm going to keep the baby."

I stared at her. "That's crazy."

Alessandra turned her tear-stained face to me. "It's a girl, Tommaso. I know it is." She put her hands on her stomach.

"I've always dreamed of having a little girl. We're going to Rome—just me and her... I'm going to call her Zoe."

I stood up. "Alessandra, stop it! You don't know it's a girl, and even if it is, you can't keep it. Lombardi's bound to notice. He's not blind. He'll send you back to Naples—with nothing!"

"I can, damn it!" Alessandra shouted. "I can! I can!" She hugged her waist. "I just have to hide it for six weeks." She reached for my arm. "You'll help me."

"Alessandra, you're so close. You can make it to Rome..."

"Shut up, Tommaso!" She clutched her stomach, rocking back and forth, the tears now running down her cheeks. "Me and Zoe... Me and Zoe."

# 41

I paced my room, eyes fixed on the clock hanging on the wall next to the armoire. Give her an hour, she said. She needed to think. Then we could talk. The second it struck nine P.M., I hurried up the hall to Alessandra's room.

When I got there, the sheets had been stripped off the bed and Alessandra was sitting on the bare mattress, her skirt hiked up, a towel between her legs. Her undergarments hung on the back of the chair. Next to her leg, gleaming in the light of the bedside lamp, was a long, thin, steel rod with a hook on the end.

A boot hook.

I stared at it stupidly for a second before it hit me.

"You're going to … "

"I can't keep her."

Her words have haunted me for twenty years. God, the inexpressible anguish in her voice—how much she wanted that child! And she could have. The truth is, we could have pulled it off—six weeks—but I was too damn selfish. I didn't want her "little Zoe" to screw up the tour. I wanted to see Paris.

"What do you want me to do?" I said.

"Just stay here with me."

I nodded my head.

Alessandra reached across the bed and squeezed my hand. Her eyes were wet with tears. "Thank you, Tommaso."

I squeezed back. "You and me, remember?"

I couldn't watch. I retreated to the bathroom. I waited, gripping the sink, my back to the half-closed door. I could hear her shifting around on the bed, making small groans, then I heard a short, sharp inhale, followed by rapid panting, then an ominous silence.

"Alessandra?" I called out, scared. "Alessandra!"

In the mirror, I could only see her lower legs. As I watched, she pulled up her knees, rose up on the balls of her feet, and dug her heels into the mattress.

"Aagh! God!" she screamed.

I spun around, yanked the door open, and ran to her bed.

She lay on her back, blood trickling down her thigh, the hook clutched in her hand. Her eyes were shut and she was panting hard. I snatched the hook from her hand, pulled her dress over her, and hurried back to the bathroom. I threw the hook in the sink, grabbed a towel and rushed back. She lay there gasping, her pale face covered with sweat. Suddenly she let out a groan and her stomach tightened and her legs jerked up again and her body shuddered, and stuff came out. I nearly vomited.

She turned to me. "The towel," she rasped.

I gave it to her. She groaned and began swabbing between her legs. When she finished she let it drop and fell back on the pillow.

"Hide it, Tommaso," she whispered.

I balled up the two blood-soaked towels and stood there, looking around. I couldn't leave them in the room. The maid would find them. I stuffed them under my coat, slipped out of the room, locking the door behind me, the key shaking in my hand, and hurried down the back stairs and into the alley behind the hotel. A waiter was smoking a cigarette against the wall. He looked at me, surprised. I hesitated, then turned and walked out to the street. The river was only a few blocks away.

When I got back to the room, Alessandra was sitting up in bed, her head in her hands, crying. I sat down beside her.

"Everything's going to be alright," I said.

# 42

The clerk at the front desk greeted Lombardi with a stack of mail when we checked in at the Hotel Kaiserin. The bell boy took our bags to our rooms and Lombardi, eager to make amends to Alessandra for the extra tour stops, took us to Café Frauenhuber, where Mozart and Beethoven drank coffee while composing music. He knew the city, and had promised us a taste of Vienna's celebrated pastries.

Lombardi studied the menu, and turned to Alessandra.

"Can that bad stomach of yours handle an *eiskaffee*? The coffee is strong, but it's poured over ice cream."

"My stomach is fine," she said. "I told you."

Alessandra was a survivor. You come from Naples, you have to be. You get knocked down, you get up. You go on with your life. We have a saying: Life is like a henhouse ladder—short and full of shit. The morning after she used the boot hook on herself, she showed up for breakfast. She was still bleeding, but she was scared Lombardi would be suspicious and demand to examine her "stomach ache." What was left inside her came out a few days later, on the train ride to Vienna. She drank this stuff I bought for her at a chemist, locked herself in the bathroom, and it ended up on the tracks. But after that her insides were all screwed up.

The waiter brought our drinks, Sachertorte for them and a Kaiserschmarrn for me. Mine was delicious.

As he sipped his coffee, Lombardi worked his way through the letters, including one from Gemelli back in Torino.

He frowned and put down his cup.

"Professor Gemelli says there's a petition circulating at the university to censure me."

"Censure you? Why?" I asked.

"They say I'm embarrassing the university by studying Spiritualist nonsense." Lombardi unfolded a newspaper clipping Gemelli had included in his letter.

"What's this?"

He started reading it to us.

Huxley hadn't wasted any time launching his counter-attack.

### Dubrovsky Exposer Dismisses
### Geneva Spiritualist Photograph

———

A French magician may have been impressed by the table levitation produced by Italian medium Alessandra Poverelli last week in Geneva, Switzerland, but Nigel Huxley, chief investigator for the London Society for the Investigation of Mediums, remains skeptical. Mr. Huxley is well-known for his successful exposure earlier this year of the infamous Russian occultist Madame Dubrovsky.

A flash-light photograph of the alleged "levitation" appeared last week in many newspapers on the Continent, prompting a warning from the veteran psychic investigator. "Publicity is the goal of any stage magician, and one can't blame Monsieur D'Argent for seizing the opportunity to promote himself. But science is not entertainment. Unfortunately, Professor Lombardi seems intent on turning his scientific tour into a traveling circus. "

Mr. Huxley recently completed his preliminary investigation of the Italian medium which he conducted in France, and the Society will soon issue its official report on that investigation. "*Signora* Poverelli is an extremely charming woman. Whether this has clouded the judgment of Dr. Lombardi and some of our Latin colleagues on the Continent, I cannot say. But everything I myself witnessed can be easily explained without resorting to the supernatural."

Lombardi tossed the clipping on the table and smiled at Alessandra. "At least Huxley got one thing right. You can be charming at times."

Lombardi signaled the waiter for another coffee, and turned to the last unopened letter. It was a *Mattino* envelope, sporting a crowing rooster.

"This one's for you, Tommaso."

## 43

It was from Doffo.

I opened it nervously. Doffo had promised to let me know if he heard anything about Pigotti coming after Alessandra. My first thought was Pigotti was on a train headed for Vienna to kill Alessandra.

But the threat wasn't from Pigotti. It was something more frightening.

> *Tommaso, I just received the enclosed letter from Pietro. The Vatican is coming after Alessandra. I will try to learn more. P.S. The Weasel is a Jesuit they use when they go after big game.*

Pietro was Doffo's boyfriend back in Rome. He would show up in Naples for a few days and they would disappear together. He was a few years older than Doffo, tall and thin, with a neatly trimmed beard. His father cleaned the bathrooms at St. Peter's. He wrote terrible poetry, but told the funniest stories—he was always making jokes about the Pope. He worked as a secretary in the Church's Office of the Holy Inquisition. In the old days, they kept a watchful eye on everybody, eager to pounce on heresy. Every village had a priest, and every priest reported to Rome. *I principi hanno le braccia lunghe.* Princes have long arms, as we say in Italy.

The rack and strappado had disappeared long before Garibaldi defeated the papal army and took Rome, but the Office still monitored and harassed enemies of the Church—and they had friends in every major newspaper in the country, eager and willing to publish any scandals they uncovered.

Doffo had blacked out the personal parts of Pietro's letter, but what remained was alarming.

> *...and here's the juiciest piece of gossip! This morning I was scribbling away at my desk just outside Cardinal Uccello's office, pretending to work, while eavesdropping on His Eminence, as usual. He was meeting with the Weasel—I'm sure you remember him. Nasty, nasty man. My ears perked up when Uccello started complaining about a Neapolitan medium named Alessandra Poverelli. Isn't she Tommaso's friend? I decided to reorganize a file in his office while they talked, and they ignored the little mouse in the corner arranging his cheeses. It seems Signora Poverelli is troubling the sleep of the Supreme Pontiff, and when His Holiness Vincenzo Gioacchino Raffaele Luigi Pecci tosses and turns all night, none of us here at the Vatican sleep well. The Pope is worried about the credibility she's providing the Spiritualist heresy, and has decided to publicly denounce her table levitations as the work of Satan. (You would think Lucifer could produce something more spectacular.) His Eminence however seemed more offended by her sex life. "She's a terrible moral example for Italian women—she's unmarried, childless and living in sin." (Sounds like fun!) He's assigned the Weasel to dig up dirt on Alessandra. He gave him a fat envelope*

*stuffed with lire and told him to start in Bari, where she was born. Poor Alessandra. If she's been naughty, the Weasel will find out. Remember what he did to Gaetano. I'll keep you informed. Tommaso's been a friend to us and, if I can help him, I'm happy to do so. Uccello keeps the juicy information in a locked drawer in his desk. He thinks he has the only key, but he's wrong.*

I looked up and they were both staring at me. I had completely forgotten they were there.

"Well, aren't you going to read it to us?" Alessandra demanded.

"Just Doffo with the latest gossip from the *Mattino* office," I replied, trying to sound nonchalant. "I won't bore you." Fortunately, just then the waiter appeared with the bill, and I hastily stuffed the letter back in the envelope.

A few centuries earlier, Alessandra would have joined Savonarola at the stake.

In 1856, Pope Pius IX had denounced mediumship as "heretical, scandalous, and contrary to the honesty of customs." The Church didn't want you dabbling in divination or talking to the dead. That was their job. They really got nervous when spirits speaking through mediums talked about a life beyond the veil which didn't include eternal damnation. Take that away and the pews empty fast.

The Italian newspapers had started to follow Alessandra's tour through Europe. She sold papers. She was Italian, beautiful, outspoken, and readers were clamoring for more stories about the "Witch of Naples." Everyone in Italy was talking about Alessandra, and the Italian Spiritualist Society was using her to promote new Spiritualist circles in a dozen cities. No wonder the Pope had nightmares.

It wouldn't take long for the Weasel to find her pile of dirty laundry.

Alessandra was living on the streets when she was fourteen, and you survive by stealing—or by selling yourself. Her husband was a gangster.

The Pope could do a lot with that information.

# 44

Weitzel's students had it all figured out.

They knew how Alessandra did her table levitation trick.

Professor Weitzel and Lombardi had done their undergraduate work together at the University of Bologna where they were rivals. Weitzel had graduated first in their class, Lombardi second.

"Frankly, Camillo, I think this whole business is nonsense," Weitzel told Lombardi as we sat in his spacious office at the University of Vienna. "But my students here are champing at the bit to take a crack at your *Signora* Poverelli. We're ready to start tonight." Heads nodded around the table. There were six of them, not much older than me, bright-eyed and sitting on the edge of their seats, eager to challenge Alessandra.

"Could we do it tomorrow night?" Lombardi asked. "We just got into town on Friday."

Weitzel stiffened. He looked sourly at Lombardi. "The department is pretty busy, frankly."

On the way back to the hotel, a crowd of church-goers were pouring out of St. Stephen's cathedral reminding us that it was Sunday. As our carriage passed down Singerstrasse, Alessandra turned to Lombardi.

"Do we have to do it tonight, Camillo?"

Lombardi frowned. "Dr. Weitzel is doing me a favor. If he wants to start tonight, we have to do it."

"That's ridiculous. Surely he can wait one day."

"Tonight!" Lombardi snapped. "No arguing, Alessandra. I'm tired too, but we have obligations."

I saw my opening.

"Why don't we go to the park?' I said cheerfully.

I wanted to ride the Big Wheel. The bell boy had told me all about it. The *Riesenrad* had been added to the park three years earlier, for the Golden Jubilee of Emperor Franz Josef. It towers over the park, soaring 65 meters into the sky above the city. I *had* to ride it.

"We're all tired," Lombardi said. "Tommaso's right. Let's go to the park and have lunch."

Lombardi rented a carriage and he sat in the back seat with Alessandra as we traveled the length of the flower-lined Hauptallee, the magnificent, main boulevard through the Weiner Prater. Lombardi worked on her, entertaining her with funny comments, and she finally started smiling again as we clip-clopped beneath the magnificent chestnut trees, the shady meadows filled with picnickers and lovers, the small ponds where little boys were launching their toy boats, and the colorful parade of humanity sharing the sunny boulevard with us—young military cadets in their red and gold uniforms strutting with their giggling girlfriends, nannies with their wicker prams, barrel organ players and accordion players, acrobats and beggars.

We rounded a curve and right in front of us was the Big Wheel.

"Can I ride it?" I asked.

"Let's all go!" Lombardi laughed, and looked at Alessandra.

"Alessandra looked up nervously at the wheel. "You and Dr. Lombardi go."

"Don't be afraid," I said. "Come."

"I'm *not* afraid!" she shot back. "It's just that … ."

" … you're afraid." Lombardi teased. "That's all right, the men will ride it, won't we Tommaso." He winked at me. Alessandra glared at him, then sat back in her seat and crossed her arms.

"I've changed my mind."

I felt a bit queasy myself when the carriage dropped us off next to the metal monster. Lombardi sent me off to buy ice creams while he got the tickets. As the line crept closer, Alessandra edged closer to Lombardi. The attendant took our tickets, Alessandra grabbed Lombardi's arm, and we crowded into the bright red cabin with ten other people. The cabin jerked forward to load the one behind us and Alessandra clung to Lombardi. Then we rose up into the blue summer sky, higher and higher till you could see the whole magnificent city spread out below us, with its green parks and the Karlskirche and Strauss's serene, blue Danube off in the distance.

Except Alessandra, because her eyes were shut.

The third time around, Lombardi finally talked her into opening her eyes. The fourth go-around, she was standing next to the window oohing and ahhing with the rest of us. When the wheel finally stopped, I hopped off and she and Lombardi took another spin, Alessandra happily waving at me each time they swooped by, Lombardi with his hand on her shoulder and a grin on his face.

Alessandra had a great time that afternoon, but she fought all evening with Weitzel.

On the way to the experiment room, we passed by a laboratory where stacks of caged dogs howled and whimpered. She asked Weitzel what was going on, and he said they were going to be used for medical research. The average Neapolitan wouldn't think twice about drowning a sack of kittens, or tying a string to a bird's leg and swinging it around his head, but Alessandra had a soft spot for animals, and they fell into a heated argument. Weitzel told her that animals don't really feel pain—they're just "machines made out of flesh," as he put it—and when she continued arguing, he suggested testily that she spend less time talking with spirits and more time studying science. By the time we got to the test room, they were shouting at each other.

Weitzel's students were waiting for Alessandra when we got there. She was quickly steered over to the table, told to sit down, and two of Weitzel's students brought out a folding pasteboard screen which they placed between Alessandra's legs and the table.

"*Cosa fanno?*" Alessandra demanded. What the hell were they doing?

They hesitated, and looked towards Weitzel who was talking with Lombardi. Weitzel walked over.

"It's part of the experiment," he told her curtly. "To keep your dress from touching the table. Professor Lombardi told you about it." He turned to Lombardi. "Didn't you?"

Alessandra glared at Lombardi. "*Cosa?*"

Lombardi looked at her sheepishly. "Dr. Negri noticed during one table levitation that your dress puffed out until it touched and partially covered one foot of the table. Theoretically, it might allow you to…"

She stared at him. Lombardi looked at Weitzel.

"Dr. Weitzel's team wants to eliminate the possibility of…"

Alessandra's eyes narrowed. "Of what?"

"Fraud." Weitzel stared back at her, arms folded.

"You're accusing me of cheating?"

Lombardi grabbed her arm. "Alessandra! Enough!" He pointed to the chair. "Sit down! Nobody is accusing you of anything. It's a scientific experiment—that's all."

They argued about the gas lights. Alessandra wanted the room darker. Weitzel vetoed it. Alessandra wanted the assistants to simply place their hands on top of hers, not hold her fingers. Weitzel vetoed it. She wanted the screen moved slightly to the left—she needed more room for her knees. They argued over that for five minutes. Finally Weitzel slammed his fist on the table and jabbed his finger in her face.

"You're stalling! You can't do anything with the screen in front of you—can you?" He looked at her contemptuously. "You're a fraud. Go back to Naples and entertain your credulous countrymen."

I expected Alessandra to jump up and slap him. Instead, she sat there, staring hard at him, her jaw set. Lombardi came over and put his hand on her shoulder.

"Alessandra…"

She jerked away from him, her eyes still fixed on Weitzel.

"I'm ready," she said.

Weitzel's assistants intertwined their fingers with Alessandra's, the gas lamp was turned down, and we started. There was no prayer, no call to the spirits. Alessandra immediately locked her gaze on the hated pasteboard screen. Five minutes into the sitting, the assistant on Alessandra's right lifted his head and sniffed the air. He looked around puzzled, sniffing again. Across the room, I suddenly caught the smell –the acrid whiff of smoldering paper. I looked over at Alessandra, then at the screen. A wisp of smoke had begun to curl from the top corner, illuminated by the flickering lamp as it climbed towards the ceiling.

At the end of the table, Weitzel stood up and wrinkled his nose.

"I smell…"

The pasteboard screen burst into flames.

"Get back! Get back!" someone shouted. Everybody started yelling, falling down, trying to escape, Weitzel flailing at the fire with his coat. Lombardi lunged for Alessandra, flames now licking at her skirt. I heard a scream and saw

Weitzel's assistant slapping his shirt sleeve which had caught fire. Weitzel stepped back, a look of horror on his face, then turned and sprinted for the door.

"Get out!" Lombardi yelled at me. The three of us stumbled into the hall, choking and coughing from the smoke. People were running up the hall carrying buckets of water. We made our way down the stairs and outside to the street where we found Weitzel and his assistants huddled together near a bench, dazed looks on their faces. Weitzel had lost a shoe in his mad scramble to escape.

Alessandra marched over to Weitzel.

"*Vafanculo!*" she said.

Then she turned to Lombardi.

"Take me back to the hotel."

The next morning, Lombardi talked with Weitzel and they mutually agreed to cancel the second test.

## 45

By the time we reached Munich, Alessandra was ready to quit.

She was still angry and upset at Weitzel's rude treatment, her cough had worsened, and the bleeding hadn't completely stopped.

It was a gray and rainy Sunday. Alessandra came down late for breakfast, and Lombardi and I were already drinking our coffee. After we ordered, he leaned forward and tried a smile on her.

"Well, sleepyhead, would you like to come with me to Baron von Weibel's castle to see the arrangements for tomorrow night?"

"No, I wouldn't," she snapped.

I tried one. I picked up the breadbasket and passed it across the table to Alessandra.

"Would *Frau* Poverelli care for a *Brötchen?*"

Alessandra reached for it just as a waiter leaned over to fill her water glass, and he spilled the pitcher on her arm.

"*Porca miseria!*" she cried. Lombardi jumped up with his napkin to dry her off, but she pushed him away.

"I don't need your help!" she said.

She threw her napkin on the table and stomped back upstairs to her room. Lombardi shook his head and sat back down.

'What's the matter with her, Tommaso?"

"She'll be alright," I said. I had already turned my attention to the giant platter of ham, sausages and cheeses the waiter was laying on the table. I was eager to start eating.

"*Buon appetito*," I said.

Lombardi sighed.

"Well, stay here and keep an eye on her today."

I spent the afternoon in the library. It was a dark and gloomy room, with heavy furniture and an empty fireplace. The room was deserted except for an elderly man dressed in a black Sunday suit and vest, with a high starched collar, sitting in a leather chair with a monocle in his eye, reading a newspaper. He looked at me sourly when I entered.

Church bells tolled in the distance and I walked over to the window. Heavy maroon curtains blocked most of the weak light from the leaden sky outside. I looked out onto the street. The rain was falling steadily, water rushing down the gutters. A newspaper boy was sitting in an archway across the street, his cap pulled down over his face, a stack of newspapers at his side. He was looking at the sole of his shoe, which had a big hole in it. He took his shoe off, stuffed a wad of paper in it, and put it back on. A carriage passed by and he hopped up, ran out into the rain and chased it down the street, waiving a paper, but it didn't stop. He dejectedly returned to his shelter.

When I turned around, the old man with the newspaper was talking heatedly in German to the desk clerk who had slipped into the room. All I caught was *schwartze*. That's what the German tourists called me when I was selling post cards back in Naples. It means black, and he obviously didn't like the idea that I was in the library. The other thing they always called us was *makaronifresser*— macaroni eaters.

The clerk whispered something in his ear, he glared at me, then got up and shuffled out, leaving the room to me.

All the magazines were in German, but I flipped through a few, looking at the photographs—the Kaiser on a horse reviewing troops, a photo of a big battleship being launched, a football team scoring a goal. I finally headed back to my room. I tapped on Alessandra's door as I passed by but she didn't answer. I figured she was sleeping.

I was wrong.

# 46

W here the devil is she?" Lombardi complained. We had been sitting there for a half an hour waiting for her to show up to eat. He looked at his watch. "7:30 already. Tommaso, go up and get her."

I knocked on her door. No answer. I knocked again.

"Go away!" It was Alessandra.

"It's me, Tommaso," I said. "Lombardi is waiting for you downstairs. You're late for dinner."

No answer. I tried the doorknob. It was unlocked, so I opened the door.

Alessandra was sitting at her desk wearing nothing but her drawers and a chemise, a bottle of wine in her hand. A second bottle, empty, lay on the floor at her feet. The closet was open, and a jumble of clothes was stuffed into a half-packed bag on her bed.

"Tommaso?" She held out the bottle. "Find a glass."

I snatched the bottle from her hand.

"Jesus, where did you get this?" I demanded.

"Room service." She lunged for the bottle. "Give it back."

I swept the empty bottle off the floor, dumped the half-finished one in the bathroom sink, and hid the empties behind the toilet. I hurried back out, grabbed Alessandra's dress from her bag, yanked her to her feet, shoved the dress into her hand, and steered her towards the bathroom.

"Get dressed!" I shouted. "Lombardi may come looking for us any minute."

"Fuck him!" she said, pulling her arm away. She stood there, hands on her hips. "Give me the bottle, Tommaso."

I should have locked the door. I heard a man's voice in the hallway outside.

"Tommaso? Alessandra?"

I watched horrified as the doorknob turned and Lombardi stepped into the room.

# 47

L ombardi's jaw dropped.

He stared at Alessandra, his face beet red, then turned his head away.

"Good God, woman, get dressed."

Alessandra walked over to the bed, sat down and folded her arms.

"Why? Time for your monkey to put on a show? Did you bring your organ?" She grabbed the pillow and flung it at him. "That's all I am. A trained monkey!"

"Stop it, Alessandra!" Lombardi picked up the pillow.

Alessandra glared at him. "I'm sick and tired of all your stupid experiments, your theories, your poking and prodding. You want to know how I levitate a table? THE SPIRITS DO IT! How do they do it? I don't know, and I don't care!"

She jumped off the bed, reached down, grabbed her shoe and flung that at him. "*Basta!*" Lombardi ducked as the boot whizzed by his ear.

"Stop it! Do you want to be sent home?"

"Sent home? You don't have to send me home—I quit!" She grabbed a corset out of her bag and started putting it on. "I'm tired of being in your freak show."

Lombardi blushed. "Tommaso, go back to your room. I'll deal with Alessandra."

Alessandra walked over to the window and leaned her head against the window.

"Oh God, I am so tired of everything."

And she began to cry.

# 48

Neither Lombardi nor Alessandra showed up for dinner. I finally ordered something, ate by myself, then returned to my room and started packing my bag. I knew Lombardi was going to terminate us. Alessandra had blown it, so close to the finish line—only Warsaw and Paris left on the tour. Two stops. Then she could have demanded her 4,000 *lire*. Instead, she was going back to Naples broke, and Pigotti would eventually find her. There was no place to hide. The Camorra had spies everywhere in the city. And when he found her, he would mess her up bad. She had gotten so close, but her dream was dead.

I was asleep when I heard a soft knock on my door.

I looked over at the clock. It was almost midnight. I heard another tap, then a faint voice.

"*Psst!* Tommaso! It's me."

I slipped on my trousers and hurried over to the door. I peeked out and Alessandra was standing in the hall in her petticoat. She slipped inside and I quickly closed the door behind her.

"What are you doing here?" I said.

"I have to talk to you."

"So it's over?" I asked her.

"No," she said. "It's…it's…" She shook her head. "Tommaso, it's so crazy…"

"What do you mean?" I demanded.

She went over to the bed and sat down. She looked dazed.

"Well?"

"After you left, he asked me to sit down and said he was tired of the tour too, and fighting with his university, and he's thinking of moving to Paris. He knows the city from his school days, and he says Renard can help him find a position."

"He's thinking of leaving Italy?"

"And his wife. He's filing for divorce"

"You're kidding!"

Alessandra looked at me. "He told me things, Tommaso. He's unhappy in his marriage. He hasn't slept with his wife for three years. I felt sorry for him, Tommaso. He's not a bad man."

Alessandra leaned forward.

"He...he has feelings for me, Tommaso. He said I'm the first woman he's met that he can't figure out—and he's a psychiatrist." She smiled. "He said I made his life exciting."

"You're pretty good at leading men around by the nose," I said.

"It's more than that, Tommaso. I've come to like him, to admire him. He's got courage, Tommaso. When he believes in something, he doesn't care what other people think. He's risking everything because he believes in me."

She paused.

"He wants me to go to Paris with him."

"You're kidding!" I was floored.

"He has an inheritance, and he still has an apartment there—from his medical school days. He said we could live together first. He said they're more open in Paris about those things. Then when his divorce came through, we could marry."

"What did you tell him?"

"I thanked him, Tommaso, and told him I would shut up and behave, and do whatever he wanted. But when the tour is over, I'm taking my money and going to Rome."

I couldn't believe my ears.

"Alessandra, you're crazy! You just won the lottery! He's got money! Food on the table, a roof over your head, for the rest of your life. And on top of that, he loves you! Holy Mother of God…"

Alessandra shook her head.

"He'll never marry me, Tommaso. Right now, I'm different and exciting, and I can help him. But he'd eventually find someone else in Paris—some woman younger and more interesting and more respectable than me. Then I'd have to start all over again. That's how men are."

Outside the window, church bells tolled midnight.

She slid off the bed and headed for the door.

"You can't rely on others, Tommaso. You can only rely on yourself."

# 49

Lombardi tried hard to change her mind.

He cut in half the number of sittings in Germany, and changed the schedule to give Alessandra every other day off. Baron von Weibel invited us to move out of the Rheinischer Hof hotel and stay at his castle, and Lombardi quickly accepted. Weibel had a lake on his estate, and Lombardi arranged for breakfast to be served late every morning in a pretty outdoor pavilion at the water's edge where he and Alessandra spent a lot of time sitting and talking.

The late summer weather had turned beautiful—sunny with blue skies, warm in the day but pleasantly cool in the evenings—and Lombardi took her riding in a carriage through the baron's oak forest filled with pheasants and wild boar, and a noisy, little woodpecker whose *rat-a-tat-tat* made Alessandra laugh out loud. When the weekend came, Lombardi surprised us by taking us to see mad King Ludwig's fairy-tale castle in the Bavarian Alps—Neuschwanstein had just been opened to the public. You've seen it in postcards, I'm sure. It sits atop a mountain like a Wagner opera set, and Alessandra wandered awestruck through the halls, hand in hand with Lombardi, marveling at the murals of medieval knights and malevolent sorceresses and shell-boats drawn across the water by silver swans. She had never seen anything like it in her life. Neither had I. Before we left, he bought her a pretty music box with a picture of the castle in winter painted on the lid, and she slept on his shoulder during the train ride back to Munich.

The sittings that week in Germany were few, but went well. Alessandra was determined to do her best for Lombardi.

The most amazing incident in Munich happened in broad daylight.

The baron had bought a Cinématographe motion picture camera that Spring from the Lumière factory in Lyon. They cost a fortune, and I had never seen a motion picture camera before. I finally screwed up my courage and asked him if I could inspect it. The next morning, he set it up on the front lawn, and was explaining how it worked, when Alessandra and Lombardi came strolling up from the lake with their picnic basket. The baron waved them over.

"Tommaso here is learning how to use the motion picture camera."

Alessandra grinned, put down her basket, and pirouetted in a circle.

I laughed. "The Baron isn't interested in filming *you* dance," I teased. "He wants to see your *basket* dance."

Lombardi had given her a bouquet of wildflowers at breakfast, and Alessandra was feeling happy. Without thinking—as she later confessed—she turned around, waved her hand like an orchestra conductor, and the wicker basket suddenly rose up and began to do a little jig. The Baron stood there speechless, mouth agape.

Miraculously, the camera was loaded, and I had the presence of mind to start cranking the handle. I ended up capturing eight seconds of the action on film. Alessandra's back is already to the camera when the film starts, but you clearly see her arm come up, then the basket dances out from behind her skirt, hops like a rabbit across the lawn, twirls around in a circle, then falls back to the grass. Later that summer, the Baron toured Bavaria, showing the film to packed houses, and the German press dubbed Alessandra the "Sorcerer's Apprentice." A professor in Berlin, who wasn't there that day, assured everyone that it was all done with wires and string.

Lombardi was ecstatic when Weibel played the film back that evening, and told me he was going to buy a motion picture camera for me to use when we got to Paris. I couldn't wait. I had visions of myself as the next Ugo Falena, directing films and entertaining thousands.

Renard had already sent out invitations to prominent French scientists to test Alessandra, *Le Figaro* had scheduled a major interview with her, and the editor of the *Parisian Illustrated Review* would be sending an artist over to the hotel to sketch the celebrated Neapolitan "Queen of Spirits." Everybody was excited and happy.

I had completely forgotten about the Weasel.

# 50

I got Doffo's second letter the day we left for Warsaw.

  Pietro had used his key to get into Uccello's desk, found the confidential report the Weasel had mailed to Cardinal Uccello following his visit to Bari, and copied it for Doffo.

  Alessandra was in trouble.

*July 16, 1899*
*Confidential*
*To His Eminence Cardinal Giovanni Uccello*
*From: Crocifisso Testa, Interrogator*
*Investigation of the Spiritualist medium Alessandra Poverelli*

*Pax Tecum.*

*On 7 July I met for two hours with Father Angelo Federico, parish priest of the village of Spinazzola in Bari, to find out what he could tell me about Signora Poverelli. Father Angelo is a simple man, of no great intelligence or learning, with only two years training in the local seminary. He has served in his current position for 27 years without promotion. He is short and fat, rather slovenly in his dress,* and lives with his housekeeper, most likely his concubine. According to Father Angelo, Alessandra's father was a Socialist agitator disliked by the villagers, and her mother an open practitioner of witchcraft who refused to have her child baptized. Her mother died when she was five and her father was publicly executed for treason by the King of Naples when she was 13 years old. Because of the family's unsavory reputation, no one in the village was willing to take her in, so out of Christian charity Father Angelo did. Satanic manifestations associated with her presence occurred frequently in the rectory, particularly when she was scolded by the housekeeper. Father Angelo suspected she was possessed by the Devil and performed an exorcism on her. I asked him if he had informed his Bishop before conducting the exorcism, and he replied that he saw no need to do so since they taught him the ritual in seminary. At this point, Father Angelo's housekeeper, who was serving the pasta, interrupted him. "He had to tie her to the bed, she was so wild. The good Father spent the whole night on his knees next to her bed, begging God to drive the Devil out. But Satan keeps his own. She was a slut, a puttana. Got herself pregnant shortly afterwards." My ears understandably perked up at this divine revelation. I asked Father Angelo if he knew who the father was. He said everyone suspected an acrobat named Ivano who came through the village with a traveling circus that summer. I asked him what had happened to Alessandra's bastard. He replied that he quietly arranged to send the pregnant Alessandra to the Santissima Bambina orphanage in Naples *to have her baby there. I assured him the Holy Father himself thanked him for this information, and for his years of hard labor in one of the more stony vineyards of the Lord. I am headed for Naples.*

*Ad Majorem Dei Gloriam.*

*P.S. Your Eminence would have been amused at the pasta presentation dreamed up by Father Angelo's housekeeper. The spaghetti was shaped in the profile of Jesus, with orecchiette for his ears.*

I stared at the letter, dumbfounded.

Alessandra had a bastard.

The Weasel would need the birth record, but he was already on that. Once he had it, the Vatican could leak it to the press, and the newspapers would go crazy. There was no way any respectable scientist could work with Alessandra once the scandal went public. Alessandra would be finished. So would Lombardi—the university would crucify him.

The only question was when the Vatican would drop the bombshell.

My guess was Paris.

I could have warned them, but I didn't. She and Lombardi looked so happy. And what would be the point? There was nothing they could do about it anyway. Besides, there was a small chance the Weasel wouldn't find anything. Twenty-six years had passed. That was a long time, and nobody kept good records on the nobodies who showed up to spend a few days with the sisters before delivering their brats, dumping their babies in an orphanage, and disappearing.

Me? I just wanted to make it to Paris. I figured I could use Lombardi's camera to shoot some photos of the new Tour Eiffel and sell them back in Naples when it was over.

You have to gnaw the bone that's thrown you.

# 51

"How do I look, Tommaso?"

"*Maronna!*" I stared at Alessandra.

How did she look? She looked spectacular—the Neapolitan cinder maid turned into a princess, ready for the reception at Countess Walewska's mansion. Polish newspapers and magazines had trumpeted her visit to Warsaw, and the city was buzzing about the mysterious Italian temptress who levitated tables.

Alessandra was squeezed into this long, beautiful, shimmering, emerald satin gown with puffy sleeves, a big bow on each shoulder, and a white satin rose on the sash around her waist. Lombardi had paid for it. He excused his generosity by telling her Warsaw society had its standards, and we don't want to embarrass the Countess. But they both knew he was still trying to get her to change her mind and move to Paris with him.

The hairdresser that afternoon had piled her long tresses on top of her head in a bun, and crowned it with a silver ribbon. But I couldn't take my eyes off her chest. The gown was cut daringly low in front.

Alessandra rested her arms on her full hips and twirled around, looking at herself in the mirror. She stopped, put her two hands on her stomach, and grimaced.

"God, I can hardly breathe in this contraption, but I do look ten years younger—tell me I do, Tommaso." She patted her bosom. "Do you think Camillo will like it?"

"If he doesn't, he's *pazzo*, crazy." I replied.

There was a knock on the door and I walked over and opened it. Lombardi stood in the hall, dressed to the nines. He sported a black tailcoat and trousers, a crisp white dress shirt with studs, a winged collar and a white silk bow tie, and black patent leather shoes. He stepped inside, took one look at Alessandra, and his jaw dropped.

"Do you think it's a bit too daring, Camillo?" Alessandra said, tugging at her dress. He stared at her. My guess is that he hadn't seen his own wife in something like that since their wedding night.

"I…I must say…it catches a man's attention."

I knew exactly what he was thinking—his attention, but also the attention of every other man in the room. Lombardi reached into his silk top hat, pulled out a small velvet box and presented it to Alessandra with a smile and a bow.

"I suggest you add these to your outfit tonight."

Alessandra opened the box and gasped.

"My God, Camillo!" She held up a pair of small, diamond ear rings. "I…I can't accept them."

Lombardi laughed. "Consider them on loan for the evening."

Cinderella was off to the ball.

## 52

K rol had Alessandra cornered.

He had pulled up his chair right in front of hers, blocking her from escape, and was describing the plot for his new novel. The Countess had introduced him as a famous Polish writer, and he certainly was verbose. I sat on a sofa next to Alessandra, watching Lombardi work his way around the crowded drawing room of her elegant, three-story *pied-a-terre* which looked out on Lazienki Park. The Italian ambassador to the Kingdom of Poland showed up with his wife, along with several Polish princes and counts, but my attention kept returning to Alessandra.

She looked pale, and fatigued.

The room was packed and humid. The servants had opened the windows wide, but Alessandra had her handkerchief out and was constantly patting the perspiration off her forehead.

"Do you believe in fate, *Signora* Poverelli?" Krol lit a cigarette, took a deep drag, then leaned forward. "I've been thinking for months about including a séance scene in my new novel, and now I have the queen of spirits sitting right in front of me. I have a thousand questions for you."

Alessandra shot me a pleading glance, and I stood up.

"You'll have to excuse her. Alessandra is fading a bit. We just arrive this afternoon and it was a long trip."

Krol ignored me. He jabbed his cigarette at her. "Do you use some special incantation to call the spirits? Do you actually see them, or do you just feel their presence in the room?"

I held out my hand to Alessandra. "We really need to get Alessandra some rest."

He pushed it away, irritated at my persistence. "All *Signora* Poverelli needs is another glass of wine. Waiter!"

Alessandra struggled to her feet. "Please, forgive me. I...I really must go."

She didn't look too steady. I took her elbow and steered her around the chair, as Krol glowered at me. Alessandra hung on to my arm.

"I feel sick. I need to find the bathroom."

As we made our way to the hallway, a balding man in a ridiculously bemedaled military uniform stepped forward and blocked our path.

"Finally let you go, did he? I've been trying all evening to meet the famous *Signora* Poverelli!" He bowed. "General Nikolai Bibikov, at your service."

I didn't know what to do. I had to get Alessandra to the bathroom quickly, but I was terrified of insulting him.

"There you are, Alessandra." Lombardi had come up behind me. He stepped forward to introduce himself to Bibikov and we escaped. Alessandra slipped into the bathroom, closed the door, and I hovered outside, pretending to inspect the paintings which lined the halls. A minute later, Lombardi came hurrying down the hall.

"Tommaso, where the devil is Alessandra? The General is waiting to meet her."

"She's feeling sick." I pointed to the bathroom. He grimaced.

"Well, as soon as she gets out, bring her to me."

Alessandra stayed in the bathroom for a long time, and when she came out, she didn't look much better, but she charmed Bibikov and managed to hang on until the reception ended at nine.

We made it outside into the cool evening air, and were waiting for our carriage to arrive, when Alessandra suddenly let go of my hand, fell to one knee, then collapsed on the sidewalk. Everybody started shouting and screaming, and Lombardi quickly bent down and cradled her head in his lap, searching for her pulse. She opened her eyes and looked at him, confused, then struggled to get back to her feet, but he held her there. I was scared to death. Someone ran to fetch Countess Walewska.

A few minutes later, the Countess ran down the steps, followed by the doorman with a glass of water, but Alessandra was already sitting up.

"I'm alright," she insisted. "It was just the heat. I'm feeling better now."

"*Signora*, please, come inside," the countess begged. "Stay here tonight." She looked at Lombardi, but Alessandra insisted she felt better, and wanted to go back to the hotel.

Later that night, I went up to visit Alessandra. She was sitting up in bed with a pillow behind her, looking pale but a lot better. Lombardi was just returning a stethoscope to his medical bag.

"I'm glad you're here, Tommaso," he said. "I've made a decision which affects both of you." He closed his bag.

"I'm canceling the rest of the tour."

"No!" Alessandra cried. She looked bewildered. "But why, Camillo?"

Lombardi took her hand.

"Alessandra, listen to me. You need rest. A month, at least. I blame myself. The traveling, the sittings every night, the need to perform—you're exhausted. Now this. I'm worried about you."

"Camillo, I'm fine!" Alessandra protested. "You'll see! Tomorrow, I'll be back to my old self." She began to cough, and Lombardi reached down into his medical bag and pulled out a bottle.

"This is laudanum. It will help you sleep tonight." He poured out a glass and gave it to her, then closed the bag. He took her hand again.

"Alessandra, I know you're worried about your fee. You don't have to. When we get to Torino, you will get your 4,000 *lire*. You've earned it."

I could see the tears well up in Alessandra's eyes. "Camillo...thank you. Thank you so much."

The tour was over. We were going home.

I followed Lombardi out into the hall, and he pulled me aside. "We're going to be in Warsaw for a while, Tommaso. She needs to stay in bed and rest. I want you to make sure she stays there."

After Lombardi left, I went back inside.

She patted the bed. "Sit down here. Next to me."

She looked at me for a long time, then she smiled. "If only I were twenty years younger...." I blushed. She fought to keep her eyes open, the laudanum beginning to take over. "You to Naples...me to Rome...I'm going to miss you terribly."

"I once dreamed about becoming the editor of the *Mattino*," I told her. "Now, it's not enough. I want to do something bigger. Maybe I'll follow you to Rome and become the editor of the *Messaggero*."

She smiled. "Wouldn't that be wonderful, Tommaso. You and me in Rome." She squeezed my hand, and her eyes fluttered and finally closed as the opium worked its magic.

Over in England, Huxley wasn't ready to let Alessandra walk away from the game.

# 53

Give Huxley credit.

He figured Alessandra out, and he played her brilliantly. The *Times* was in on the plan, but Huxley chose the bait, and set the hook.

We left Warsaw for Torino on Aug 10, 1899, my seventeenth birthday. I bought a bottle of Polish *wodka* the night before we left, drank half of it, and boarded the train with a terrible hangover. Lombardi had kept Alessandra in Warsaw for almost two weeks, then arranged a first-class sleeper for her on the Nord-Sued Express on the trip home. By the time we reached Zurich, she had made a remarkable recovery. The cough was still there, but color had returned to her face, along with her appetite. Lombardi kidded that she was "costing him a fortune" in the dining car.

At every stop along the way, reporters peppered Lombardi with questions, demanding to know why the tour had been suddenly cancelled. Not everybody bought his story that Alessandra's health was in danger. In Paris, *Le Petit Journal* breathlessly trumpeted that Weitzel in Vienna had caught Alessandra using matches to start a fire so she could terminate a failed sitting—a rumor Huxley planted.

We arrived back home on Sunday, and Lombardi put us up in the administrative guest house at the asylum until he could get to the bank to arrange our train tickets and Alessandra's payment. The impossible dream she had confessed to me that night at the Piazza del Plebiscito was about to come true. She could start a new life—without Pigotti, and with 4,000 *lire* in her purse. She would run her own life.

At ten o'clock the next morning, the "Kaiser" came looking for us. Frau Junker was as sour as ever.

"You will come with me. Dr. Lombardi wants to see you in his office."

When we got there, Lombardi was sitting behind his desk with a scowl on his face. Behind him was a cabinet of curiosities filled with fossils and stones. A row of ivory skulls mounted on iron rods sat on a side table—probably the props Lombardi had used in his famous Darwin lecture in Rome. A young, clean-shaven man in a sharp-looking, brown suit and silk tie lounged in a chair in front of Lombardi, a notebook and pen in his hands. He jumped up when Alessandra entered the room.

"*Signora* Poverelli?"

Lombardi gestured to him. "This is Mr. Harold Carter, Rome correspondent for the *London Times*. He insists on asking you a few questions."

Carter flashed Alessandra a boyish grin. "*Che piacere vederti.*" So pleased to meet you. His Italian was excellent. He bowed and kissed her hand. Huxley had picked the right messenger.

Frau Junker brought over two chairs, Lombardi dismissed her, and we all sat down.

"*Signora* Poverelli…" Carter started.

"Alessandra is fine," she replied with a smile, brushing back her long black hair.

"Thank you…Alessandra, then." He opened his notebook. "Our newspaper recently interviewed Mr. Nigel Huxley, an investigator for the London Society for…"

"We're quite familiar with Mr. Huxley," Lombardi interjected.

"I understand. I wanted to ask *Signora*—I'm sorry, *Alessandra*—here, if she had seen the interview."

"I haven't," Alessandra replied. "And I don't care what that *cazzo* says."

Carter laughed. "I understand. I won't read you the article. But I was hoping to get a comment from you on his offer to test you in England."

Lombardi stood up. "Alessandra has nothing left to prove. She's passed enough tests."

Carter ignored him. He held up a newspaper clipping and looked at Alessandra.

"In the interview here, Mr. Huxley explains how you *could* have produced the phenomena he witnessed at the sitting on Ile Ribaud. He suggests you come to England and demonstrate your paranormal powers. If you can, he says the Society will happily join its Continental colleagues and declare your powers genuine. Will you consider it?"

Lombardi slammed his fist on the table.

"She's not going to England, damn you!"

Alessandra wheeled on Lombardi. "Don't tell me what I can or can't do, Camillo!"

Carter kept his gaze on Alessandra. "If I could read you the last paragraph of the story? ... "

"Go ahead," Alessandra said.

Carter unfolded the newspaper clipping and read it. "I am confident our vulgar, little Neapolitan trickster will decline to be tested in England ... "

"Vulgar little trickster?" Alessandra was on her feet, fists clenched. Carter looked at her. "I apologize, *Signora* ... Should I continue?"

"Go on."

" ... She is a cheat. An extremely talented one, but a fraud nonetheless. I'll wager 100 pounds sterling ... "

"His own money?"

"Apparently, yes."

"Nothing will give me more pleasure than emptying that *stronzo*'s wallet." Carter smiled.

"Then you accept…"

"She can't afford a trip to England," Lombardi roared, "and I'm not paying!"

Carter folded the clipping. "That won't be necessary, Professor. The Society is offering to pay all travel costs—first class—as well as Alessandra's expenses while in England."

Lombardi pointed to the door. "Wait outside. I need to discuss this further with *Signora* Poverelli."

Carter picked up his hat and bowed to Alessandra. "It was a pleasure to finally meet you. When you get to England, please give Mr. Huxley my regards."

As soon as Carter left, Lombardi slammed the door.

"Alessandra, listen to me! This is crazy! You need at least another two, three weeks of rest. You've just gotten over…"

"I feel fine, damn it!"

"But you're not fine! Listen to your cough! I've been to England. It's rainy and damp. Terrible for your cough. And the travel—five days at least. For what? A hundred pounds?"

Lombardi went to his desk, yanked open the drawer, and pulled out his cheque book.

"I'll give you the hundred pounds. Here!" He started writing the cheque.

Alessandra came over and grabbed the pen. "I don't want your money, Camillo! I want his!" She flung the pen across the room. "A trickster? A fraud? I'll show the damn English who the fraud is!"

"Then I'm going with you."

"No! This is between me and him."

"It's not just between you and him! My reputation is at stake too! If you fail…"

"I won't fail."

"Alessandra, please—please. I'm begging you. "

"I have to, Camillo."

I saw my opportunity and grabbed it. "I'll go with her to England," I said. I had never been there, and I didn't want to go back to Naples. I wanted to see the world.

"Well then at least take Tommaso, Alessandra. I'll pay for him." Lombardi dropped into his chair and sighed. "This is crazy." He shook his head. "I'll wait for you in Paris, at Renard's apartment."

# 54

"Where is he?"

Alessandra was angry.

We stood in the cavernous station, surrounded by our luggage, looking around for the Thomas Cook agent the Society has promised would meet us when we got to London. The boat train from Dover arrived at Victoria Station, and we had to get over to King's Cross Station to catch the train to Cambridge.

"Huxley is behind this," she groused.

"Maybe we came in on a different track," I suggested.

"No! He planned this!" She stamped her foot angrily.

I looked up nervously at the station clock. We had been waiting there for 30 minutes, and we had less than an hour to find the other station. I pulled out the English phrase book Lombardi had given me in Paris the night we left for Calais.

"No problem. I can get us there," I said. I waved to a porter. "We'll take a cab." Lombardi had also slipped me five pounds British sterling for an emergency, and this was certainly one. I had no idea how frequently trains ran to Cambridge, and someone was supposedly waiting for us there. What if we missed them too?

Alessandra was still complaining when we got into the cab and the driver snapped the horse's reins and we rolled out into the busy street.

"I don't think he understood your directions," she said. "Maybe he'll take us to the wrong place. Maybe you should show him the word in the book."

I was getting exasperated. On the two-hour ferry ride across the Channel, she was in a constant panic. Lombardi had taken care of her all through Europe, but now it was just me and her.

"You're the one that wanted to come to England," I snapped.

"And the minute I get Huxley's money, we're out of here." She pulled her window curtain shut and crossed her arms. "I hate England."

Not me. I glued my face to the window and gaped at the sights. Naples was a big city, but London was ten times bigger, four million people, the capital of the world. The noise and din and bustle, the jammed streets and sidewalks—big shot *Inglesi* industrialists in their fancy suits and vests and top hats and bowlers, stylish ladies clutching the hands of their immaculately dressed children, shouting men walking around wearing sign boards advertising soap and cigarettes, women selling bouquets of flowers, chimney sweeps and oyster carts, beautiful parks and tall statues and stately buildings with lions guarding the steps. I had never seen anything like it in my life. The streets were even more jammed than the sidewalks, and we slowly plowed our way through a sea of vehicles—double-decker busses drawn by teams of horses, men on bicycles, tradesmen's carts loaded with coal and beer barrels and cabbages, all fighting to cross the same bridge we were. We queued up and nudged forward on the policeman's whistle, as the driver of a hansom cab loudly demanded right of way for his aristocratic fare. I watched a gang of street urchins dart in to grab some oranges off a grocer's cart, escaping through the stalled traffic as he shook his fist and cursed them. It was a wonderful show, and Alessandra missed it.

We barely made it to the station on time, and I gave the driver a shilling—way too much from the way he beamed and thanked me, but it was Lombardi's money and besides, I didn't have time to wait for the change. We hurried through the station, found the track, and boarded at the whistle. When we plopped into our seats, Alessandra finally took a deep breath and turned to me.

"God, Tommaso, I'm so glad you're here with me."

We were both relieved when we stepped off the train in Cambridge and heard a cheerful voice cry out in excellent Italian from the other end of the platform.

"Good morning! You must be *Signora* Poverelli." A small man with a briar pipe in his mouth hurried over and offered her his hand.

"I'm Archibald Mallory, from the Society. Welcome to Cambridge, and please forgive my poor Italian! I'll be your translator during your stay here."

Mallory had spent two years in Florence as a student many years earlier, and taught Italian poetry at Trinity College. He turned to me and grinned.

"You must be Tommaso Labella, the photographer. I saw your famous photo, and I personally found it impressive in terms of evidence—although my opinion is a minority within the Society. Speaking for myself, nothing would give me greater pleasure than establishing the reality of a spiritual realm. If our attempts to verify scientifically the intervention of another world prove futile, it will be a terrible blow—a mortal blow to humankind's hopes for another life."

A porter grabbed my bag and Alessandra's portmanteau, and Mallory led us around to the side of the station where a stunningly pretty young girl about my age sat in a carriage.

My jaw dropped. She was like something out of Botticelli's Birth of Venus—hazel eyes, creamy white skin, and light chestnut hair that fell in soft curls on her shoulders.

"*Buongiorno! Mi chiamo Elsa,*" she said, and flashed me an impish smile that made my heart skip a beat.

Mallory laughed. "My daughter, Elsa. She's going to assist me this week."

Elsa held up a book and giggled. It was an English-Italian dictionary.

I held up the Italian-English phrase book Lombardi had given me—which I had studied on the ferry ride over to England, thank God.

"My name is Thomas," I replied in English. "I am very pleased to make your acquaintance."

I didn't wait for Mallory to tell me where to sit. I hopped into the back seat with Elsa. I couldn't believe my luck. Mallory helped Alessandra up into her seat and we set off.

"Your trip went well?"

"Horrible," grunted Alessandra. I blushed. Her rude response was embarrassing.

"I'm so sorry to hear that," Mallory said. "Was there something...?"

"There was a bit of a mix-up in London," I volunteered. "No one was there to meet us..."

"And it wasn't accidental!" Alessandra interjected. "Huxley had a hand in that, I'm sure."

Mallory looked at her, surprised. "I apologize on behalf of the Society for the problem in London. I will certainly look into this matter."

I jumped in to stop Alessandra from going through her whole litany of complaints.

"Forgive us. It's been a long trip, and the sea in the Channel coming over was pretty rough. Alessandra got a bit seasick..."

Alessandra glared at me.

Elsa was pretty good in Italian. "*Mal di mare?*" She smiled and pointed to herself. "Me also." She imitated a woozy person, her tongue hanging out, her eyes crossed. " ... even on a lake." Then she pantomimed a perfect puke.

I burst out laughing.

Mallory turned to Alessandra. "My apologies, *Signora*. I've been seasick myself, and it is a distinctly unpleasant feeling."

Alessandra ignored him. She sat there sullenly in her seat and stared at the road ahead as we made our way through the center of the town. Cambridge wasn't noisy and exciting, like London, but it was very pretty, with a lot of picturesque churches, a busy marketplace, and lots of students walking around. When we passed by the university, Mallory pointed out Trinity College where he taught. It had a great iron gate, and a medieval clock tower, and was founded by King Henry the VIII in 1546.

"Old," Mallory said with a smile, "but not as old as your University of Naples. I'm afraid you've got us beat by three centuries."

"I'm thinking of attending the University of Naples," I said, trying to sound nonchalant. Alessandra rolled her eyes, but I ignored her.

"*E' vero?*" Elsa said, excitedly. Really? "*Che bravo!*" Good for you!

We finally turned off the main street and Mallory pointed his whip down a hedge-lined allée where a massive three-story manor sat surrounded by tall chestnut trees.

"Farnam House," Mallory announced. "You'll be staying here, as guests of Professor Henry Tyndall and his wife Maxine. He's president of the Society. Both of them speak some Italian, though hers is better."

"Do you live nearby?" I asked. I wanted to see Elsa often.

"Don't worry—we live just a few streets down from here, and we'll be here every day."

"Where will *Signor* Huxley stay?" It was Alessandra.

"He comes up from London tomorrow, in time for the reception. He'll be staying at our house."

"As long as he doesn't stay with us," Alessandra snapped.

Professor Tyndall was awaiting us as our carriage pulled up. He looked to be in his early sixties, with a long, untrimmed white beard, and his manner was rather stiff and slightly pompous. He quickly passed us to Maxine. Her auburn hair was pulled back tight and flat against her head, giving her a slightly masculine look. She was a principal of a woman's college at Cambridge, where English women could study just like men, though they couldn't earn a degree, of course. She was a lot younger than him, and came from a wealthy and powerful family—her cousin was England's Prime Minister. Her Italian was excellent, and she had a sense of humor.

Alessandra insisted on going straight to her room, but Elsa, Archie and I joined Maxine in the sitting room where a light tea of scones and pastries had been laid out for our arrival. As a servant filled my cup, I complimented Maxine on her Italian.

"*Signora*, how did you become so fluent in our language?"

She reached across the table and took a cigarette out of a silver box. "I had a boyfriend in Florence." Mallory laughed.

"Maxie, you shouldn't do that to poor Tommaso. Tell him the whole story."

"Well, it's true!" she protested. She lit her cigarette and leaned back in her chair.

"I spent a year in Italy, Tommaso, when I was 18, though I'm sorry to say I never made it to your Naples. My mother wanted me to study art. I wanted to study mathematics and physics. In the end, we compromised. I studied da Vinci's catapults, and Michelangelo's David." She grinned. "I rather enjoyed studying *him*."

"Now, Maxie, Elsa's here with us…"

"Oh pooh! Archie," she said. "She's not going to faint."

"I've seen a photograph of the statue, father," Elsa protested. "In a library book. He's quite…handsome."

Maxine laughed. "You'd better keep an eye on Elsa this week." She pointed her cigarette at me. "She'll be spending a lot of time with this rather handsome Italian boy—and he's not a statue."

I turned red. Maxine let me escape.

"Elsa, give Tomas a tour of the house so he won't get lost while he's here. Henry and I need to talk to your father about the schedule for this week."

I'm glad I got the grand tour. The manor was huge, with two wings, ten bedrooms, a library, billiard room, picture gallery, drawing room, dining room, hallways and stairways, kitchens and servants' quarters. I also got a quick peek at Henry's gloomy, oak-paneled, private study where a large portrait of a dour Queen Victoria hung on the wall behind his desk, reminding Englishmen to do their duty.

We passed by Alessandra's room and I thought of knocking and seeing if she wanted to join us. But the room was silent, so we slipped down the back stairs and out into the late summer sunshine onto the great, green lawn. Manicured flower beds lined a stone path that led down to the river Cam where a small wooden boat floated on the placid water under a shady willow tree.

"*Andiamo!*" I laughed. Let's go. I jumped in the punt and grabbed the pole that's used to push the boat along the shallow riverbed. Elsa gathered up her skirt and hopped in behind me, and we were just about to shove off when I heard an angry voice.

"Tommaso! Tommaso!" Alessandra was hurrying down the path and she didn't look happy.

"Where have you been?" she demanded. "I've been looking all over for you! Come up to the house and show me where the bathroom is."

"Just ask someone," I said. I really wanted to take Elsa out on the punt.

"I can't speak English!"

"The word is 'water closet.'"

She glared at me. What could I do. I finally turned to Elsa and shrugged my shoulders. Elsa was a good sport. I helped her back onto the river bank.

"*A domani.*" She smiled brightly. "Tomorrow."

When we got back to the house, I directed Alessandra to the bathroom.

"You know, it wouldn't hurt you to learn a few words of English," I said to her.

"I don't want to learn English," she shot back. "I want to get this over with and go home." She slammed the door.

# 55

Alessandra didn't belong in England.

She hated the Sunday afternoon reception. The clock on the mantel showed one PM and we had been standing in the receiving line for a half-hour. Through the open French doors of the drawing room, I could watch the crowd of guests out on the lawn sitting at flower-decked tables sampling cucumber sandwiches, and berries and cream. A badminton net was stretched across the lawn and a half-dozen guests were batting a shuttlecock around, while their boisterous *bambini* competed in croquet. The English worship sports. They believe it's one of the reasons England rules the world. The Duke of Wellington, who defeated Napoleon, reportedly visited Eton School a few years after his victory and, after watching the boys cheerfully bloody each other's noses on the football field, declared "It is here that the battle of Waterloo was won." I'm sure Huxley believed that as he pounded his university opponents in the boxing ring.

Alessandra hadn't eaten a thing for breakfast. She had come down late the morning after we arrived, and resisted Maxine's attempts to engage her in conversation. When she learned there would be a reception for her, she balked, and I had to insist she attend.

"I'll go," she finally said, "but I don't want to stand next to Elsa. It reminds me how fat and old I am."

Lombardi offered to buy her some new clothes for her trip—he knew how snobbish the English were—but she turned him down. She was only going to England for a few days, she said, and she didn't give a damn what they thought of her clothes. She was also terribly superstitious—new clothes might bring bad luck.

So she stood there in the reception line that afternoon wearing her dowdy, black séance dress, looking like she was attending a funeral instead of a garden party, while all the English women glided by in their loose, white summer dresses and lace collars, wearing wide-brimmed sun hats decorated with flowers. Alessandra had new shoes at least, but they were tight, and her feet hurt, so she kept playing with her foot, which was embarrassing. Flanked by Henry and Maxine, she stood there grimly shaking the hands that were thrust at her, mumbling "*piacere*"—though she certainly didn't *look* pleased to meet them. I'm sure some of the guests that day came simply to gawk at her. Huxley had arranged a big story in the *London Times* about the arrival of Italy's notorious Queen of Spirits, and his confident promise to expose Alessandra "if she turns out to be the clever fraud one suspects she is."

Me? I was enjoying the whole show, bowing and throwing out "Delighted to meet you!" and greeting the good-looking women with a kiss to the hand, Continental style, which made them simper and Elsa roll her eyes. "Romeo!" she whispered, but I noticed she moved closer to me.

There was a commotion and I saw Henry extend his hand to an aristocratic looking gentleman with a silver cane.

"Lord Hartford! How kind of you to come." He turned and bowed to the slim, elegant woman clutching Hartford's arm. "Lady Hartford! You delight us with your presence."

Maxine Tyndall gathered her skirt, bent her knees and performed a graceful bow.

"My Lord."

Alessandra should have had the sense to just stand there, or simply extend her hand. Instead, she panicked. She leaned forward in a comical half-bow, tripped, and toppled into Lady Hartford, who let out a cry, stumbled backwards, and would have ended up on her *culone* if Henry hadn't reached out and grabbed her. Mallory quickly helped Alessandra to her feet, but the damage had been done. Lady Hartford gave her a withering look.

Everyone was staring at Alessandra. Out on the lawn, two little girls giggled and flopped on the grass, mimicking Alessandra. I wanted to crawl in a hole and disappear.

"*Brava, Signora*. A bit more practice and you've got it."

I turned around and Huxley was standing there with a Pimm's Cup in his hand and a smirk on his face. Alessandra glared at him. He raised his glass.

"Welcome to England—I can't tell you how delighted I am to have you here."

Keeping an eye on Alessandra, Huxley leaned forward and whispered in my ear.

> *Il ragno, la mosca*
> *l'ammazza-za!*
> *se la mette in bocca*
> *e si ingozza-za*

It's a famous child's rhyme in Italy. The English have their own version.

> *Come into my parlour*
> *Said the spider to the fly...*

# 56

Dinner that evening was a disaster.

As we headed downstairs, I reminded Alessandra to use her silverware. Neapolitans like to say "Fingers were made before forks," and I noticed Alessandra was using hers way too often the whole tour.

Elsa had assured me that Huxley would be seated at the opposite end of the table. Alessandra was still smarting from her encounter with Huxley at the reception, and I knew she was spoiling for a fight. I wanted to enjoy Elsa, not spend my evening playing referee.

"And don't drink more than one glass of wine," I warned.

"I don't need your advice, Tommaso," Alessandra replied. "Is Elsa coming?"

The tone of her voice annoyed me. "Of course. Why do you ask?"

A maid was hurrying up the stairs as we started down. She stepped aside as we passed. Alessandra glanced at me.

"I…I just wanted to know if you will be sitting next to me."

"Alessandra, you're the guest of honor. You'll be seated next to Mr. Tyndall."

"But he doesn't speak Italian."

"Elsa's father will be on the other side. He'll translate for you."

As we reached the bottom of the stairs, I heard a girl's voice.

"*Buona sera*, Tommaso!"

Elsa was standing at the front door in a blue satin dress, a white ribbon in her chestnut hair, and a mischievous smile on her face. She looked fabulous. Archie Mallory followed her through the door.

I left Alessandra and hurried over.

"Good evening, Miss Mallory," I smiled and bowed. "How do you do? You look positively smashing this evening."

I had spent the afternoon studying my English phrase book. It was a long shot, but you never knew. Girls are funny. If they fall for you, they do what they want—their mothers be damned.

The tall windows in the Tyndall's dining room looked out over the great lawn where the reception had been held. Chinese lanterns lit the twilight, and down at the water's edge, a small wooden punt sat in the dusk. Swallows flitted through the evening sky, and through the open windows you could hear the chirp of crickets. There were fourteen of us seated at a long, mahogany dining table fragrant with roses, bright with candles, and crowded with silver, bone china, and linen napkins. A full champagne glass sat next to each dinner plate. Henry rang a silver bell, and the serving staff came out and lined themselves against the wall.

"Ladies and gentlemen, if I may propose a toast!"

Mallory brought Alessandra to her feet, and Elsa poked me in the ribs. I blushed and stood up. We all raised our glasses.

"To Home, Country and Queen!—and to our guests from Italy, *Signora* Poverelli and Master Tommaso Labella." Everyone hurrahed, clinked their glasses, and we sat down.

Elsa made a face. "Unfair. I get lemonade."

"We have a traditional English dinner tonight for our foreign guests," Henry continued. He wagged his finger at Alessandra. "No macaroni tonight." Everyone laughed.

"You must try everything," Elsa teased. "*Mangia tutto!*"

The celery soup was boring, but I pretended to like it. Alessandra, across the table, flashed me a sour look when she tried her's, then pushed it away. Elsa patted her lips delicately with the napkin after every spoonful, and I noticed how she placed the spoon on the side of the bowl when she finished, as a signal to the servants. After the soup bowls were taken away, a servant came around with glasses of sherry, and Alessandra grabbed one off the tray. She leaned across the table.

"With your permission, Signor Labella," she said mockingly.

"Make sure you eat something," I warned. She hadn't eaten anything at the reception, and I knew the wine would go to her head.

Instead, she ended up pushing her food around her plate. I had trouble with the food myself. It was heavy and salty—a slab of beef, potatoes, heavy gravy, with various mustards and horseradish. Tyndall served up a claret with the roast. He had a large wine cellar, and was proud of it.

"My favorite Bordeaux, Master Labella" he said, as the maid placed a glass in front of me. "Chateau Latour."

Uncle Mario had once mentioned the name of a local wine to me, and I wanted to impress Elsa. I took a gamble.

"If you ever get to Naples, you must try our *Lacryma Christi*. Tears of Christ. Made from grapes grown on the slopes of Mount Vesuvius. A bit sweet for my taste, but popular with the ancient Romans."

Mallory laughed out loud and translated my opinion for everyone. Henry frowned.

"Lacryma Christi, eh? Can't say I've heard of it. But I'll do that."

Elsa stared at me. I nonchalantly swirled the claret in my glass and studied it.

Score another for Romeo.

Across the table, Alessandra had already downed half her glass, and Commodore Turnbull was getting annoying. He was the British Naval attaché to Italy, just back from Naples with his dumpy wife Henrietta. Alessandra later told me they reminded her of the Croppers, who had adopted her from the orphanage.

The pompous Commodore didn't think much of the Italian Navy, and as he forked down his potatoes he wasn't shy about sharing his opinion with us.

"Your Umberto-class battleship is not a bad little boat. Of course England manufactures the guns and engines." He pushed peas onto his fork and pointed at Alessandra with his knife. "The *Re di Sardegna* can do twenty-plus knots. Damn good design." He downed his peas and started slicing his beef. "Helps the Eye-talian Navy run for it when the fighting starts," he chuckled. "You're better lovers than fighters."

Elsa spoke up. "The world could use more lovers and fewer fighters."

Henrietta jumped in.

"We were hoping for a posting to Rome. You don't have a proper English club in Naples, like you have in Rome or Hong Kong. It's just a reading room with a few London papers. Dull as dishwater. At least in Rome you have the hunt clubs, and Sunday picnics at the Villa Borghese, and the balls and receptions are much more fun."

I could see Alessandra getting irritated.

"Bloody noisy—Naples," growled Turnbull, dipping his bread in a lake of gravy. "We had an apartment on the Chiaja, 500 francs a month. Supposed to be the nice part of town. But the din! Egad, morning to night! Rattle of carriage wheels on that lava pavement, the tramp, tramp, tramp of the infantry, donkeys braying, organ grinders camped outside your window; hawkers screeching in their unintelligible language trying to sell you something."

"And the help! The stories I could tell you! " Henrietta exclaimed, stabbing a potato and stuffing it into her mouth. "You want to make sure you only hire someone with a letter stating they were discharged from a foreign family of distinction. But even then they're dreadfully incompetent. The maid could hardly speak a word of English. And the cook— he was an absolute thief! He'd run off to the market to buy a chicken, and come back claiming it cost two shillings. We found out he paid half that, and pocketed the rest. They'll rob you blind!"

The embarrassed Mallory translated, and Alessandra glared at Henrietta.

I shot Alessandra a warning look.

Henrietta babbled on.

"And the sun! Goodness! You have to use a parasol everywhere you go if you want to keep your skin white. Otherwise you'll come home looking like a nigger. "

Henry attempted to move the conversation in another direction.

"Elsa, when is your father going to send you to the Continent to do the Grand Tour? Maybe Master Tommaso here could squire you around Naples."

Elsa blushed. Henrietta jumped back in.

"Make sure you visit the Piazza del Plebiscito, Elsa. The Commodore always had a laugh there—didn't you dear?" She attacked the remaining potato on her plate. "The Commodore likes his cigars, and when he finished one he would toss the butt into the street so we could watch the half-naked ragamuffins fight over it."

It was true. You grab the butts, remove the tobacco, and when you collect enough you wrap it in a piece of paper and you've got a perfectly good cigar—something the little guy can afford. I used to hawk a tray of them around the piazza myself, before Uncle Mario hired me.

The dinner ended with a selection of cheeses, like the British do. It was the first time I had ever smelled Stinking Bishop, and I almost gagged. Lombardi wanted us to try Limburger cheese when we were in Munich, but we refused. Stinking Bishop is even worse, believe me.

"Don't be a coward," Elsa teased. She cut off the rind, and put some on a biscuit. "Hold your nose and try it." I did, and it wasn't bad, but I'll stick to mozzarella.

Henry served port with the cheese, but Alessandra didn't need another drink. She had already finished a glass of champagne, a glass of sherry, and two glasses of claret, all on an empty stomach. When the maid offered her a port, I tried to wave her off. Alessandra scowled at me, and grabbed a glass, spilling some on Mallory's jacket. I was livid.

"Excuse us," I said. I got up, and hurried around to Alessandra's chair. I pulled her out of her seat, and steered her towards the hallway. When I got her there, I lit into her.

"Stop it!" I told her. "No more wine! You're drunk, and you're making an ass of yourself!"

She pulled away, and staggered backwards. "I'm *not* drunk. And I don't give a shit about those English pricks. They can go fuck themselves." She stood there, arms folded, staring at me. Finally she said, "I have to take a piss."

I returned to the table, hoping the dinner was just about over. A few minutes later, Alessandra returned. The maid had left her a small serving of Stinking Bishop, and Alessandra picked up the plate and sniffed it. Everybody at the table was looking at her.

She made a face, then turned to Mallory.

"This cheese smells like a goat fart."

Henrietta put down her knife. "What did she say, Archie?" Mallory blushed.

"She said she doesn't ... like the cheese."

"WHAT DID SHE SAY?" It was Lady Hackett at the other end of the table. Huxley leaned into her ear trumpet, and said in a stage whisper loud enough for everyone at the table to hear, "SHE SAID THE CHEESE SMELLS LIKE A GOAT FART."

Everyone stared at their napkins, as a giggling maid slipped into the kitchen to tell the rest of the servants what the crazy Italian lady had said.

## 57

Alessandra was confident the spirits would show up that night.

They always had in the past when she called them. They would help her put on a show, humiliating Huxley and sending her home with an extra hundred pounds sterling.

"We can leave tomorrow, Tommaso," she assured me as we headed down to the sitting. She had received a telegram from Lombardi that morning and she was sky high.

> *I believe in you. Waiting for you in Paris. Love Camillo.*

Her heart was already in France, which made me nervous.

When we entered the library, we found everyone sitting around the table waiting for us –Elsa and her father, Maxine who would act as stenographer, and Huxley and Henry who had their heads together in conversation.

Henry jumped up and showed Alessandra to her chair.

"Lord Carraig, Chairman of the Society, and his wife Lady Carraig, have decided to join our circle tonight," Henry announced. "They will be here shortly. They're coming from a dinner with the Duke of Westminster. While we wait, perhaps I can recap the rules all parties have agreed to for the test." He picked up a piece of paper from the table and put on his reading glasses.

"First, there will be someone positioned under the table with a lamp—Mr. Mallory here—for the duration of the sitting." Over Huxley's vehement objections, the Society had accepted Alessandra's one precondition for her trip to England—that she wouldn't be tied down. In return, Alessandra was forced to allow someone under the table to control her feet and knees. That would let Henry and Huxley concentrate on controlling her hands.

"Second, there will only be three sittings—one tonight and ... "

Alessandra cut him off. "I'll only need one."

I winced. She was much too confident.

"Third, each sitting will run for 90 minutes only."

Huxley had insisted on a time limit. He was smart. He knew it usually took Alessandra time before she settled down, and he wanted pressure on her from the moment it started.

"Under these test conditions, the Society is interested in scientifically observing any phenomena you have reportedly produced in the past—raps, taps, touches, apports, the movement of objects, a table levitation, a materialization like that reported by Dr. Negri in Genoa."

Alessandra looked at Henry. "A table levitation like the spirits did for Dr. Fournier in Geneva– would that be enough?"

"The Society would concede. I assure you." Henry looked to Huxley for confirmation.

Huxley hesitated. "All four feet off the floor?"

Alessandra gave him a hard stare. "If I do, you pay me?"

Huxley smiled. "You have my word. One hundred pounds sterling."

"Your own money?"

Huxley looked amused. "A personal cheque, drawn on my private account at the Union Bank of London."

Henry interrupted them. "Really, Nigel. I don't think a personal wager is appropriate here."

Huxley ignored him and continued to stare at Alessandra.

Henry persisted. "This is highly irregular. Maxine?"

"What do I think?" Maxine smiled and pulled out her cigarette case. "I think I'll put five on Alessandra."

# 58

His Lordship arrived a few minutes before 8:00.

Lord Carraig appeared to be in his fifties, a tall, thin Englishman with a meticulously clipped moustache, wearing a bespoke suit from Savile Row which fitted him like a glove. Lady Carraig looked like she had drunk her fair share at the Duke's dinner. She tripped over the rug, took her seat next to me, grabbed my hand and closed her eyes. I could smell the alcohol on her breath.

Between the moonlight shining through the large French windows of the library, and the light from Mallory's oil lamp under the table, the room was bright enough to read the numerals on the mantel clock.

Alessandra started off strong.

Ten minutes into the sitting, a tattoo of three soft raps sounded from the direction of the book shelves.

Elsa squeezed my hand. She had heard them too.

"I heard three raps," Lord Carraig announced.

"Objection," Huxley said. "I heard only two."

Maxine, sitting at the opposite end of the table, logged the event.

"8:10 PM. Two, possibly three, raps on south wall."

According to Alessandra, "low spirits" produced the raps, pinches and levitation of small objects. They were mischievous, earth-bound discarnates who couldn't let go of the material existence, and refused to move on. She would often feel them crowding around her minutes after the prayer finished. They needed to work together to make something happen. A few, like Savonarola, didn't need other spirits to do stuff.

Moments later, we all heard a sharp rap that distinctly sounded like it came from *under* the table. Hanging onto Alessandra's left hand, Henry leaned down.

"Archie?"

"No movement of *Signora*'s knees or feet," came a soft whisper from under the table. Maxine shorthanded it to her log. "8:12 PM. Rap heard under the table. Medium's knees and feet were under continuous control."

Less than a minute later, Lady Carraig spoke up.

"I felt a touch on my elbow ... "

Then Lord Carraig. "I felt a shove on my back."

Alessandra jumped up and everyone in the circle scrambled to their feet, still holding hands.

"Spirits, we know you are here," she shouted. "SHOW US MORE!"

Huxley looked nervous.

Mallory cried out from under the table, "What's going on?"

"Stay there!" Henry shot back.

I felt a rush of excitement. Alessandra had uttered those exact same words at Rossi's house in Naples, the night I took my famous photograph. *Show us more!* Right after that, the table had levitated into the air. It was going to happen again.

"SHOW US MORE!" she shouted.

"Watch the table," I told Elsa. I held my breath.

Nothing happened.

The table remained on the floor.

We stood there, all of us, looking stupid, for fifteen or twenty seconds, until Huxley finally turned to Alessandra.

"Perhaps we should all sit down now?" he sneered.

Alessandra stared at the table, a look of disbelief on her face. We all sat back down and Alessandra resumed her pleadings—*Spirits come! Spirits come!*—but there was an edge of panic in her voice now. The minutes continued to slip away—five, ten, fifteen—until we finally heard the soft bong of the clock on the mantel.

9:30 P.M. Time up.

Across the table, Huxley smiled smugly.

## 59

Alessandra was nervous. I could tell.

At breakfast the next morning, she ate little and said less and wanted to retreat to her room afterwards, but I convinced her to take a walk in the garden. It was a glorious, sunny August morning.

"You'll do better tonight," I assured her, as we made our way through a trellised archway into Maxine Tyndall's magnificent, formal rose garden which flanked the east side of Farnam House. Maxine bred her roses for competition, and showed them at the Royal National Rose Society's annual exhibition. Red and white tea roses bordered the brick walk, and a bright orange butterfly flitted across our path, but Alessandra didn't seem to notice. She plodded along, head down, ignoring my attempts to cheer her up, until we reached an iron bench next to a sundial and I made her sit down.

"What is the matter with you?" I demanded. "You've still got two more chances. You'll do fine." In truth, I wasn't thinking about Alessandra—my mind was on Elsa. She was coming over after lunch and I was excited.

Alessandra stared at the gravel at her feet.

"The spirits, Tommaso—I could feel them at first. Not strongly, but they were there. Then they faded away. I couldn't feel them anymore." She nervously fingered the *corno* around her neck. "Everything feels wrong here."

She turned to me. "Maybe I made a mistake coming here."

"It's a little late to do anything about it now," I shot back.

She reached out for my hand. "Tommaso, please, don't be hard on me."

I felt ashamed.

"I'm sorry," I said. "But why didn't you call on Fra Girolamo?"

"I…I was afraid to."

"Why?"

She hesitated. "Maybe he won't come." She wrung her hands. "Maybe he hates this place, like I do."

"But he's always come when you've called before."

Alessandra stared straight ahead. "Maybe he won't hear me. We're so far from home."

"Well, it's not the end of the world if he fails to show up. You go home without Huxley's hundred pounds, that's all."

She jumped to her feet. "And let Huxley win? Never!"

"Well, do it or don't," I finally said, annoyed. "I don't care."

We continued down the path past the Tyndall's glass-house where rakes and hoes and pruning shears were neatly hung in a wooden cabinet, and a gardener was filling a basket with white roses. When he saw us, he smiled, stepped outside, tipped his hat and handed Alessandra one of the roses.

"See," I teased as we set off again, "not everyone in England is against you."

She stuck her tongue out at me.

We finally reached the river and plopped down on the grass under a tree. A convoy of ducks paddled up to the bank hoping for a handout before giving up and drifting off. Alessandra finally spoke up.

"Do you think I could live in Paris?"

I looked at her. "Paris?"

"Camillo says it's cold there in the winter. He says it even snows sometimes, and there's ice on the sidewalks." She laughed. "Imagine me slipping and falling on my big backside."

"You're reconsidering his offer?" I was surprised. She had sounded so sure back in Warsaw. She picked up a pebble and tossed it into the water, watching the ripples run away.

"I don't know. Everything is so confusing..."

# 60

"A*ndiamo,* Tommaso!" Let's go!

I looked out the drawing room window and there was Elsa on a bicycle, laughing and pedaling around the gravel driveway alongside the house, her long dress flying out, one hand holding on to her white straw hat. She looked fantastic.

"Coming!" I yelled.

On my way out, I passed by the billiard room and Mallory waved to me. Huxley had just lined up a long shot, and with a crack sent the ball straight across the green felt, potting it in the far pocket. Mallory raised his cue. "I don't stand a chance, Tommaso," he laughed. Huxley ignored me, moving on to the next shot.

When I got outside, a servant stood next to Elsa, holding two bicycles.

Elsa gave me a big grin. "Where's Alessandra?"

"She had something to do," I said. In truth, I hadn't mentioned the bicycle ride to her. I wanted it to be just me and Elsa.

"Do you know how to ride a bicycle?" Elsa asked.

"Me? Of course!" I lied, grabbing the handlebars.

It was my first time on a bicycle. I pushed off and wobbled around in a crazy circle fighting to keep my balance, nearly running over the terrified maid before flipping over the handlebars and falling on my *culone*. Elsa started laughing. Red-faced, I jumped up and shoved off again, this time doing better—I'm not an acrobat but I've got good balance. As she applauded, I even managed a quick "no hands" to show off for her before skidding to a stop next to her bicycle.

"Ready!" I grinned, and we set off together towards Cambridge town.

The weather was humid and sticky, and soon my shirt was soaked in sweat, but Elsa pedaled at a strong pace. The road into town was busy—lots of carts and carriages and people trudging along with bundles and bags, which we had to dodge as Elsa and I chatted away. At one point, a small dog raced out of a yard and tried to bite Elsa's boot, but I cut him off with my bike and Elsa flashed me a grateful smile. I felt like I was making progress.

When we reached the university, we hopped off the bicycles and I bought us ice creams from a street vendor and we sat together on a bench under a tall tree enjoying our "penny licks" as the English call them.

"Alessandra is missing a treat," Elsa said, running her pretty pink tongue around the glass, determined not to waste a smidgen of her vanilla ice.

She handed me her empty glass. "Is she alright, Tommaso? She seems so unhappy."

"She'll be alright," I said. "She's just not used to England."

Elsa hesitated. "I'm ashamed no one from the Society was there to meet her in London. I'm sure that didn't make her feel very welcome. Mr. Huxley sent the Cook agent to the wrong station—to the Waterloo Station. My father told me he can't understand how Mr. Huxley could have gotten it wrong."

"Alessandra is convinced he did it on purpose. She doesn't like him."

"Good! I don't like him either," Elsa replied. The anger in her voice took me by surprise.

"I agree he's not very pleasant," I said.

"It's more than that."

I waited for her to continue. Finally she spoke.

"He…he's always…touching me, Tommaso." She shivered. "My father won't believe me….everybody thinks he's such a nice man…" She turned to me, her eyes blazing. "I hope Alessandra humiliates him! Then maybe he'll quit, and go away, and leave me alone." She turned away but I could see tears in her eyes.

I didn't know what to say. The whole thing was so unexpected.

We rode back to Tyndall's house in silence. On the way back, dark clouds gathered, the air became heavy and sultry, and the rumble of thunder announced a coming storm. Before we could reach home, the downpour caught us, drenching us to the bone. When we finally arrived at Farnam House, servants ran out of the house with umbrellas to take our bicycles, and a maid stood inside the door with towels to dry ourselves off. As we walked down the hall, Elsa turned to me.

"I'm sorry," she whispered. "I shouldn't have told you. I didn't mean to spoil your afternoon."

I wanted to reach out and take her in my arms, but I was too embarrassed.

"Will you be all right?"

"Yes," she nodded. "Thank you."

The upstairs hall was dark and gloomy, except when a flash of lightning momentarily lit the hall. When I got to Alessandra's room, I knocked on the door.

"Who is it?" came a startled voice from inside the room.

"Alessandra, it's me—Tommaso."

I heard feet hurrying across the floor, a key was turned in the lock, the door was opened a crack, and Alessandra peered out.

"Tommaso! Where were you?" she cried. "I've been looking for you all afternoon."

I stepped into the room. "Elsa took me for a bicycle ride." I could see the disappointment on her face. "We would have invited you," I added hastily, "but it looked like rain. I didn't want you to get a cold. You're lucky you didn't come. We got soaked."

Alessandra shut the door and locked it.

"I'm scared, Tommaso!" she said as she dragged me towards her bed.

Tarot cards were spread out on the sheet, illuminated by the flickering of a bedside candle.

"Put the cards away," I said. "You'll do fine tonight." Whenever Alessandra got really nervous about something, she always pulled them out. That's the problem with Italians. We're too superstitious.

"No!" she exclaimed. "Look!" She sat down on the bed, clinching her fists, tears in her eyes.

Six cards were laid out in a half circle, Neapolitan style. In the center, face up, sat the seventh card—a burning tower, with a woman falling to her death. Everybody in Naples knew what that meant.

Catastrophe.

# 61

I could tell she was scared.

Alessandra made the sign of the cross when we entered the séance room – something I never saw her do before.

The plan was simple. She would call Savonarola. *Babbo* Giro would hear her, and come, and possess his beloved, and produce an astonishment to humiliate Huxley, just like he did at Ile Ribaud.

As soon as we were seated in the library, and Mallory took his position under the table with the oil lamp, Alessandra immediately bent her head, and closed her eyes, and began mumbling the disturbing incantation she used in Naples.

"*Babbo … Babbo! … Per favore! Per favore!*"

Please, Father, please!

Henry Tyndall looked amused. Huxley had told him about Savonarola but, like Lombardi, he didn't buy the absurd idea of spirit possession by a mad monk from the medieval ages. But Huxley, controlling Alessandra's other hand, bit his lip nervously.

"*Babbo … Babbo! … Per favore! Per favore!*"

Over and over.

"*Babbo … Babbo! … Per favore! Per favore!*"

As the minutes ticked away and nothing happened, Huxley relaxed.

Alessandra readjusted her position in her chair, then scrunched her eyes even tighter. Her plaintive begging resumed. Louder. More insistent.

Suddenly, her shoulders slumped, and her head fell forward and rested on the table.

I felt a rush of relief. I *knew* what would happen next—I had seen it in Naples, and at Ile Ribaud. She would remain there motionless for a minute, then there would be violent shudders as Savonarola's spirit took possession of her body, then...

Alessandra slowly lifted her head and turned towards Huxley. He shrank back into his chair, hand raised to shield himself from the chilling look of the discarnate monstrosity we both expected.

But I was the one who let out a gasp.

Instead of Savonarola's menacing gaze, the eyes were Alessandra's, and they were filled with tears.

"He can't hear me," she whispered.

Then she stood up and walked out of the room.

For a second, Huxley looked bewildered, then a leer of triumph spread across his face.

Mallory poked his head out from under the table. "What's going on?"

Henry turned to me. "The sitting is over?"

I looked towards the door.

"I... I think so," I replied.

Henry pulled out his gold pocket watch, glanced at it, then turned to Maxine. "Please record that *Signora* Poverelli voluntarily terminated the second sitting at 8:15 PM..." He snapped the case shut and slipped it back into his vest pocket. "...and that during the second sitting, there occurred nothing worthy of note."

When I got upstairs, I saw a maid fleeing down the hall. I knocked on Alessandra's door and opened it. Alessandra was angrily pacing the room.

"I found the maid rummaging through my closet when I came up," she declared.

"Maybe she was doing some cleaning," I suggested.

"At eight o'clock at night?"

"What did she say?"

"She said she was changing the pillows. The hell she was!" Alessandra walked over and slammed the door. "She was looking through my bag." I steered her back to the bed and made her sit down.

"Look," I said. "You're tired. You had a rough night. But you've still got one more sitting. Get some sleep. Savonarola will show up tomorrow night. You'll see."

Alessandra stared out the window.

"No he won't," she finally said.

A tear rolled down her cheek and she wiped it away. "He's abandoned me, Tommaso. I don't know why, but he has."

# 62

You have to understand – she was desperate.

She was going to lose to Huxley, and she couldn't endure the humiliation. What had he written? *She's a fraud. An extremely talented one, but a fraud nonetheless.* Alessandra had come to England seeking revenge, to prove him wrong. Instead, she had produced nothing.

I had gone to bed at eleven, and her knock woke me from a deep sleep. I sat up in bed, confused. Moonlight filled the room as I slipped out of bed and stumbled over to the door. When I opened it a crack, Alessandra was standing there, fully dressed. In her hand, she clutched her leather hatbox.

"What's going on?" I said, bewildered.

She slipped inside and closed the door. "I need your help."

I pointed at the hatbox. "What's that for?"

"Come with me."

"I don't like this," I said. She was up to something crazy, and I didn't want any part of it.

"You have to trust me, Tommaso." She hurried over to the closet, pulled out my coat, and thrust it in my hand. "Please!" What could I do?

"Where are we going?" I grumbled, slipping on my boots. She went over, put her ear to the door, listened for a second, then opened it.

"Follow me," she whispered.

The hall was dark and deserted, and we slipped down the staircase, past the library, and out the side door into the garden. We halted there for a second to let our eyes get used to the dark. I still had no idea where we were going. It was chilly outside, and the moon was riding high in the sky above our heads, the grass on the lawn still glistening wet from the afternoon thunderstorm. Behind us, the mansion rose up in the dark. It must have been after midnight.

"What are we doing out here?" I hissed.

Just then we heard what sounded like the click of a door, and Alessandra quickly dragged me into the shadow of the house. We crouched there in the dark, holding our breath, our ears straining for the sound of footsteps or a voice—anything—but it was silent again. After a few minutes, Alessandra grabbed my arm and we hurried across the lawn until we reached the glasshouse. The iron door creaked loudly as we opened it, and from the mansion I heard the warning bark of Hercules, Tyndall's Rhodesian Ridgeback. I prayed nobody got up and let the beast out to investigate.

Once inside, Alessandra grabbed a pair of pruning shears and slipped them into her skirt pocket. I tried to stop her and demand an explanation, but she was out the door again. We hurried back across the lawn, then turned down a narrow path that ran deeper into the garden. Finally she stopped, opened the hatbox, and pulled out a small oil lamp—which I had seen at her bedside earlier that night.

"Light it," she ordered. "But keep the wick low." I did as I was told.

She quickly started cutting roses and tossing them into the hatbox. She was careful to take only one from each bush, and always from the back, where the missing bloom wouldn't be noticed. I stood there, holding the lamp, my mind racing—what was she going to *do* with the roses? I knew it had to do somehow with the final sitting, but how?

Then it hit me. Flower apports were common in séances. The Spiritualist newspapers were filled with stories about them.

The "spirits" were going to leave behind rose petals which we'd find scattered on the table when the sitting finished and the lights were finally turned on.

"You're going to fake an apport," I said. "Aren't you?"

She didn't answer me.

"Don't do this," I said. "You'll get caught. Please. I'm begging you."

"I won't let him win!"

"You're crazy. You're risking everything!"

"I have to!"

I should have grabbed the shears and flung them into the bush, but in the end I didn't. She was going to do it— with me or without me. We snuck back to the house and I slipped into my room, my stomach in knots.

Alessandra's first husband had been a magician.

I could only pray he trained her well.

# 63

M r. Huxley will not be joining us tonight."
We were standing in the hallway of Farnam
House the next morning, Henry in his wading boots, a fly
fishing rod in his hand. Maxine handed him his tweed fishing hat, and he plopped it on his head. She raised prize roses.
He was president of the local angler's club, and his prize
pike hung over the fireplace in the library.

I thought maybe I hadn't heard him right. "Mr. Huxley's not coming?"

"Bout of indigestion. He had two of Mrs. Mallory's
famous lemon syllabubs for dessert last night." He chuckled.
"That will send you off to the WC, eh Maxie?"

Henry picked up his creel.

"Last chance to catch a real fish, Master Labella—
wicked teeth, razor sharp gills. A true fighter! That's your
English pike." Henry had been inviting me all week to go
fishing with him, but I was focused on landing Elsa.

"Thank you," I said, "But I promised Alessandra I'd
go for a walk with her this morning."

"Capital idea." he replied. "Settle her down." He
frowned at me. "I must say I've been disappointed in her
performance. Frankly, I expected a better show, given all the
hoopla coming from Dr. Lombardi and his colleagues."

"She'll do better tonight, sir," I promised.

"She better," Henry warned. "Last chance for your *Signora*." He patted his vest pocket for his cigars. "Mr. Huxley has asked Mr. Mallory to take his place sitting up at the table. He'll be delighted, no doubt. Bloody uncomfortable sitting on the floor." He stuck a cigar in his mouth and headed for the door. "Well, cheerio!"

Maxine headed back to the library and her magazine and I stood there. Whatever chance I had of convincing Alessandra to drop her crazy scheme was gone. Without Huxley there, she would certainly roll the dice. I trudged up to Alessandra's room to give her the stunning news.

As I expected, she was thrilled.

"My God, Tommaso! Huxley won't be there tonight?" She grabbed me by the shoulders and started dancing me around the room. "You'll see. We can do this!"

I pushed her away. "Leave me out of this!" I said. "I don't want any part of your crazy plan. You're stupid! You're risking everything!"

"Tommaso..." I could see the hurt in her eyes.

I took her hand. "Alessandra, please, I'm begging you." I said. "No tricks. Do your best, whatever happens happens, we go home. Lombardi is waiting for you. If it doesn't work out you've still got Rome and 4,000 *lire*. Fuck Huxley and his hundred pounds."

"I can't, Tommaso. I...I can't let him win." She looked at me. "I can do this. You have to trust me. I've worked it all out. The flowers will be..."

"Stop," I said. "I don't want to know." I stood there, looking at her.

"Do your best," I finally said, and headed for the door.

# 64

Just before we stepped into the library that night, Henry pulled us aside.

"I dropped off a bottle of Dr. Bateman's Elixir Salutis to Mr. Huxley this afternoon for his dyspepsia. He leaned in conspiratorially. "I *really* wanted to show him the fish I caught. Four pounds, six, by Jove!" He grinned. "Nigel may know a bit about fisticuffs, but he couldn't catch a fish if his life depended on it."

He pulled out his snuff box and took a pinch. "Found him in bed surrounded by tea pots and rhubarb pills. Anyway, we were talking and he told me he was concerned that some of our `Continental friends will dismiss the Society's experiments as unfair—too rigid. He wants no excuses." He turned to Alessandra. "He suggested we skip the clock tonight, and provide you with a more sympathetic circle of sitters, as well. He wants you at ease tonight, allow you to do your best. After some consideration, I agreed with him. Sporting chance and all that, eh wot? So we've invited two ladies from the local Cambridge Spiritualist Church to join us tonight."

We heard a loud voice call out.

"*Signora* Poverelli! *Signora* Poverelli!"

Henry smiled and pointed to a plump matron hurrying across the room towards us, waving a newspaper in her hand. "That's Mrs. Goody. Let's see what she has to say to you."

Mrs. Goody could hardly contain her excitement.

"What an honor, *Signora*!" She thrust the newspaper into Alessandra's hand. "We've read so much about you. The *Spiritualist Light* has been following your tour of Europe all summer." She clutched her bosom, breathless with excitement. "I can't believe we will be sitting with you tonight! Can you, Abigail?"

Her elderly companion, gripping a cane, waved a tiny hand from a library chair across the room. She looked like she was in her seventies.

"We've brought along a song book," Goody gushed, dragging it out of her purse and putting on her spectacles. "Abigail and I may not always sing on tune, but we sing loud enough to raise the dead." She tittered. "That's a little joke of ours."

Elsa discretely tugged my arm and we slipped past them into the library. "She got that right," Elsa giggled. "My father's taken me to some of their Saturday services."

Mallory was standing in the corner, chatting with Maxine. It seemed strange not to see Huxley with them, eyeing us suspiciously. Maxine waved us over.

"I suspect our Elsa is going to miss Master Labella here when he returns to Naples."

Elsa blushed.

Henry called across the room. "When you're ready, Mr. Mallory, we can begin." He came over and put his hand on my shoulder. "I'll be blunt, Master Labella. Every medium the Society has investigated to date has turned out to be either a fraud or a bust. I know many people view our investigations as foolish, even laughable. But we remain hopeful—it only takes one white crow to upset the law that all crows are black."

Elsa pulled me close, her bright eyes shining with excitement.

"Alessandra's our white crow. Isn't she, Tommaso."

# 65

I kept my eyes fixed on Alessandra all night.

I *knew* she was going to do it, but when she finally made the move, I *still* didn't see it. Nobody else did either. It was amazing.

The lamp was under the table, but the wick had been trimmed. Alessandra was patient. She wasn't on a clock. She let the minutes plod by — long stretches of silence, the excitement wearing off, people starting to yawn. At the same time, she herself constantly moved about in her seat, rearranging her position, asking Mallory and Henry to release their grip for a few seconds to allow her to "scratch her nose." Twice she had us all conveniently stand up so Mrs. Goody could lead us in a rousing hymn. Henry wasn't Huxley—he was an amateur. He allowed so many diversions, so many opportunities to set up the move.

We had been sitting there for almost an hour when Alessandra suddenly sat up in her chair.

"They're here," she announced. "I can feel their presence. Spirits, show us a sign!" She jumped to her feet and swept her arms heavenward.

A second later, Mrs. Goody spoke up. "I feel something!"

She reached up, patted her head, then gasped in surprise. "Why they're ... flowers!"

Everyone looked up. Rose petals were fluttering down from the gloom above her head, into her hair, onto her shoulders.

Mallory ducked under the table for the oil lamp, raised it, and everyone stared in astonishment at the table top, now littered with rose petals. Abigail reached out with her bony hand to scoop up a souvenir from the Other Side.

"A gift from the spirits!" she croaked, gaping up at the ceiling.

"An apport!" squealed Mrs. Goody. "Good heavens!"

Elsa stared at the petals, mouth open wide, then broke into a grin. "Oh my God!" she exclaimed. She jumped up and kissed me. "Tommaso! Oh, I'm so happy!"

Mallory reached out and grabbed Alessandra's hand. "Signora!" he cried. "*Brava! Brava!*"

Henry sat there stunned, trying to comprehend what had just happened. Finally, he stood up. "Rather remarkable," he said. "I don't know what else to say." He turned to Maxine and frowned. "Wait till Nigel hears about this."

I looked at Alessandra and she gave me a quick wink. How she managed to toss the rose petals into the air without being seen, she never told me. My guess is they were in her sleeve all along. It was a hell of a performance, but I wanted us gone before Huxley recovered from his bout of indigestion.

We needed to grab the money and run.

## 66

I was going to miss Elsa.

I hadn't managed to steal anything more than a kiss, but I had been making progress. One more week and I would have gotten in her knickers, believe me. I dreamed about her that night, and was awoken the next morning by the sound of her laughter out in the hall.

"Tommaso, wake up!"

For a second, I imagined I was still dreaming, but it was definitely her cheerful chirp, followed by Alessandra's voice. "We're going for a walk before breakfast!" I looked over at the clock on the mantel. It was already eight, and outside my window the sun was up. I quickly threw on my shirt and pants, ran my hand through my hair, and opened the door. Elsa stood there grinning, hands on her hips, sporting a pretty red skirt and smelling of lilacs.

"Sleepyhead!" Elsa grabbed my arm and pulled me outside.

Alessandra had a smug, triumphant look on her face. I didn't blame her. Huxley had her on the ropes, the bell was about to ring, but she had slipped the knockout, caught him with a surprise punch of her own, and put him on the canvas. She looked like her old self—confident, happy, cocky.

"We're going home, Tommaso!" she said, giving me a big hug. "I can't wait to see Camillo!"

"Wasn't Alessandra fantastic last night, Tommaso?" Elsa exclaimed. She dug into her skirt pocket and pulled out a rose petal. "I'm going to keep this for the rest of my life." She turned to Alessandra. "My father is so happy! At breakfast this morning, he said you have given humanity hope."

"So the Society is conceding?" I asked.

"My father expects them to. He said he sees no other conclusion that can be drawn. They'll have to draft an official report, of course."

"Have they talked to Mr. Huxley yet?" I asked, trying to sound nonchalant. "I know he's not feeling well."

"He looked so much better this morning. He's meeting with father and Henry in the library right now."

"Good," laughed Alessandra. "I hope he brought his hundred pounds."

We walked outside and into the sunshine. It was a beautiful, late summer morning, the air perfumed with the smell of freshly-cut grass. A maid was waiting in the driveway with Hercules, the Tyndall's hound. She curtsied and handed Elsa the leash. Like Alessandra, Elsa loved dogs, and always walked him when she came over. The two of them fussed over him like he was a baby, cooing and patting him, and took turns holding the leash as we strolled the gardens.

As we passed by the glass house, the gardener gave us a distinctly unfriendly look, and turned his back to us as we passed by. Elsa and Alessandra were too busy chattering away to notice it, but I saw it. I wasn't sure what it meant, but I found it odd.

We finished a leisurely circle of the house and Elsa turned to me.

"I'm starving. Race you back to the house!" she said, and took off with Hercules.

"Tommaso's last!" Alessandra shouted. She grabbed her skirts and started running, me on her heels. I sped past Alessandra, but Elsa was too fast. We all ended up winded and laughing at the front door, ready for a hearty breakfast of bangers and mash. Alessandra hung back for a moment, letting Elsa enter first. Then she wheeled around and leapt into my arms.

"Oh God, Tommaso! We did it!"

And then everything came crashing down.

# 67

It's still painful to recall what happened next.

Henry and Maxine were sitting in the library on the edge of their seats, whispering with Mallory, when we hurried by on our way to the dining room. Alessandra called out and waved, but nobody looked up. That's when I knew something was terribly wrong.

We entered the dining room and discovered Huxley sitting there, a cup of tea in his hand. Behind him stood Bridget, the upstairs maid Alessandra had surprised in her room the night of the second sitting, "changing the pillows" as she claimed. She had a smirk on her face. She was also concealing something behind her ample butt.

Huxley put down his cup.

"Be a good little girl and run along, Elsa. Your father is waiting for you in the library."

Elsa hesitated, then looked at me. "Be right back," she said, and left.

Huxley folded his arms and leaned back in his chair.

"*Buongiorno, Signora* Poverelli."

Alessandra glared at him. "Where's my money?"

Huxley faked a pout. "How rude! Aren't you going to ask me how I feel? After all, I've been ... sick." He chuckled.

Alessandra stared at him.

"No? Ah well. As you can see, I've managed a miracu- lous recovery. I couldn't let you leave England before I could say goodbye." The smile disappeared. He leaned forward, his mouth drawn back in a snarl. He raised his hand. "Bridget?"

Bridget stepped forward, pulled a box from behind her back, and set it on the table.

Alessandra gave a cry.

It was her hatbox.

"Bridget was cleaning your room while you were out walking this morning, and found this in the back of your closet. Shall we see what's inside?" Huxley opened the top and pushed it across the table. My stomach turned over.

It was all there. Pruning shears, rosebuds, cut stems, clods of dirt, mud smears. All the evidence Huxley needed to destroy Alessandra.

Huxley closed the box. "Bridget will testify that she saw you sneak out of the house with it on Tuesday night, followed you, then watched you return with it—am I cor- rect, Bridget?

"As you said, sir."

Alessandra stared hard at Bridget, but Bridget stared right back, defiant.

It all made sense –the click of the door we heard that night was Bridget. Right then and there, I should have in- sisted to Alessandra that we abandon the whole crazy scheme, but I hadn't.

Huxley pulled out his cigar case and reached in his pocket for a match.

"Bridget observed you the whole time you were here. She was in my employ, by the way—an arrangement I made before you even arrived in England."

"Fuck you," said Alessandra.

I swallowed hard. "Was Mr. Mallory in on this?"

"No. " Huxley lit his cigar, took a deep puff, inspected the glowing tip, then studied Alessandra for a moment. "Your kind are so predictable. I suspected you were planning to use the rose petals in your last sitting. But I was afraid if I were there, you might think twice, might settle for…a draw instead."

He leaned forward. "I didn't want that. I wanted to show the world what you really are. So I made it easy for you. I faked my little stomach ache, had Henry invite that simpleton Mrs. Goody to take my place. I suggested he get rid of the clock, so you had all the time in the world to set up your pathetic little trick." He sneered. "I *wanted* you to cheat!"

He stuck the cigar in his mouth. "And you took the bait."

"*Bastardo!*" Alessandra leaned forward and knocked the cigar out of his mouth. "*Ti faccio un…* "

I grabbed Alessandra. "Shut up!"

It was over. I was embarrassed, and furious at Alessandra.

Huxley stood up and smiled. "There's no need for you to go upstairs –the Tyndall's have already packed you bags. You'll find them waiting for you in the carriage at the back door." He reached into his pocket, pulled out an envelope, and offered it to Alessandra.

"Not the hundred pounds you expected, *Signora*—just a train ticket to send you back where you belong."

Alessandra grabbed the envelope, then leaned forward and spit on his suit.

I grabbed her and hustled her out of the room. All I wanted to do was get to the train station. As we hurried past the library on the way to the carriage, I saw Elsa sitting in an armchair, crying. I wanted to tell her I had nothing to do with it, that it was all Alessandra's idea, that I had tried to stop her. I didn't want her to remember me as a cheat.

It was the last time I saw Elsa.

Huxley delivered one final twist of the knife, with the help of a telegram he wired ahead to the *London Times* the minute we fled Farnam House in disgrace. By the time we reached the Dover docks late that afternoon, newspaper boys were already hawking papers with Alessandra's photo emblazoned on the front page along with big, black headlines—I could only make out "Italian" and "Huxley" but I could guess the rest.

The ferry horn was sounding as we hurried towards the gangway, a newsboy hanging on my arm, pestering me to buy a paper. All of a sudden, he recognized Alessandra. He stared at her in disbelief, then let out a yell.

"The dago! The dago!"

He danced around, pointing at her and making faces as every newsboy on the pier came running. Alessandra fled up the gangway. I dug into my pocket, gave him a coin, grabbed a paper and followed her to our cabin. When I got there, I shoved the paper in her face.

"Are you happy now?" I shouted. "Lombardi warned you not to go to England. But you wouldn't listen! I warned you not to play tricks, but you wouldn't listen! You could have quit while you were ahead. Now you're an international joke."

So was Lombardi.

The ferry's engines rumbled to life, the deckhands slipped the lines, and we cast off for France. The Paris newspapers probably had the story already.

"Camillo's gonna kill you when he finds out."

# 68

Alessandra looked terrible.

She sat in her seat, a tear-soaked handkerchief clutched in her hand, silently staring out the window as the night train from Calais sped towards Paris. I was worried about her.

She didn't eat anything on the ferry back to France, and gave me a scare when I found her standing alone at the stern of the boat, clutching the rail, the sea just a small jump away. The empty expression in her eyes scared me enough that I steered her back to the cabin and kept her close to me the rest of the trip. I was feeling pretty bad myself, after how I had behaved in Dover. She needed a friend, and I had failed. When we boarded the night train to Paris, the conductor had kindly inquired whether the lady was ill, and whether I would like him to tell the porter to bring Alessandra a glass of brandy once we left the station. I thanked him, and when it showed up I made her drink enough to sleep an hour before she woke again to stare out the window.

I reach over and hugged her.

"It's going to be alright," I said. She squeezed my hand, then buried her face in the pillow and wept.

A somber Renard was waiting for us when we pulled into the Gare du Nord station at midnight. A light rain was falling on the rooftops of Paris as we rode in silence through the city to his mansion on Boulevard Haussmann. A servant met us at the door, and we made our way to the library where Lombardi was waiting for Alessandra.

He was slumped in a chair, head in his hands, a half-empty bottle of cognac on the table, a copy of *Le Figaro* in his lap. The French papers had the scandal already. Her photo was on the front page.

"Camillo!" Alessandra rushed across the room and collapsed at his feet. She looked up, tears streaming down her face. "Oh God, forgive me!"

He reached down and shoved her away.

"Forgive you?" he shouted. "After what you've done? You've ruined us both!" He flung the newspaper at her. "I'm the laughingstock of the university!" He fell back into his chair. "No one will believe us now." He drained his glass, flung it across the room, then reached down and yanked Alessandra to her knees.

"Tell me!" he demanded. "Was everything a fake? My mother? Did you fake her too? Tell me the truth, damn you!" He raised his hand to strike her but Renard stopped him.

"No! Your mother was real!" Alessandra clung to his arm. "She was there!" She turned to me, her eyes pleading. "You saw her, didn't you, Tommaso? Tell him!"

"I did," I said.

"The spirits do exist!" Alessandra wiped the tears from her face. "But they abandoned me in England. Even *Babbo* Giro," she whispered. "He always comes when I call. I must have done something to make him angry."

Lombardi rose from the chair.

"*Babbo* Giro didn't abandon you. How could he? He never existed."

He started for the door. Alessandra jumped to her feet, panic in her eyes. She grabbed his arm.

"Camillo, where are you going?"

"Out," he replied coldly.

"But when are you coming back?"

"I don't know."

Renard looked at me. "Stay with her." He followed Lombardi out the door.

Alessandra rushed to me. "He'll come back, Tommaso, won't he? Oh, tell me he'll come back."

"Yes," I lied. "Just give him some time to think." I got her over to a chair and sat her down, then put my coat around her shoulders and held her tight. "He'll be back."

I was sure it was over.

## 69

We waited five hours.

Alessandra sat in the dark, empty room, staring vacantly into space, rocking herself back and forth, whispering to herself. "He'll be back ... He'll be back ... He'll be back ...."

Over and over.

At some point, a servant came in with a silver tray of food but it remained next to her, untouched. She didn't respond when I asked her if she wanted a blanket, or a glass of water. She just held herself and kept rocking back and forth.

"He'll be back ... He'll be back ... "

I finally fell asleep, holding her hand in mine.

The first faint light of dawn was coloring the sky outside the library window when we heard the doorknob turn. Alessandra gave a cry and ran to the door. Renard stood there, a somber Lombardi behind him.

"Camillo! Thank God, you've come back!"

Alessandra reached out her arms to him, but Lombardi drew back. Renard steered her back to her chair. "Sit down, Alessandra. Dr. Lombardi has something to say to you."

Lombardi walked to the fireplace and stood there, his back to Alessandra.

"Our fates are now entwined," he announced, his voice trembling. "I cannot redeem my reputation unless I redeem yours." He leaned on the mantel, head bowed, then turned around and faced her.

"Dr. Renard and I will demand that the Society allow you one final test—to be conducted in Italy. We will ask Dr. Negri, Dr. Fournier and von Weibel to support us. In return, you will agree to accept—without question or debate—any conditions Huxley and the Society wishes to impose. Do you understand?"

Alessandra nodded her head mutely.

"Your fee is forfeit. The scandal is a violation of your contract."

"I don't want the money, *caro*," she whispered. "I just want you to forgive me."

Lombardi picked up his coat.

"You don't deserve it, but if you manage to pass Huxley's test, you'll be paid 1,000 lire. Then we're done with each other. I'm returning to Torino to see what I can do to save my position."

Alessandra followed him to the door.

"*Caro* ... please ... don't ... "

He suddenly whirled around, tears blinding his eyes.

"I would have done anything for you, Alessandra!"

He kissed her fiercely, then he was gone.

## 70

Naples hadn't changed in the four months we were gone. It was still the same shithole.

Alessandra stumbled down the steps of the train lugging her bag. I followed her, massaging my neck. We were both stiff, sore and hungry.

After Cambridge, Naples hit you hard. The garbage, the yelling and arguing, the noise, the stench. We fit right in—we both stunk. We had slept on station benches between trains, and we were flat broke. I never saw Alessandra so low. She ate almost nothing on the three-day trip back, staring out the window, sleeping fitfully, waking every hour to ask me where we were. When we reached Marseilles, I used the last of our money to buy some olives and stale bread, and a bottle of cheap red wine which we passed between us.

"The game's not over," I said, trying to cheer her up. "Lombardi will force Huxley to give you one last shot. You'll get your 1,000 *lire* and be off to Rome, leaving me behind."

I didn't believe it, of course. Huxley wasn't about to give Alessandra a second chance. It was over.

A *carrozzella* driver called to us as we stumbled out of the station into the September heat, but I waved him away. We didn't have the fare. We would have to walk to Doffo's place. It was scorching, no breeze, and my feet hurt. Fortunately Doffo was there when we knocked on the door.

"Tommaso!" he cried. "You're back?"

We squeezed into the room and I dumped our bags on the floor. Doffo shared his tiny apartment with three other guys from the *Mattino*—double bunks, nails for clothes hangers, cracked mirror, a small table and some wooden chairs, pile of dirty clothes in a basket. He ladled out a glass of water from a clay pot and passed it to Alessandra who drank it down greedily.

"I saw the story," Doffo said, sneaking a glance at Alessandra. "What happened?"

"She made a mistake. I'll tell you the story later."

"What are you going to do next?"

"Ask Venzano to take me back."

Doffo grimaced. "Too late. They already hired another photographer."

"He likes me. I can write. I'll become a reporter."

I looked over and Alessandra had fallen asleep in the chair, still clutching the empty water glass in her hand. Her shoes and skirt were covered in dust, her head was cradled in one arm, and matted, tangled hair covered her face. She looked old.

"I hate to ask you this, but can we stay here tonight?"

"I can probably talk the guys into letting you stay one night. She can have my bed, and we can sleep on the floor." He nodded at Alessandra. "What will she do now?"

"Find a job."

"She can always go back to doing séances."

"No. Pigotti would eventually hear about it and come after her. She has to find some other line of work." I looked at Alessandra. "That's life. God I'm thirsty." I walked over and slid the glass out of Alessandra's hand, filled it with water and gulped it down. "Has Pigotti been around?"

"The newspaper? More than once. Asking people where Alessandra had gone." Doffo looked at me. "She didn't tell him that she was leaving? Or where she was going?"

"No."

"Why?"

"One, he wouldn't have let her go. Two, she stole his money."

"You're kidding!"

"If Pigotti learns she's here, she's dead. And he'll probably kill you too."

Doffo laughed. He had been beaten up twice in Rome by thugs hired by politicians he skewered in his cartoons. He didn't scare easily.

"A lot of people would like to kill me. He can get in line."

## 71

My heart jumped into my throat.

The guy looked just like Vito, Pigotti's enforcer. The squat, beefy guy who beat the bushes looking for me the night I met Alessandra at the Piazza del Plebiscito.

He was standing on the sidewalk in front of the *Mattino*, hands in his pockets, smoking a cigarette. I hurried into the building. Once I was safe inside, I glanced over my shoulder, but nobody was following me.

Alessandra's exposure and humiliation in England made every newspaper in Italy. Pigotti wasn't especially smart, but it didn't take a genius to guess that Alessandra would return to Naples. So you put a guy outside the *Mattino*, maybe Rossi's place too, all the old haunts, and wait for her to show up—or for me to show up. I was on the tour with her. Good chance I'd know her plans. I walked back to the door and peeked out. Whoever the guy was, he was gone. I chalked it up to nerves. A lot of guys in Naples looked like Vito.

I walked up the stairs to the fourth floor. Julieta was nasty as ever when I showed up outside Venzano's office.

"Well look who's back home," she smirked. "Where's *Signora* Seduta Spiritica? I heard our little séance queen ran into a little trouble in England. Caught cheating. What a surprise!" She pointed to a chair. "Wait here."

Venzano's voice boomed out from his office. "Tommaso? Is that you? Get in here."

I flicked off Julieta and entered the office. Venzano was at his desk, reworking a headline.

"Boss!" It felt great seeing him again.

He leaned back in his chair and smiled. "I was wondering when you would show up. Alessandra come back with you?" I closed the door behind me, and took a chair.

"She's here in town. But her husband is looking for her, and he's not happy."

"Doffo told me he's come around looking for her." He put down his pencil. "So Lombardi's girl was a fraud all the time?"

"She was stupid. But she's not a fraud. There's no way she could have faked some of the things she did."

"Then why did she cheat?"

"Huxley baited her into going to England where she was a fish out of water. Couldn't speak the language, hated the food, surrounded by people who wanted her to fail."

"That makes a difference?"

"She's not a machine. She performs best when she's surrounded by friends."

"Why didn't Lombardi go with her?"

"She wouldn't let him. It was between her and Huxley. She didn't want his help. Then when she couldn't produce anything, she panicked. She couldn't stand the idea of him winning."

Venzano shook his head. "Too bad. I'm going to miss her. She made a lot of money for us. " He held up a copy of the *Mattino*. The front page was a blow up of Alessandra's face, eyes closed, grimacing, cropped from the famous photo I took at Rossi's house. Underneath was a single word in huge black letters—*Exposed!* Venzano tossed it on the desk.

"We sold 5,000 copies."

It was the opening I was hoping for.

"The story's not over," I said, trying to sound confident. "Lombardi told me he's going to force Huxley and the English to do a final test."

Venzano's eyes widened. "Tell me more."

"He and Renard are going to rally scientists here on the Continent. One final test—here in Naples. He'll be announcing it soon."

Venzano grinned ear to ear. I had him.

"Take me back, and you'll have the inside story. I know everybody. Lombardi trusts me. And you've seen my writing."

"I can't pay you what Lombardi did."

"I can help you sell a lot of papers," I said. "Just double my old salary." I had learned a few tricks from Alessandra.

Venzano laughed. "Deal."

"I need one more thing."

"What's that?"

"A place where Alessandra can stay until the test— some place in town Pigotti won't find her. She also needs a job. She's broke."

Venzano looked at me for a long moment, then picked up his pen. He scribbled out a note, folded it, and pushed it across the desk. He glanced towards the door and dropped his voice.

"A lady friend of mine," he whispered. He winked. "French woman. She's always looking for domestic help. They're always quitting on her. She lives up in the Vomero, near Castel Sant'Elmo. It's a classy neighborhood. Guys like Pigotti wander in there, the police rough them up and kick them out. Alessandra will be safe there."

# 72

It *was* Vito. And for a fat guy, he was fast.

I was a block from the *Mattino,* heading back to Doffo's place, when I heard running footsteps behind me. I spun around and Vito was in my face. He lunged at me, grabbing my shirt, but I twisted out of his grasp and took off. I ducked down a side street but it was a dead end. I looked around helplessly as Vito came charging around the corner. He tackled me, knocking me to the ground, then grabbed me by the collar and dragged me to my feet.

"Got him, boss!" he said.

"Hold on to the bastard!"

I looked up and Pigotti was hurrying down the alley. When he reached me he jerked me into a little courtyard and shoved me up against the wall.

"Where the fuck is she?" he snarled.

"Where is who?" I said.

He punched me in the stomach and I doubled up, gasping for breath. It felt like I had been kicked by a horse. My head started spinning, and I fell to my knees. I could taste blood in my mouth.

"Get him up," Pigotti ordered.

Vito yanked me to my feet. Pigotti grabbed me by the neck.

"Where is she—my wife?"

"I don't know." I said.

"Fucking liar! You went everywhere with her. You think I didn't read the newspapers while that fat Jew was running around Europe fucking my wife?" He slapped me hard. "I knew she would fuck up, and he would dump her, and she'd end up back here with nothing."

He tightened his grip around my throat, and leaned in close. His breath stank.

"She's here. She came back with you."

"She didn't..."

He kneed me in the balls and I fell to the ground again. He kicked me in the ribs.

"Liar! Where is she?" he screamed.

I was afraid he was going to kill me.

"She...followed Lombardi...back to Torino," I gasped. "...went...to his house." It was the only thing I could come up with.

"Bitch!" Pigotti slammed his fist against the wall. "Whore! I'll kill her! I'll kill them both!"

From a window above my head, I heard a man's voice call out, "Hey, what's going on down there?"

"Boss, we gotta go," Vito said. I heard them run back towards the street.

I rolled over on my back and lay there, gasping for breath.

## 73

Go away! We're not hiring."

The maid slammed the door in our face.

I banged on the door. When she opened it this time, I jammed the door open with my foot and forced into her hand the note Venzano had given me.

"It's for Madame Dubonnet. From her friend, *Signor* Venzano. You better deliver it or you're in trouble." She stared at the note suspiciously, then looked at me.

"Wait here."

Alessandra and I sat down on a small wooden bench. My ribs still ached, and I had a cut on my forehead, but Alessandra had cleaned me up pretty well. The servants' entrance in the back of Madame Dubonnet's mansion was surrounded by a high wall and the watchman at the big iron gate kept his eye on us.

"How are you doing?" I whispered.

"God, Tommaso, I need this job," Alessandra replied.

"Where's Bastet?"

"Right here." She pulled the lucky charm out of her dress pocket and kissed it. She still looked tired, but her spirits were on the rise. She was a survivor.

The door opened and a man dressed in a long tailed coat and striped trousers looked down at us.

"Who's Alessandra?"

Alessandra jumped to her feet. "I am, *Signore*."

He stared at her, then looked at Venzano's note. "You're looking for employment?"

"Yes, *Signore*"

"What do you do?"

"I do laundry, *Signore*."

"Who did you work for before?"

I jumped in. "She worked for *Signor* Venzano—the editor of the *Mattino* newspaper. You have his letter."

He turned to me. "And who are you?" he demanded sourly. The snooty maid stood next to him, glaring at me.

"I work for *Direttore* Venzano. He told me to bring her here."

He folded up the note, put it in his pocket, and turned to the maid. "Leave us."

He closed the door and stood there, arms folded.

"I don't know how your *Signor* Venzano knows Madame. It is not my business. But she has instructed me to find you a position." He pointed to a shack leaning against the side of the wall. "There's the laundry. Thirty *lire* a week –ten back to me. You sleep there."

"Why do you get ten?" I protested.

The butler wheeled on me.

"Screw you, boy!" He turned to Alessandra. "If you don't want it, I'll be happy to tell Madame you turned down the job."

Alessandra stepped forward. "I'll take it, *Signore. Mille grazie.* When do I start?"

He glared at me, then adjusted his bow tie.

"You start now. Madame has a big party tonight. " He stepped back inside the house and slammed the door.

"Fuck you," I muttered.

Alessandra rolled up her sleeves. "I've done this before, Tommaso. I can do it again." She reached out and embraced me. "You better be going. Thank you for everything."

"Give Lombardi two months," I said. "You'll see. He'll be back here, with Huxley…"

Alessandra looked away, and I watched a tear run down her cheek.

"Camillo may come back, Tommaso, but he won't be coming back for me."

# 74

Huxley underestimated Lombardi.

He thought the little professor would slink home and quietly resign his position at the university, but Lombardi came out swinging in an interview he gave to *La Stampa* newspaper. Yes, Alessandra had failed her test in England, Lombardi admitted. But she successfully passed *thirty two* tests conducted by skeptical scientists in five different Continental countries. Baron von Weibel in Munich had captured on film a dancing basket. And what about my photographs in Naples and Geneva? And Monsieur D'Argent's endorsement?

> "Are our powers of observation, our experiments, our methods to prevent fraud inferior to those exercised by British investigators?" Dr. Lombardi demanded. "I don't believe that, nor do my colleagues in Italy and France, Switzerland and Germany who tested *Signora* Poverelli and found her powers genuine."

Yes, Alessandra had "made a mistake" in England, but it wasn't a fair test. She was exhausted from three months of constant traveling and testing. She had collapsed in Warsaw, and he had prudently cancelled the tour. As soon as Huxley learned about her weakened condition, he launched his demand that she travel to England without delay to sit for them.

> "Mr. Huxley's motive was obvious," Lombardi declared. "He was determined to see her fail, because she had embarrassed him in France."

Alessandra arrived in England, she was weak and ill, and was met with unrelenting hostility and skepticism. Her powers failed, and in her desperation to avoid embarrassment she succumbed to temptation.

> "No one regrets that foolish decision more than *Signora* Poverelli herself," Dr. Lombardi explained. "All she asks is a chance to redeem herself."

Lombardi brought to the interview a petition signed by fifteen Continental scientists. Alessandra deserved one final test. The Society could set the rules—but the test should be held in Italy. Renard's name topped the petition. Negri, Fournier, and von Weibel had also signed it. Gemelli was the only person from Lombardi's university to sign it, but Sapienti added his prestige to the petition.

It worked.

On Sept 17, *La Stampa* ran a front-page editorial backing Lombardi's demand for a retest. Rome's *Messaggero* echoed the call a day later, joined by the *Corriere della Sera* in Milano. Then newspapers all across Italy joined the fight—Genoa, Bologna, Florence. It's easy for an Italian to hate the British. Besides, it was a story that could sell a lot of papers.

Down in Naples, Venzano doubled his coverage in the *Mattino*.

Doffo came up with a series of clever cartoons viciously lampooning John Bull as a pompous, arrogant bully—when the British consul in Naples showed up at the opera, he was booed by the audience. That earned Doffo a standing ovation in the newsroom and box of Havana double coronas from Venzano.

I pummeled Huxley with an article about Ile Ribaud—a breathless, I-was-there account describing how Huxley had tried to intimidate Alessandra on the train, and how she spat in his face (she slapped him, but spitting sounded more dramatic), and how our gallant Italian sailors had chased the effete Brit back to his first class cabin. How the sneaky limey had snuck into Alessandra's room when she was gone and rummaged through her bags, how he was left dumbfounded by Alessandra's astonishing answers to his Machiavellian history trick, and how the spirits yanked the chair from under him and dumped him on his ass—"*with a squeal of surprise, the British Torquemada flailed his arms and tumbled backwards, landing with a thump on the well-padded seat of his tailored English trousers...* "

Venzano loved it. We were selling 3,000 papers a day and crushing the *Piccolo*. Our newsboys started yelling "Alessandra! Alessandra!" every time a new edition came out. People came running.

Up in Paris, Renard blistered Huxley in an interview in *Le Figaro*. They had all agreed to sign a joint statement if Alessandra produced unexplainable phenomena at Ile Ribaud, but the duplicitous Englishman reneged. Perfidious Albion! Skepticism was welcome, but "*Science requires an open mind, and humility in the face of new facts. Monsieur Huxley has demonstrated neither in his investigations.*"

But we were getting nowhere. The Society sniffed its nose at the criticism and the clamor for a new test. We were foreigners, and the British don't take criticism from foreigners.

Then Sir Arthur Conan Doyle sent his famous letter to the editor of the *London Times*. The celebrated British author was a member of the Society, and had even conducted a ghost investigation himself. He was just beginning his conversion to Spiritualism at that time. He chided Huxley for his behavior in France, quoting his famous detective Sherlock Holmes who told Watson in one of his novels, "When you've eliminated the impossible, whatever remains, however improbable, must be the truth." Get on with it, he growled. The Society needed to accept the challenge, create an experiment where fraud was impossible, then let *Signora* Poverelli show what she could do.

On November 2nd, All Souls Day, Venzano walked into the news room with a huge grin on his face.

"*Attenzione*! *Attenzione*! Listen up, everyone."

Typewriters stopped clattering, editors stopped screaming, writers stopped scribbling. We all looked up. Venzano waved a copy of the *London Times*.

"Congratulations, gentlemen. They're coming to Naples."

"Who's coming to Naples?" shouted someone in the back of the room. Venzano roared with laughter.

"The *Inglesi*, you idiot! *Signor* Huxley and the London Society for the Investigation of Mediums!" The Society had agreed to one sitting, the week before Christmas, winner take all. He flung the *Times* into the air. "We're going to sell a lot more papers, gentlemen."

The very next day, Venzano called me into his office and handed me a telegram he had just received from Lombardi. Lombardi was coming to Naples and wanted to see Alessandra.

"Bring me the story," he smiled. "I'm saving you a spot on the front page."

## 75

Madame Dubonnet's maid opened the front door a crack and peered out at me.

"Go around the back," she hissed. "You're not allowed to call at the front door." She started to shut the door. Then she saw Lombardi standing there, dressed in his suit and tie, walking stick in hand.

"Begging your pardon, *Signore*," she exclaimed, her face turning red. "I most certainly did not mean you." Bewildered, she looked at me, then at Lombardi. "Is Madame Dubonnet expecting you, sir?"

"I have not come to call on Madame Dubonnet," Lombardi declared. "I'm here to see *Signora* Poverelli." The maid looked at him blankly.

"Alessandra," I said. "Your laundress."

"Oh!" she said. Flustered, she turned and called into the house "Monsieur Gronchi! Monsieur Gronchi!"

She turned back to us, nervously wringing her hands, then decided to usher us into the parlor. Madame Dubonnet had money. The room was beautifully decorated with antique French chairs and Persian carpets, and a vase of red and white geraniums graced the marble mantel. A delicate walnut escritoire sat in front of a tall, silk-curtained window where Madame Dubonnet undoubtedly sat to pen her *billets-doux* to Venzano when her husband was off traveling.

"How may I assist you, *Signore* ...?"

We turned and there stood the butler who had stiffed me the day Alessandra came begging for a job. This was going to be fun.

Lombardi handed him his card. "Professor Camillo Lombardi. I'm here to see *Signora* Poverelli. Bring her here immediately," Lombardi ordered.

Gronchi stared at me dumbfounded, then turned to Lombardi and bowed. "*Si, certamente, Signore.*"

I hopped up off the sofa. "I'll go with him," I said to Lombardi. I couldn't wait to see her again. I had stayed away because I was afraid Pigotti had put a tail on me.

As we hurried down the hallway, Gronchi grabbed me by the arm.

"She stole some money from the gentleman, no doubt. Is that why you're here?" He wagged his finger at me. As soon as this matter is settled, I want you both gone!"

When we got to the laundry, Alessandra was on her knees, bent over a washtub, surrounded by baskets of dirty sheets. She had lost weight, her face pallid and thin. She didn't even look up when we stepped inside. Her hands were red and raw, and her hair stringy and damp from the heat sent up by a big copper kettle of boiling water behind her. She wiped her brow with a forearm and returned to her scrubbing. On a string around her neck hung Bastet the cat.

"Get up, woman!" Gronchi kicked her with his shoe. "Follow me!"

Alessandra looked up.

"Tommaso?" she cried. She struggled to her feet and hugged me. She looked at Gronchi, then me. "What's going on?"

"Shut up and follow me!" Gronchi snarled. He turned and headed back to the house. Alessandra wiped her hands on her skirt and hurried after him. I bent over, picked up the bar of soap Alessandra had dropped, and followed them back to the parlor.

"Here she is, *Signore*," Gronchi announced. He pushed Alessandra into the room. Lombardi was standing at the window, his back to us. He turned and Alessandra gasped.

"Camillo … ?"

She started towards him then stopped, and fell on her knees. She reached forward.

"Oh Camillo! Forgive me!" Tears streamed down her cheeks as she opened her arms to him. "Forgive me!"

Lombardi reached down and pulled her up into his arms, kissing her fiercely, tears of joy on his face. He cradled her in his arms. "Let's start over, shall we?"

Gronchi stood in the doorway, gaping at them.

I walked over, pulled out the bar of soap from my pocket, and shoved it into his hand.

"The lady quits. Do your own fucking laundry."

## 76

I stared at Huxley through the viewfinder of the camera.

The last time I had seen him in England, he was wiping Alessandra's spit off his suit. I'm sure he thought it was the last he would see of her. Instead, here he was in Naples, among the unwashed, forced to face her one last time.

Huxley had arrived on December 8, the Feast of the Immaculate Virgin, the start of the Christmas season in Italy. The Queen Victoria Hotel was decorated English-style for the holidays—greenery on the mantels and a Christmas tree in the lobby. In the piazza outside the hotel, shepherds and angels were hovering over a Nativity crèche waiting for baby *Gesù bambino* to arrive, and the *zampognari* with their bagpipes were starting to panhandle outside churches.

"Who's Huxley talking to?" Fabio asked. Venzano had hired Fabio to replace me as a photographer.

"The guy on the left is from the *London Times*," I said. "The fat guy in the bad suit is an American, *New York Herald.*

"*Ma va' là!*" he whistled. "You're kidding me! All the way from America?"

"The desk clerk told me they've got 20 reporters booked in the hotel—Italy, France, England, Austria, Switzerland—shit, *two* from Germany."

"*Bonjour*, Tommaso."

I felt a tap on my shoulder. It was Henri from the *Tribune de Genève*. He had done the great story on Alessandra's sitting in Geneva with D'Argent.

"Where's Monsieur Lombardi? I want to do an interview with him and Alessandra."

"Sorry, Henri. They didn't come." I thumbed towards Huxley. "They don't need to hear this blowhard."

Henri tucked his pencil into his notebook. "I don't know—he looks pretty confident."

Claudio from *La Stampa* was taking a piss in the men's room when I walked in.

"So Tommaso—our Alessandra's going to show the Brits a few tricks?" He finished and walked over to the wash basin. "The guy from the *Times* told me the London bookies like Huxley. I told him I had 500 *lire* that said they were full of shit." He ran a comb through his hair and shoved it back in his pocket. "Tell Alessandra the boys at *La Stampa* are behind her."

A gruff voice piped up from the stall. "The English can kiss my Italian ass."

Claudio winked at me. "Carbone—from the *Messaggero*." He turned to the stall. "Wipe your ass and grab your pen, Geppetto. The show starts in five minutes."

Every chair was taken when I got back. The *Piccolo* photographer had jammed in next to Fabio, and I elbowed him out of the way. The three German reporters had camped out in the front seats after breakfast—all business, those guys. The Italian reporters, as usual, were lounging around in the back of the room, yakking away.

"*Buongiorno*, gentlemen."

Huxley's booming voice cut through the chatter and everyone fell silent.

"Most of you know who I am. Nigel Huxley, chief investigator of the London Society for the Investigation of Mediums. You know why we are here. To test *Signora*

Alessandra Poverelli—again. The Society has agreed to one final test, here in this hotel, on December 21st. We will be returning to England the following day, where we will celebrate the Christmas holidays—and the termination to this ridiculous charade."

"Charade?" It was Claudio from the back of the room.

A look of exasperation crossed Huxley's face.

"*Signora* Poverelli is a fraud. She has no supernatural powers –she has tricks. She was exposed in England. That should have been the end to it, but she sells newspapers, so you scandal-mongers demand a retest." He sneered. "Well, the story ends in two weeks, because your little, jumped up Neapolitan trickster will produce nothing. I guarantee it."

The German reporters were bent over their notepads, scribbling furiously.

Huxley gestured to a trio of men standing off to the side. "These three gentlemen will ensure that *Signora* Poverelli gets away with nothing."

He had assembled a hell of a fraud squad. Archer was a professional magician with thirty years on the London stage, and an expert in what Huxley called "the psychology of deception." He would be watching Alessandra for any misdirection or substitution of hands. Hardwicke was a sandy-haired Scotsman who specialized in mechanical devices used in séances to produce raps and taps and levitations. According to Hardwicke, sometimes they were built into the furniture, but usually they were smuggled into the room by a confederate of the medium. He had even written a book on them—*Gambols with the Ghosts. Tricks for Producing Spiritualistic Effects*. Farthing was an older, soft-spoken man who ran the Society's Glasgow office. He had spent two decades investigating mediums in Scotland.

"We caught *Signora* Poverelli in England—and frankly, it wasn't all that difficult," Huxley sneered. "We are prepared to embarrass her again."

Scattered boos and catcalls erupted from the back of the room. Huxley ignored them.

Henri raised his hand. "Will Dr. Lombardi be in the room during the sitting?"

Huxley nodded. "Yes—as an observer only. We are allowing him to choose two additional observers.

"Has he chosen them ?"

"One will be Dr. Charles Renard. The other will be Tommaso Labella, the photographer from the *Mattino* who accompanied *Signora* Poverelli everywhere on her tour. However, he will not be allowed to bring his camera or other mechanical devices into the sitting room."

Carbone caught the insinuation. "Mechanical devices? Are you suggesting... "

Huxley smiled. "Suggesting what? That master Labella is a confederate of *Signora* Poverelli? That he brought an equipment bag into the room for every sitting Dr. Lombardi conducted on the Continent, a bag which was never inspected, which carried a trick apparatus to assist *Signora* Poverelli in producing her fraudulent raps and her levitations? ... "

I felt my face flush.

He paused, his timing impeccable. Everyone in the room was hanging on his words.

" ... No, I'm not."

The bastard just had.

"Now, if you will follow me up to the fifth floor, gentlemen," Huxley announced. "We have prepared a special stage for *Signora* Poverelli's magic show."

The séance room was a madhouse. The hotel furniture and bed were gone, and a team of English workers were busy removing the carpets, installing iron bars on the windows, and changing the door lock. Huxley had rented the two adjoining rooms as well, to prevent a confederate passing something through an adjoining wall to *Signora* Poverelli in

290

the séance room. Archer and Hardwicke had inspected each room from floor to ceiling, tapping walls for hollow spaces and loose panels; searching for any cracks, vents and openings to the outside. Anything found was closed and sealed. The street side of the séance room was five stories up—not that it mattered, since the windows themselves would be barred. The hallway outside would be patrolled during the séance by Mr. Farthing.

Huxley led us over to a large wooden crate sitting against the wall. A burly laborer had crowbarred the top off , and two workers were lifting out a table.

"The séance table, gentlemen. Built in England for this test."

"Can't trust these Eye-talians," Carbone cracked, drawing a laugh from the reporters.

That triggered a lecture by Hardwicke. "Standard precaution for any serious investigation," he harrumphed. "Let the medium provide the table and they've got you. They'll hide a telescoping reaching rod in a hollowed out cavity, or leave a slightly raised nail to use as a lifting hook, or round the bottom of legs to make the table easier to rock or tilt when the medium leans on it. I've seen it all."

Huxley knocked on the table top. "The same size and weight as the table *Signora* Poverelli supposedly levitated in Master Labella's famous *Mattino* photo. We are challenging *Signora* Poverelli to perform that same levitation she performed for Dr. Rossi, under the same lighting conditions—but this time using *our* table."

He steered us to the center of the room where the hotel manager was nervously watching an electrician screwing an odd-looking metal plate to the wooden floor. Huxley rested his hand on the manager's shoulder. "I have apologized to Mr. Bates here for our extensive modifications to his hotel. I have assured him that everything will be removed when we are finished with *Signora* Poverelli."

Huxley tapped the metal plate with the toe of his shoe. "*Signora* Poverelli's feet will rest throughout the sitting on this rather ingenious device developed by Mr. Hardwicke."

Hardwicke beamed at the compliment. He took a puff on his pipe. "I rather suspect *Signora* Poverelli uses her knees to lift the table, and the toe of her boot to tap nearby sitters and simulate spirit touches. She might even slip off a boot in the dark and employ her toes to pinch a sitter or place an object in a lap." He frowned. "We've even caught mediums who demand complete darkness for their sittings up and moving about the room performing their mischief. We can't allow that rubbish."

He pointed his pipe at the apparatus. "*Signora* Poverelli will rest her feet on this metal plate. It allows some ordinary moving of the feet, such as is inevitable in a long sitting, but if a foot is completely taken off the plate, an electric bell will ring. Perhaps one of you chaps would like to test it?"

"*Ja*, I will." The reporter from the *Berliner Tageblatt* stepped forward and gingerly placed his shoe on one of the plates. The electrician connected the wires and nodded to the German who lifted his foot.

*BRIING-G-G-G-G!*

The startled reporter jumped back and everybody broke out laughing. After Huxley finished and we were walking back downstairs, Henri pulled me aside.

"What do you think?" he asked nervously.

"Don't worry," I said. "Alessandra will come through— just like she did in Geneva."

But in my heart, I didn't believe that.

Alessandra was exhausted. She coughed non-stop now and couldn't sit for more than fifteen minutes in a chair before pain in her back and legs forced her to lie down on a couch. She would be tied to a chair, surrounded by people who wanted her to fail, and would have one shot.

She no longer believed – in Savonarola or herself.

## 77

They spent a lot of time together that last month.

After he rescued Alessandra from Gronchi, Lombardi moved her into a quiet, private apartment off Piazza Dante, and visited her faithfully every day. He was worried about her health, and insisted she rest and eat regularly. He hired a cook to fix her favorite food—bread soup, *scagliozzi*, *pasta fasuli*—and every evening they walked together in the gardens of the *Accademia*. She touched his hand when she talked with him, and leaned on his shoulder on the way back home.

Lombardi hadn't forgotten how Alessandra loved Negri's little seaside neighborhood in Genoa, and how she stood at the window for a long time, staring out, letting the breeze caress her face. A week before the final showdown with Huxley, Lombardi took her to Peppino, a little *ristorante* Venzano patronized in the Mergellina, on a small hill terraced in bougainvillea overlooking a little harbor.

He wanted me there that night, and told me why.

I couldn't wait to see Alessandra's face.

Alessandra wore the shell cameo of Venus that Lombardi had given her in Munich, but her skin was pale and her cheeks hollow. She walked slowly, and winced when she bent to sit down.

We sat on the terrace and talked as the sun slipped into the western sea and the stars filled the sky above our heads. During the dinner, Alessandra kept a shawl around her shoulders to keep the chill away and Lombardi talked of the coming new year and the dawn of a new century. If scientists were courageous in their pursuit of truth, the science of mental power would dominate the 20th century the same way the science of mechanical power dominated the 19th century. There was so much to learn. Whatever happened in the upcoming test, he believed Alessandra's powers were genuine.

When the meal was over, and the coffee and *sfogliatelle* arrived, Lombardi reached into his coat pocket and pulled out a telegram.

"I received this from Dr. Renard last week."

It was an invitation to Lombardi to move to Paris. A French industrialist had bequeathed 25,000 francs to Renard's Institut Métapsychique to explore mediumship "without prejudice and with the same dispassion Science brings to the examination of any observed phenomenon which excites the imagination of mankind." Lombardi would be named director of the new research program.

He looked at Alessandra. "I've accepted his offer. I leave for France January second. "

The pain in Alessandra's eyes was unmistakable.

Lombardi reached into his coat pocket, pulled out a second piece of paper, and pushed it across the table to Alessandra.

"Come with me, Alessandra."

She stared at the document. I could see a Ministry of Justice seal at the top.

"What...what is it, Camillo?"

"A divorce decree. My marriage is over. I'm going to start a new life in Paris." He took her hand in his and kissed it. "Come with me. Live with me. But only if you want."

He reached into his jacket pocket one last time and handed Alessandra a linen envelope with her name written on it.

"This is for you—whatever you decide."

Alessandra looked at him.

"Go ahead," he said." Open it."

Alessandra opened the envelope. Inside was 10,000 *lire*.

"For you, if you decide you still want to move to Rome, to find an apartment of your own, with a flowerpot on a sunny windowsill, and a cat to keep you company."

Alessandra looked at me, then at Lombardi.

"Camillo … I … I … " She stared at the money.

"You don't have to decide tonight," he said. "We'll talk after the test."

## 78

I found the envelope on my desk at the *Mattino* the next morning.

I hung up my coat, slid into my chair, and opened it.

> *Signora Poverelli is in grave danger. The personal nature of this threat precludes it from being disclosed in writing. Tell Signora Poverelli to come to the Chapel of San Gennaro tonight at midnight. A side door on Via dei Tribunali will be left unlocked. She is to come alone.*

I stared at the note, my head spinning.

Was it a trap by Pigotti?

Possible. He could easily pick a lock and lay low for her in the cathedral, but the handwriting seemed too elegant, the phrasing too refined for an illiterate street thug like him. I waved the envelope at Carlo, the reporter who sat next to me in the newsroom.

"Who dropped this off?"

"A priest." He kept pounding his typewriter.

"A priest?"

Carlo looked up. "He was wearing a cassock."

I should have put two and two together, but I had drunk a lot the night before.

"Thanks," I said. "If Venzano comes looking for me, remind him I'm at Court all day—the Colonna murder."

I shoved the note in my pocket and headed for Alessandra's apartment.

I knew one thing—if Alessandra decided to go, I was going with her.

## 79

The cathedral was dark and empty as we stumbled down the nave.

I never liked the place. When I was six years old, my mother took me to the Chapel to see the miracle of the blood, along with half of Naples. A priest holds up this silver reliquary containing the dried blood of decapitated San Gennaro, and everybody prays hard, and the blood turns to liquid. Sometimes it even boils. You can see it with your own eyes. It scared the shit out of me. When we got home, I told my mother I never wanted to go there again.

Ahead of us, we could see the flicker of votive candles coming from the Chapel. When we reached the door I stepped into the shadows.

"I'll stay here," I whispered.

Alessandra nodded and turned into the chapel. I peered in. The Chapel was empty except for a solitary nun kneeling at the communion rail, praying her rosary before the statue of the Blessed Virgin Mary. Alessandra looked around, puzzled, then looked back at me. I shrugged my shoulders. We were a few minutes early.

Alessandra advanced towards the nun.

"Sister … ?"

The nun kissed her crucifix, rose from her knees, then turned and looked at Alessandra. She was young, in her twenties maybe. But her face was hard and her voice harsh. She pointed to a pew.

'Sit down," she ordered.

Alessandra hesitated, then did what she was told.

"You are in danger of losing your immortal soul. Satan is using you to lead the faithful astray."

Alessandra looked at her bewildered. "Who are you?"

"Your daughter—conceived in lust, abandoned at birth, and raised by the kindness of the good sisters of Santissima Bambina."

Alessandra sat there for what seemed an eternity. Then she stood up and reached out her hand to her daughter. "*Tesoro mio!*" she said softly. My treasure.

In the candlelight, I could see the tears in Alessandra's eyes.

The nun pulled back.

"I do not want to know you," she said curtly. "I am only here to bring you a message from the Holy Father in Rome. The Devil is using you to cause thousands of simple Christians to abandon their childhood faith for the heresy of Spiritualism. The Holy Father will reveal your sin to the world—and expose us both to shame—unless you withdraw from the test."

The Weasel had it figured out. If Alessandra quit, she would be declared a fraud, her every miracle suspect. The sheep would turn once again to the Shepherd for guidance.

But Alessandra hadn't heard a word.

"I never abandoned you," she said softly, a tear running down her cheek. "They wouldn't let me keep you." She wiped the tear away with her sleeve. "What did they name you?"

"My name is of no importance. It is enough to know that I pray for you, and the boy you led astray. Be not

deceived! The lust of the flesh bringeth forth sin, and forni-
cation bringeth a punishment of eternal damnation!"

"The boy?" Alessandra sounded bewildered.

The nun looked at her with scorn. "My father, Ivano—
the circus acrobat you slept with. The holy sisters told me
the shameful story."

Alessandra staggered backwards.

"Is that what they told you?" She crumpled to her
knees and slammed her fists on the floor, her howls of rage
filling the Chapel as Sister Magdalena fled past me.

I ran to Alessandra and pulled her to me and held her
as tight as I could, trying to stifle her screams, terrified that
the sacristan would come running with a kitchen knife. But
no one came. I rocked her back and forth in my arms until
she finally exhausted herself and I pushed her hair back and
kissed her forehead, my fingers stroking her tear-stained
cheek.

"Alessandra, everyone makes mistakes in life," I said.
"You were young."

She sat there in silence, in the gloom, her head down.
When she finally spoke, her voice was flat, emotionless.

"I saw the circus. Ivano taught me how to juggle. Then
he left. That's all that happened. I never slept with him."

I stared at her. "Then who's the father?" She looked at
the floor.

"Father Angelo."

The shock I felt that night I still feel, twenty years later.
Alessandra wrapped her arms around herself, the tears well-
ing up in her eyes once again.

"He…he said I was possessed by the Devil. He tied
me to the bed by my hands and my feet, so I couldn't move.
Then he knelt down and said some prayers, then…then he
got up and walked over to the door, and bolted it. I tried
to free myself from the ropes… I was screaming and crying…He…took off his robe and got on top of me…lifted

my ... my dress ... and ..." She beat her hands on her knees, rocking back and forth.

"Oh God, Oh God!" Tears streamed down her face.

"I couldn't get away Tommaso. I couldn't get away."

Alessandra locked herself in her apartment and wept for two days.

I told Lombardi she had gone back to Bari to visit her father's grave. When she finally came out, she told me she was going to do the sitting. She never told Lombardi about the Church's threat. She would lose her daughter, and she was coughing up blood on the way to the hotel on the night of December 21, 1899, but she had searched her heart and found the answer.

She loved him.

When our carriage pulled up at the Queen Victoria Hotel that night, half of Naples seemed to be crowded into the Piazza Amedeo, desperate to catch a glimpse of the famous Alessandra. The society swells were already inside the hotel, but Alessandra's class were jammed elbow to elbow on the pavement outside, craning their necks to catch our arrival—porters and street sweepers, fishmongers and match sellers, beggars and whores. They had come to cheer their Cinderella.

By now, everybody in Naples knew her rags to riches story, her humiliation in England, and her fight for one last chance to redeem herself.

The *Mattino* and the *Piccolo* had launched a circulation war the day Huxley announced he was coming to Italy, and had worked the story for eight weeks, each newspaper dishing up breathless stories and daily updates until everybody in the city was rushing out to buy the latest edition as soon as it hit the streets. Doffo presented it as a prizefight. He drew a poster showing a boxing ring with a fat John Bull knocked on his butt with Alessandra, wearing bloomers sporting the flag of Italy, raising her gloves in triumph. Below it ran "Italy vs. England! December 21! Read the *Mattino*!" Venzano had our newsboys plaster it on the walls of every public building in town. The archbishop of Naples unwittingly helped those who couldn't read a paper. The Sunday before the showdown, he instructed every parish priest in the city to denounce Alessandra as an agent of the Devil. Cooks and maids and laundresses who hadn't already heard the lady of the house chattering about Alessandra over the breakfast table suddenly found out, swelling the ranks of the curious. Everybody wanted to see her.

When Alessandra stepped out of the carriage, supported by Lombardi, a great cheer rose up. Surprised, she waved her hand as Renard circled around and steadied her other arm, nervous about the amount of blood she had coughed up in her handkerchief on the way over.

I was alarmed at a guy near the hotel entrance who looked like Vito. But before I could get a second look, someone in the crowd stepped in front of him, blocking my view.

The lobby was packed with newspaper reporters, and photographers. Carbone from the *Messaggero* grabbed me as soon as I stepped inside. He pulled me into a corner.

"I need to talk to you privately after this is over."

"About what?" I said.

"Our guy at the Vatican got some information this morning. About Alessandra. From someone high up." He looked at me, and shook his head. "Not good."

My heart sunk.

"No problem," I said, trying to sound confident.

Across the room, Venzano was waving at me. Fabio had set up his camera near the staircase and Doffo stood next to him, peering through his thick glasses at a sketch he had just completed. *Signora* Damiano had brought her Naples Spiritualist circle—all twenty of them—and they quickly surrounded Alessandra, grabbing her hand to wish her success. Rossi wasn't among them. After Huxley exposed Alessandra in England, he felt betrayed. He wrote a *mea culpa* published by the *Piccolo*, declaring he had been deceived. Cappelli stayed in Palermo.

The Italians turned out in force to support Lombardi—Sapienti and Parenti from Torino; Negri, Baldinotti and Pirelli from Genoa. Baron von Weibel had rushed down from Munich, bringing his film of Alessandra's dancing basket to show the press. But it was Fournier who gave Alessandra the greatest boost that night—he brought little Zoe.

"*Tante* Alessandra!" she cried, pushing through a sea of legs and running into Alessandra's arms. She flung her arms around Alessandra's neck and kissed her as Alessandra hugged her tightly, tears in her eyes, before releasing her back to her father. But not before Fabio captured the shot for the *Mattino*.

As we started upstairs, where Huxley was waiting for Alessandra, Claudio from *La Stampa* yelled out, "How's your girl, professor? Gonna show us something tonight?"

Lombardi turned around and addressed the crowd of reporters.

"I have the greatest confidence in *Signora* Poverelli. She is ready."

But she wasn't, and Lombardi knew it.

The day before, he had handed me a statement to be given in advance to the *Mattino*.

*The failure of Signora Poverelli tonight to produce phenomena suggestive of the reality of a psychic force as yet unrecognized by Science, a force which I and many reputable scientists have personally witnessed multiple times, will undoubtedly cheer skeptics. It provides them with an excuse to deny its existence, an opportunity to dismiss Signora Poverelli as a charlatan, and an encouragement to universities to censure and dismiss anyone who persists in investigating this mystery. For myself, I remain fully confident that such a force exists, Signora Poverelli's gift is real, and I will continue to pursue proof of its existence.*

I handed it to Venzano the day before the test. He asked me what I thought. I told him the truth.

"It's over," I said. "She's finished."

## 81

Huxley humiliated Alessandra one last time.

When we reached the fifth floor, a sour-looking matron with a suspicious eye steered Alessandra into the side room Huxley had set up for the required pre-test inspection. Alessandra was stripped naked, her clothes inspected for secret pockets or hidden hooks on her sleeves or bodice, then Huxley's assistant took her time using her fingers to probe every cavity in Alessandra's body –her mouth, her *fica* and even her *culo*.

Lombardi and Renard only received a quick pat down, but Huxley had ordered Archer to give me the works.

"Behind the curtain, Labella," he barked.

"Why?" I protested.

He sneered. "Afraid we'll find something?"

He made me take off my jacket, shirt and shoes, turned my pants pockets inside out, and ran his hands up the inside my legs, giving me a shot in the *coglioni* before telling me to put my clothes back on. I wanted to kill him.

I took my chair against the far wall, next to Lombardi and Renard. Huxley didn't want us anywhere near Alessandra when the lamp was turned down. Huxley's short-hand writer was already busy at her desk next to the shuttered and barred window, adjusting the wick on the oil lamp which would provide the room's only illumination once the sitting started.

When Alessandra shuffled into the room, my heart sank. I could see the fight was gone from her. Farthing led her over to the table and Hardwicke positioned her feet on the electrical plate.

"Don't lift them off the pad," he warned her, then he took his seat.

Farthing headed for the door to take his guard position out in the hall. Archer let him out, then locked the door and slipped the key in his pocket.

Huxley grinned. It was the moment he had been waiting for since Ile Ribaud.

"The rope, Mr. Archer."

Archer reached into his jacket pocket, pulled out a pair of silver cords, and handed them to Huxley who held one up to Alessandra's face and sneered.

"A first for you, I believe."

Huxley began tying her right hand to the chair. "Shall we see what miracles you can produce when you're properly restrained?" He wound the cord tightly around her wrist a half dozen times, and finished it off with a complicated knot. "A warning, *Signora*. Pulling against it will only make the rope tighter."

I could see the rising panic in Alessandra's eyes as Archer handed Huxley the second rope. Huxley took his time fastening the line around her left wrist. Alessandra started to tremble, and began to tug at the ropes.

Huxley paused, annoyed. "Shall we proceed?"

Alessandra took a deep breath, then nodded her head and shut her eyes tight. Huxley returned to the task, carefully checking each loop for slack, then gave the binding one last yank, slipped into his seat at the end of the table, and Archer turned off the overhead electric light.

In the flickering flame of the oil lamp, I could see Alessandra shaking now. Her breaths were becoming sharper, quicker, shallower. Suddenly, Alessandra stopped and drew back, as if surprised. Her eyes were locked shut, but she was looking at something.

"No ... No!"

Archer glanced nervously at Huxley. He waved his hand dismissively.

"Just an act."

Alessandra's head began to whip left, then right, like she was trying to avoid someone from getting too close to her face.

From kissing her.

"Don't! Please! Please, Father! I beg you!"

It was the voice of a thirteen-year-old girl about to be raped.

I jumped up.

"Take the ropes off her." I shouted.

"Tommaso!" Lombardi grabbed my sleeve. "Sit down!"

"Take the ropes off! NOW!"

I pulled away and started for Alessandra.

A scream rose from her throat.

"NO! OH GOD, NO!"

Alessandra's back arched, her head jerking backwards with each thrust, *ah, ah, ah, ah* ...

"Stop it!" Huxley yelled. "Stop this acting!"

He reached out and slapped her.

Alessandra's head flew back, then fell forward and hung there, her wrists still tied to the chair. Then her eyes slowly opened, and turned towards Huxley.

## 82

"WHO DARES STRIKE MY BELOVED?"

It was the last time in my life I heard the hiss of that monster. A creature of her mind, like Lombardi believed? If only it were!

Alessandra raised her right arm, and the rope binding her to the chair snapped like sewing thread. Then her left arm jerked upwards, ripping off the chair arm, which hung there, swinging from her wrist like a scythe.

The stenographer let out a scream, and Hardwicke and Archer scrambled to their feet.

The sickly, green eyes slowly swept the room, until they came to rest on Huxley. Then they flared, like an ember struck with a poker.

"UNBELIEVER! THE TIME OF RECKONING HAS COME!"

"It's ... it's all an act ... nothing to be afraid of." Huxley stood up and bared his teeth at Alessandra. "You don't scare me!"

An invisible hand yanked him off his feet and flung him across the room, his arms flailing wildly, slamming him against the wall. Huxley slid to the floor and lay there stunned, blood streaming from his nose.

Hardwicke and Archer bolted for the door. Huxley rolled over and started crawling on his hands and knees after them. Archer frantically searched his pocket for the key, and jammed it in the lock.

"Open! Open! Damn you!"

Out in the hall, I could hear Farthing shouting.

"What the devil is going on in there?"

The door wouldn't open.

Archer and Hardwicke scrambled across the room and crouched behind a chair. Huxley screamed, and we watched in horror as he was dragged backwards by his foot, kicking at some invisible hand, then pinwheeled across the floor and slammed against the wall a second time.

*"AND THE LORD REACHED OUT HIS HAND..."*

Alessandra lifted her hand and the séance table rose to the ceiling, hung there, then came crashing down—legs snapping, splinters of wood flying across the room. Alessandra bent down, picked up a leg from the shattered table and started across the room.

I remember shadows and shouting, the clanging of the electric bell, the screaming of the stenographer, Farthing pounding on the door, and Alessandra, lit by the lamp flame, heading for Huxley.

He was slumped against the wall, a gash across his forehead, one eye closed. When she reached him, he raised his fists and pawed the air with a few feeble punches.

Alessandra lifted her club high in the air.

*"...AND GOD SMOTE HIM FOR HIS ERROR AND THERE HE DIED."*

I put my hands over my eyes.

"Alessandra, NO!"

Lombardi's scream echoed in my ear.

Alessandra hesitated, then turned her head towards us, and in the lamp light I finally saw Savonarola *himself*—the sickly, putrid flesh, bloated and swollen, like a corpse pulled from a river, a writhing pot of maggot and worm, and those watery, slime-green eyes burning with hatred for our wretched world of sinners, doubters, disbelievers.

The ghoul turned back to Huxley and raised his club over his head. It started down, then suddenly stopped in mid-air—mercifully held back by what, I don't know—and Alessandra collapsed to the floor like a discarded rag.

Lombardi reached her first.

Her eyes were open but they saw nothing. Blood flowed from her mouth and ears, her breathing ragged, her pulse feeble.

"We need to get her to a hospital!"

We heard a crash, the door flew open, and Farthing burst into the room. He flipped on the electric light and stared, mouth agape, at the battered Huxley, then at the demolished table.

"What the bloody hell!"

## 83

"Out of the way! Out of the way!"

We fought our way down the stairs, past gawking maids and startled guests, Lombardi and Renard carrying Alessandra between them. A reporter came charging up the stairs and I shoved him aside.

"One more floor!" I shouted. We were almost there.

"My medical bag —Negri has it!" Lombardi yelled. "Get it!"

We hit the lobby and newspaper reporters rushed us, shouting questions, flash guns going off, people yelling and screaming.

"Let her breathe!" Lombardi shouted. "Please, give her room!"

I spun around, trying to spot Negri. Where the hell was he! My eyes swept the room, and I saw Damiano and Parenti, and Fournier lifting Zoe onto the bell desk to keep her from being trampled, and then Negri, standing on the piano bench, gaping at Alessandra. He didn't see me. I started for him.

Then I heard Doffo scream.

"Pigotti!"

Doffo was frantically waving his hands.

"Pigotti!"

I looked in the direction he was pointing.

Pigotti was shoving his way through the milling crowd towards Alessandra, a pistol in his hand. "He's got a gun!" someone shouted. People started screaming, backing away, falling over chairs to escape.

There was nothing I could do. I was too far away.

I watched the crowd part, Pigotti shove Renard out of the way, then raise the gun and aim it at Alessandra. Lombardi looked up, saw the gun, and stepped forward, shielding Alessandra.

The roar of the gunshot echoed off the wall.

Lombardi staggered backwards, and a bright red patch of blood slowly spread across his starched white shirt. Someone tackled Pigotti, knocking the gun from his hand, and he went down kicking and screaming, swallowed up by the angry crowd.

# 84

Alessandra never got to see Lombardi buried.

She was in the hospital for five days, and the Jews bury their dead quickly. Renard found a synagogue on Via Cappella Vecchia and the rabbi handled everything. Dr. Lombardi's wife and family had disowned him, so nobody from Torino came down for the service. Renard and I attended, and afterward we went over to his rented apartment with the rabbi to collect Lombardi's things. Inside his closet, I found his personal diary, covering the year 1899 and his investigation of Alessandra.

The last entry, written the morning of December 21, was a poem to her.

> *Rise up my love and come away with me*
> *The flowers appear on the earth and the time*
> *of singing has come.*

I slipped the diary into my pocket for Alessandra.

It would mean a lot to her.

Alessandra was released from the hospital the day after Christmas, and we took her back to Piazza Dante. By then she knew that Lombardi was dead. I stayed with her until New Year's Day, then accompanied Renard to the train station. Huxley had already left for England. The newspapers were focused on the shocking murder of Lombardi, and

Huxley and his team had slipped out of Naples without talking to the press about what had happened upstairs that night. As he boarded his carriage for Paris, Renard handed me an envelope –money to pay the rent on Alessandra's apartment for another month. He shook my hand.

"Write me, and let me know how she is doing."

On the eve of the Feast of the Epiphany, I gave Alessandra Lombardi's diary, the page folded back to his last words to her. We were sitting at the table talking about him, when we heard a knock on the door. It was Venzano.

He hurried over and handed a telegram to Alessandra.

"La Befana left this in my stocking." He smiled. "But I believe it's for you."

Back in London, Henry Tyndall had issued an official statement to the *London Times* regarding the Society's investigation in Naples. Huxley hadn't signed it, but the other three had.

> *"With great intellectual reluctance, though without much personal doubt as to its justice, we the undersigned are of the opinion that we have witnessed in the presence of Alessandra Poverelli the action of some kinetic force, the nature and origin of which we cannot attempt to specify, through which, without the introduction of accomplices, apparatus, or mere manual dexterity, she is able to produce the movement of objects at a distance from her and unconnected to her in any apparent physical manner."*

Huxley resigned his position with the Society a week after returning to London. He never paid Alessandra her hundred pounds sterling.

Two months later, Hardwicke delivered the team's final report to the Society's Board of Directors. Renard sent me a copy. What *was* the source of that mysterious force which smashed a wooden table to smithereens, and tossed a six-foot, 200-pound man across the room like a rag doll? With fraud and trickery eliminated, Hardwicke noted, there remained but two possibilities—an unknown power of the human mind, like Lombardi believed, or an "intelligence external to the medium."

He couldn't bring himself to say spirits of the dead.

As I stood in the rain yesterday and watched Alessandra's coffin being lowered into the grave, it occurred to me that Alessandra already had the answer.

Eventually, we'll all know.

# 85

A ntonio is a fast writer.

It's three P.M. now, and he already has the first two articles for the Sunday edition written and sent to layout. I'll go down to the darkroom later tonight to choose the lead photo from Giorgio's assembled pile.

After Lombardi's murder, Alessandra left Naples and moved to Rome. She never married, but found her sunny apartment and got a cat, just like she had always dreamed of. Her vindication in Naples allowed her to support herself by giving private séances. Ironically, her apartment was just around the corner from the Vatican, but the Church stopped pursuing her once she disappeared from the news. Pigotti? He's rotting away in a prison in Naples. Ten years earlier, he would have gone to the gallows, but Italy abolished capital punishment in 1889.

I quickly worked my way up the *Mattino* ladder with Venzano's support, and a decade later moved to Rome to work for the *Messaggero* as sub-editor then managing editor, then the big seat. Alessandra and I saw each other often, and she always came to my house for Christmas. Doffo's here too. I brought him up to Rome as soon as I became editor, and he's busy skewering everybody. I've given him free rein to go after what Garibaldi famously branded "that pestilential institution called the Papacy." He and Pietro have a place now. Pietro still works for Cardinal Uccello, and keeps Doffo supplied with secrets and scandals.

Alessandra stayed in her apartment until her consumption finally forced her into the hospital. I used my pull to get her into a private sanitarium in Trastevere, across the Tiber, but close enough to the *Messaggero* office that I could visit her every day.

On Monday, I'll take the train to Paris to meet Monsieur Pathé and pitch him on my idea of making a film about Alessandra's life.

I told Alessandra about it the night she lay dying. She had lost a lot of weight, and the long sleeves of her dress now hid ulcers instead of Pigotti's cigarette burns. But the ruins of her beauty were still visible, in her long black hair, untouched by grey, and in her eyes.

"Who will play me?" she whispered.

"How about Pina Menichelli?" I said, reaching out to take her hand.

She smiled. "Wouldn't that be wonderful." I knew she would like that. She had seen Pina in *Il Fuoco*, and the vamp had become her favorite actress.

"But first we have to convince Monsieur Pathé," I said. "Wish me luck."

Alessandra began to cough violently, and Maria appeared at the door with fresh handkerchiefs. Alessandra waved her away, and fell back into her chair, exhausted.

"My bureau..." she said, pointing to her bedroom. "...small blue box..."

I went in, found the box and brought it to her.

"Open it, Tommaso" she said.

Inside was a silk purse, and inside that was a tiny cat figurine carved in alabaster. Alessandra looked at me and smiled.

"Take Bastet with you."

Just before midnight, she took a turn for the worse, and the doctor pulled me into the hall and warned me the end had come. She died early the next morning, her hand in mine, as the sun flooded through her window and the light in those luminous eyes of hers faded away.

Bastet's here in my pocket.

I'll let you know what happens.

**END**

# Author's Note

*The Witch of Napoli* is a work of fiction. Its inspiration was the true-life story of controversial Italian medium Eusapia Palladino (1854-1918). Parapsychologists cite Palladino's table levitations as some of the most baffling and impressive feats of psychokinesis ever observed and recorded. In the many historical books, newspaper stories and scientific reports dealing with her life, you'll find many memorable quotes, descriptions and observations expressed in the unique language of the 19th century. I managed to slip a few of them, slightly adapted for my story, into my novel. They include:

*"Her large eyes, filled with strange fire, sparkled in their orbits, or again seem filled with swift gleams of phosphorescent fire, sometimes bluish, sometimes golden. If I did not fear that the metaphor were too easy when it concerns a Neapolitan woman, I should say that her eyes appear like the glowing lava fires of Vesuvius, seen from a distance in a dark night."* – Monsieur Arthur Levy penned this evocative description of Palladino after attending a séance with her in 1898 at the house of celebrated French astronomer Camille Flammarion. The astronomer later included Levy's description in a book he published in 1907 entitled "*Mysterious Psychic Forces: An Account of the Author's Investigations in Psychical Research, Together with Those of Other European Savants.*"

"As a child, she saw eyes glaring at her in the darkness, and was frightened one night when invisible hands stripped off her bedclothes." – Eusapia Palladino's mentor and champion Dr. Cesare Lombroso shares this gossip about Palladino in his 1909 book entitled *After Death—What? Spiritistic Phenomena and Their Interpretation.*

"I was like a wild animal, a forest bird, and these foolish stranieri wanted to make me into a prissy English girl. They dressed me in pinafores and starched blouses, wanted me to take a bath every day, to comb my hair, to use a fork at the table." – Eusapia Palladino reminisces in a short autobiographical essay about her life, published in 1910.

"Here in Naples, we have a woman who belongs to the humblest class of society. She is nearly forty years old and very ignorant. But when she wishes, be it by day or by night, she can divert a curious group for an hour or so with the most surprising phenomena. Firmly held by the hands of the curious, Alessandra levitates furniture, holds it suspended in the air like Mahomet's coffin, and makes it come down again with undulatory movements, as if they were obeying her will. She produces raps and taps on the walls, the ceiling, the floor far distant from her. She can make musical instruments – bells, tambourines – positioned in a corner of the room far beyond her reach play without touching them." – Dr. Ercole Chiaia of Naples first alerted Dr. Cesare Lombroso to Eusapia Palladino. This is an excerpt from the oft-cited letter he wrote to Lombroso in 1888 inviting Lombroso to investigate Palladino.

"A luminous hand with exquisite delicacy applied itself to his lips, preventing him from continuing." – Dr. Giuseppe Venzano attended a séance with Palladino in Genoa in 1907 during which a deceased lady friend of his materialized in the room.

*"If there ever was an individual in this world opposed to the claims of spiritism by virtue of scientific education and, I may add, by instinct, I was that person. But I glory in saying that I am a slave to facts. …I see nothing inadmissible in the supposition that, in hysterical and hypnotized persons, the stimulation of certain centres of the brain, which become powerful owing to the paralyzing of all the others, may give rise to a transmission of cerebral or cortical forces which can be transformed into a motor force. In this way, we can understand how a medium can, for example, raise a table from the floor, pinch someone by the beard, strike him or caress him – phenomena frequently reported during séances. Do we not see the magnet give rise to an invisible force which can deflect a compass needle without any viable intermediary? What is needed is the development of instruments to establish the reality this occult force. We were unable to detect existence of the X-ray until science gave us photography and the vacuum tube. Once we had the necessary instruments, doubt was dispelled."* – Selected comments made by Lombroso during his investigations of Eusapia Palladino.

*"She has the hyperaesthesic zone, especially in the ovary. She has the hole in the esophagus that women with hysteria have, and general weakness, or paresis, in the limbs of the left side. She exhibits a persistent cough from tuberculosis, a disease endemic in Naples. It is easier for her to be magnetized than hypnotized. Methodical passes of the hand over her head can free her from headache (cephalea), and quiet her agitation of mind, and upward magnetic passes can provoke her in a state of semi-catalepsy, just as passes in the reverse direction can remove distortions of her muscles and paresis….She experiences a desire to produce the phenomena; then she has a feeling of numbness and the gooseflesh sensation in her fingers; these sensations keep increasing; at the same time she feels in the lower portion of the vertebral column the flowing of a current which rapidly extends into*

*her arms as far as her elbow, where it is eventually arrested. It is at this point that the phenomenon takes place...like they had been dipped in lye."* – For an extensive and often amusing series of "scientific" observations Lombroso made about Palladino, see his book *After Death—What? Spiritistic Phenomena and Their Interpretation.*

*"I did not consider it worthy of the dignity of a savant, and a naturalist, to be present at such spiritistic séances. I shared that degree of distrust and suspicion which should always accompany the observation of the abnormal..."*– Comment made by Lombroso following his conversion.

*"...not only because they are reported by persons worthy of credence, even by scientists, but because I also have experimented."* – Comments made by Dr. Enrico Morselli, Professor of Psychiatry at Genoa University, Italy, who studied Palladino and later wrote about his psychic experiments in his book *Psicologia e Spiritismo.*

*"It feels like a cat is climbing my right arm towards my shoulder... Somebody is tickling me...something just pulled my beard... I'm feeling a true hand, flesh and bones are felt, the skin of the hand, warm, mobile fingers are all perceived....the hand gives off a light...I can see her bust and arms while both her hands are held by ... Absurd as the phenomenon of a materialized hand may seem, it seems to me to be very difficult to attribute the phenomena produced to deception, conscious or unconscious, or to a series of deceptions. It is inconceivable to suppose that an accomplice could have come into the room, which is small, and was locked and sealed during the progress of our experiments. We were making no noise, we could light up the room instantly. We must accept the evidence as we find it."* – Comments made by various investigators who attended sittings with Palladino and experienced phantom touches and hand materializations.

*"If all attempts to verify scientifically the intervention of another world should be definitely proved futile, this would be a terribly blow, a mortal blow to all of our hopes for another life."*– One of the reasons Frederic W.H. Myers decided to help co-found England's venerable Society for Psychical Research (the model for my fictional London Society for the Investigation of Mediums).

*"It allows some ordinary moving of the feet such as is inevitable in a long sitting, but if a foot is completely taken off the plate, an electric bell will ring."* – Renowned British physicist, inventor and psychic investigator Sir Oliver Lodge describes a device used to control a medium's foot movements.

*"With great intellectual reluctance, though without much personal doubt as to its justice, we the undersigned are of opinion that we have witnessed in the presence of Alessandra Poverelli the action of some kinetic force, the nature and origin of which we cannot attempt to specify, through which, without the introduction of accomplices, apparatus, or mere manual dexterity, she is able to produce the movement of objects at a distance from her and unconnected to her in any apparent physical manner. "* – Conclusion reached by the Society for Psychical Research following its famous investigation of Eusapia Palladino in Naples in 1908.

# Suggested Reading

Alvarado, Carlos. "Eusapia Palladino: An Autobiographical Essay." *Journal of Scientific Exploration*, Vol. 25, No. 1, pp. 77–101 (2011)

Alvarado, Carlos: "Eusapia Palladino: A Short Bibliography." http://carlossalvarado.edublogs.org/page/13/

Blum, Deborah. *Ghost Hunters: William James and the Search for Scientific Proof of Life After Death*. Penguin Group. (2007)

Bottazzi, Filippo. *Mediumistic Phenomena: Observed in a Series of Sessions with Eusapia Palladino*. ICRL Press. (2011translation)

Carrington, Hereward. *Eusapia Palladino and Her Phenomena*. B. W. Dodge. (1909)

Carrington, Hereward. *The American Séances with Eusapia Palladino*. Kessinger Publishing LLC (2006) (Reprint)

Dingwall, Eric. *Very Peculiar People*. University Books, (1962)

Feilding, Everard. *Sittings with Eusapia Palladino & Other Stories*. University Books. (1963 reprint)

Feilding, E., Baggally, W. W., & Carrington, H. "Report on a series of sittings with Eusapia Palladino." *Proceedings of the Society for Psychical Research*, 23, 309–569. (1909)

Flammarion, Camille. *Mysterious Psychic Forces: An Account of the Author's Investigations in Psychical Research, Together with Those of Other European Savants.* Small, Maynard Publishers. (1907)

James, William. "An Estimate of Palladino." *Cosmopolitan Magazine,* (1910)

Lodge, Oliver. "Experience of unusual physical phenomena occurring in the presence of an entranced person (Eusapia Paladino)." *Journal of the Society for Psychical Research,* 6, 306–336, 346–360. (1894)

Lombroso, Cesare. "Eusapia Paladino and Spiritism." *Annals of Psychical Science,* 7, 167–180. (1908)

Lombroso, Cesare. *After Death – What? Spiritistic Phenomena and Their Interpretation.* Small, Maynard Publishers . (1909)

Morselli, Enrico. "Eusapia Paladino and the genuineness of her phenomena." *Annals of Psychical Science,* 5, 319–360, 399–421. (1907)

Palladino, Eusapia. "My Own Story." *Cosmopolitan Magazine,* (1910)

"Palladino Reported as Dead in Rome" (Obituary) *The New York Times,* May 18, 1918, p. 13.

Starner, William. *Dolce Napoli,* Charing Cross Publishing (1878)

Schmicker, Michael. *Best Evidence.* (2nd Edition): iUniverse. (2002)

Wiseman, R. "The Feilding Report: A Reconsideration." *Journal of the Society for Psychical Research,* 58, 129–152. (1992)

# About The Author

Michael Schmicker is an investigative journalist and nationally-known writer on scientific anomalies and the paranormal.

He is the co-author of *The Gift, ESP: The Extraordinary Experiences of Ordinary People* (St. Martin's Press, hardcover, paperback, e-book (USA); Rider/Random House (UK). His first book, *Best Evidence*, has emerged as a classic in the field of scientific anomalies reporting since its first publication in 2000. His writings also appear in three anthologies, including *The Universe Wants to Play* (Anomalist Books); *First of the Year 2009* (Transaction Publishers), edited by former *Village Voice* writer Benj DeMott; and *Even the Smallest Crab Has Teeth* (Travelers Tales).

Michael began his writing career as a crime reporter for a suburban Dow-Jones newspaper in Connecticut, and worked as a freelance reporter in Southeast Asia for three years. He has also worked as a stringer for *Forbes* magazine, and Op-Ed contributor to *The Wall Street Journal Asia*. Michael has been a featured guest on national broadcast radio talk shows, including twice on Coast to Coast AM (560 stations in North America, with 3 million weekly listeners). He reviews books for the *Journal of Scientific Exploration*; serves on the Board of Advisers of the Rhine Research Center; and is a member of both the American Society for Psychical Research as well as England's venerable Society for Psychical Research.

He lives and writes in Honolulu, Hawaii, on a mountaintop overlooking Waikiki and Diamond Head crater.

Visit his official author website:
www.michaelschmicker.com

# Bonus Excerpt

Keep reading for an excerpt from *The Gift: ESP: The Extraordinary Experiences of Ordinary People,* Michael's non-fiction investigation of the paranormal mysteries of precognition, clairvoyance and telepathy.

# A Fire at the Pentagon

Shortly after the shocking, Sept. 11, 2001 terrorist strike on the United States, my co-author Dr. Sally Rhine Feather received a call from a well-educated, forty-year-old woman named Marie living in North Carolina. A few weeks before the attack, she and her husband had been vacationing in Washington, D.C. Their planned sightseeing itinerary had included all the usual stops, including the Pentagon, but the weather had been very hot and humid, the traffic heavy, so they skipped the Pentagon.

"When we exited the city, my husband was driving," she wrote. "I was sitting next to him in the front. I was just trying to close my eyes to relax for a minute. Then he told me, 'Well, when we come around the bend up ahead, you should get a good view of the Pentagon because our road goes right by it.' It was one of the things we had said we wanted to do when we visited Washington. So I opened my eyes to look, and when I looked to the right, there it was. But it had huge billows of thick, black smoke pouring out of it, just huge clouds of smoke. I didn't see fire, I saw smoke, like a bomb had gone off, billows and billows of black smoke going up in the sky.

"I yelled out and slammed my hands on the dashboard. My poor husband didn't know what was happening. I mean, I really screamed out loud. His first thought was that we were going to be in an accident, and I was warning him he was going to hit someone. But it was pretty open space on the highway, and nobody was cutting in front of us or anything at that moment."

When Marie saw the black smoke, it created such an intense, emotional feeling that she lost her breath. She was almost hyperventilating. Then suddenly, she felt like she was literally falling into the Pentagon itself – which was why, she explained to Dr. Feather, that she slammed her hands against the dashboard. She described the feeling as being on a roller coaster the second you crest the top and plunge forward and down. The combination of her vision and falling forward overwhelmed her. She described it as sensory overload.

"I truly felt like we were in danger, even though we were actually on the highway and a couple of miles away from the Pentagon. I thought it was on fire. My husband said the Pentagon was not on fire, and then I finally realized that in fact it wasn't. And as fast as it had started, it stopped. It had all happened in a few seconds."

Marie was understandably confused and shaken by the experience. A pretty woman with dark, curly hair, Marie holds a business degree. She has had psychic experiences most of her life, but this one was different. Seeing something that was not there had never happened to her before.

Two weeks later, Marie's frightening precognitive visual hallucination came true. At 9:45 A.M. on Sept. 11, 2001, just one hour after American Airlines Flight 11 slammed into the North Tower of New York's World Trade Center, American Airlines Flight 77 smashed into the Pentagon, killing 184 people and setting off fires that generated billows and billows of thick, black smoke.

Parapsychologists are still searching for a better term for what Marie experienced than an ESP "hallucination". Hallucination is a negatively loaded term, connoting abnormal psychology. Both ordinary hallucinations and ESP hallucinations are characterized by the mistaken impression that the object or person perceived by one of the five senses is actually present there in physical reality. But the two types of hallucinations differ in several important ways. The ordinary hallucination produces fantasy, nonsense and verifiably false claims and usually occurs in people who are mentally or physically ill or in a drugged state. The ESP hallucination delivers accurate, factual information that can be subsequently checked out and verified and is experienced by sane, healthy, normal people like Marie.

Dr. Feather received dozens of calls and emails in the following weeks and months after Sept. 11, 2001 from people describing similar spontaneous precognitive experiences which seemed to foreshadow the terrible events of that day. Many came in vivid and dramatic dreams. Others reported during waking hours of getting strange intuitions or bodily feelings of something being terribly wrong, suggesting that they had some psychic awareness on an unconscious level of the approaching events. In a few cases, the experiences seemed so realistic that the people felt they were actually living through the events themselves.

Now let's move backward sixty years to 1941.

*Attack on Pearl Harbor*

The two most dramatic disasters in the history of the United States are the 2001 terrorist attacks on New York and Washington, D.C. and the 1941 Japanese attack on Pearl Harbor in Hawaii that launched World War II. Sixty years separate Marie's ESP experience from the following one, but the two precognitive experiences share some striking similarities. The story, found in the collection of 30,000 spontaneous ESP cases on file at the Rhine Research Center, was sent by a woman living in California in December 1941.

"It happened when I was in high school. I wasn't feeling well, and I came home early. It was about 2:00 or 3:00 in the afternoon. I lay down on a couch in the living room and took a nap. This is what I dreamed:

"I was standing on a hill in the predawn darkness, shivering in the wind. I was looking at a large building below and ahead of me. An American flag was flying over it, and I knew it was a barracks. I knew there were men inside asleep. I even knew how many men there were, 400 and something. For some reason, I had a terrible premonition, and I shook more with fear than with cold. I didn't know what was going to happen, but I knew something awful was, and I wanted to cry out a warning, but I couldn't.

"Then I heard a groaning sound, at first far off and then closer. I looked up, and there were squadrons of planes overhead. In a few seconds I knew why I had been afraid, because when they were directly over the building, they started dropping bombs, hundreds of them it seemed. The noise was deafening, and the flames leapt up at the dark sky. I could feel the ground shake under me but, most frightening of all, I could see inside that building. I could see the men caught in their beds, caught and ripped and burned and killed, and yet horrible as that was, that was not what caused the great feeling of panic that swept over me. The thing that was racing through my mind at that moment was a single thought, 'But why? We are not at war!' With that phrase playing in my brain over and over, I awoke, gasping with fear.

"I had never had a dream so vivid. I went into the kitchen where my mother was preparing dinner and told her about it. I wasn't in the habit of telling my dreams to people, because they were always obviously silly things not worth telling, but for some reason this was different, and that night I told my Dad, too.

"Well, you can probably guess what comes next. That was on Thursday. On Sunday morning, December 7, I was listening to the radio when suddenly they interrupted with a special news bulletin. The Japanese had struck Pearl Harbor before dawn, the men were caught in their barracks, 400 and something, and we were at war.

"As is the case of those first bulletins, they are rather short and incomplete, and they tell you to keep listening for further reports that will come later. In this bulletin, they didn't have an account of all the damage done, but they said that as far as they knew at the moment, the greatest loss of life had occurred when one of the barracks suffered a direct hit. They told how the men were caught there before they were even fully awake, and he gave the number as 400 and something, which was the number I had dreamed. The description followed everything exactly as I had seen it. The only thing I had not known was the identity of the enemy."

Reports like these suggest that ESP is remarkably stable and consistent in terms of form and content. Whether they come from Portland, Maine or Portland, Oregon, some of the experiences are basically identical." Consider this case sent to the Rhine Research Center:

*"Something Has Happened to My Mother!" (I)*

"One Sunday afternoon, several members of our family were eating dinner at my grandmother's house. Suddenly, and for no apparent reason in the midst of pleasant family dinner chatter, my mother stood up and screamed 'My mother! My mother! Something has happened to my mother!' We were all shocked... About fifteen minutes after her experience, the phone rang, and she received the information from her father that her mother had indeed died fifteen minutes previously. My mother was not aware that her mother was ill, or even that she was in a hospital (where she expired)."

And now the almost identical experience of another woman who wrote to the Rhine Center:

*"Something Has Happened to My Mother!" (II)*

On Thanksgiving Day, a woman was a guest for dinner and was surrounded by happy people. Nevertheless, around 11:30 in the morning, when conversation consisted of nothing more serious than chitchat about the Thanksgiving dinner, she suddenly knew without a doubt that her mother, who lived far away in California, was in great distress. She tried not to disturb the party of fourteen people and managed to finish dinner. But her thoughts were perfectly clear. She knew her mother had passed away. She excused herself and went home. When she got there, a message awaited her. Her mother had died about 9:30 in the morning, making the time of the mother's death and the daughter's reaction about the same. The mother was aged, but she had not been ill, and the daughter had no reason to expect her death.

Both women, in the middle of their pleasant dinners, had sudden intuitions that something terrible had happened to their mothers at that very moment. Both women were absolutely convinced that the information they received from their sixth sense was correct. And shortly afterwards, both women received messages confirming their ESP. Parapsychologists have found spontaneous ESP experiences basically identical to those above in ESP case collections stretching back to the 1880s...

# Critical Acclaim for The Gift: ESP: The Extraordinary Experiences of Ordinary People

"The authors take us through some amazing anecdotal evidence of ESP in this very readable account."

> – Fred Alan Wolf, Ph.D., Discovery Channel's resident physicist and American Book Award-winning author of *Taking the Quantum Leap*.

"… insights and experiences we all may experience, but which are not often shared with others."

> – John Edward, author of the *New York Times* bestsellers *Crossing Over* and *One Last Time: A Psychic Medium Speaks to Those We Have Loved and Lost*

"…an astounding array of spontaneous psychic experiences that stretch the human definition of reality. It should be read by anyone interested in understanding the limits of the human mind and consciousness."

> – Joe McMoneagle, author of *The Stargate Chronicles: Memoirs of a Psychic Spy*.

"A wonderful book, filled with fascinating stories from the world's largest collection of ESP cases."

–Rupert Sheldrake, Ph.D., author of
*The Sense of Being Stared At and Other
Unexplained Powers of the Human Mind.*

"… speaks directly to the needs of millions of people who are concerned with the personal meaning of their ESP experiences."

– Jeffrey Mishlove, Ph.D., President of
Intuition Network.

"There is no better introduction to the controversial world of ESP and why it continues to be a fascinating and frustrating enigma."

– Stanley Krippner, Ph.D., Professor of
Psychology and co-editor of *Varieties of
Anomalous Experience.*

"A fascinating and readable book reminding us...that our greatest treasure is not things, but the human mind."

– Charles Tart, Ph.D., author of *Altered
States of Consciousness.*

# One Last Thing...

If you enjoyed The Witch of Napoli, and think others will too, please consider posting a review on Barnes & Noble or Amazon.

Aloha and all the best, Michael

CPSIA information can be obtained at www.ICGtesting.com
Printed in the USA
LVOW11s2250220315

431597LV00004B/215/P

9 780990 949022